THEODORE TERHUNE STORIES

Seven Clues in Search of a Crime
House with Crooked Walls
A Case for Solomon
Work for the Hangman
Ten Trails to Tyburn
A Case of Books
And a Bottle of Rum
Dead Pigs at Hungry Farm

Seven Clues
in Search of a Crime

BRUCE GRAEME

With an introduction by J. F. Norris

 Moonstone Press

This edition published in 2021 by Moonstone Press
www.moonstone press.co.uk

Introduction © 2021 J. F. Norris

Originally published in 1941 by Hutchinson & Co Ltd

Seven Clues in Search of a Crime © the Estate of
Graham Montague Jeffries, writing as Bruce Graeme

ISBN 978-1-899000-26-5
eISBN 978-1-899000-27-2

A CIP catalogue record for this book is available from the British Library

Text designed and typeset by Tetragon, London
Cover illustration by Jason Anscomb

Printed and bound by CPI Group (UK) Ltd, Croydon, CRO 4YY

Contents

INTRODUCTION

Theodore I. Terhune, Bibliodetective

Bookseller detectives as series characters are far and few between in the Golden Age of Detective Fiction. While the unique subgenre of "bibliomysteries" (detective novels in which collecting books and manuscripts figure prominently in the plot) were popular as early as the 1920s in America—with titles including *The Colfax Bookplate* (1926), *Into the Void: A Bookshop Mystery* (1926) and *The Whisper on the Stair* (1924), as well as several novels by Charles J. Dutton—rarely did these books feature a character who appeared in more than one novel. It wasn't until after the Second World War that mystery writers began to create bibliomysteries with a recurring series character. Henry Gamadge, created by Elizabeth Daly, appeared first in 1940 and is perhaps the bibliodetective best known to devotees of vintage detective fiction. Gamadge, however, is primarily an authenticator of old manuscripts; actual books rarely appear in the novels. Theodore Terhune, who makes his debut in *Seven Clues in Search of a Crime*, is a genuine bookseller who owns his own shop. He literally stumbles onto his first crime when riding a bicycle to work. When he inadvertently thwarts an attack on a young woman and prevents the theft of her handbag, he immediately gains a reputation for being a detective. This accidental heroism will lead him to a full range of adventures, involving theft, con-artistry and murder, over a series of eight mystery novels.

Terhune, who sometimes goes by the nickname Tommy, is also a mystery writer and tells us that he has had the privilege of having stories published in the American magazine *Saturday Evening Post*, a crown jewel for first-time writers eager to appear in the "slicks". Significant for the entire series is that the Terhune novels regularly feature plots involving books, book collectors and the art of writing fiction. Equally unique is that each book is radically different in tone and subject matter. Bruce Graeme was one of the finest narrative experimenters of the Golden Age, and the Terhune series reflects the author's eclectic knowledge and predilection for unusual atmospheric touches. Terhune's adventure in *Seven Clues* will involve a trip to New York City and Albany, a professional criminal for hire, attempted murder on board a passenger ship, a mysterious person nicknamed "Blondie", an automobile accident and learning the true identity of a tyre salesman. The bibliomystery plot is introduced when Terhune is asked to find out who stole some pages from a handwritten and illustrated manuscript on heraldry in the MacMunn family. As the title suggests, over the course of the novel Terhune discovers seven clues, a combination of physical objects and information gathered from his clever interviews, that foreshadow a crime yet to be committed.

Later in the Terhune series Graeme will explore a variety of other subgenres while still managing to make books and book collecting part of his plots. *House with Crooked Walls* (1942) is a send-up of Gothic horror stories consisting of grotesque Poe-like sequences, a secret-filled haunted house and apparently supernatural events. *Work for the Hangman* (1944) is a brilliant example of the detective novel morphing into an inverted suspense thriller and incorporates the pioneering convention of murder by proxy, a plot device that pre-dates by six years Patricia Highsmith's classic use of "trading murders" in her debut novel *Strangers on a Train* (1950). In *Ten Trails to Tyburn* (1944), a series of anonymous short stories are sent to Terhune and his policeman friend Murphy, the aim being to help them discover the reason behind a mysterious death that may in fact be a deviously concocted murder.

In each of these novels other characters from the village of Bray-in-the-Marsh serve as Theodore Terhune's friends and assistants in the solving of crime. Graeme is perhaps one of the first mystery writers whose characters grow and change over the chronological history of the series. Among those first introduced in *Seven Clues*, readers will continue to meet Lady Kylstone, a local aristocrat whose secretary Helen is the young woman in peril. Alicia MacMunn hires Terhune to look into the mystery of the heraldic manuscript, and her cynical daughter Julia will come into her own as Terhune's primary Watson (and sometime girlfriend) in later books. A crew of other local business owners, pub regulars and fellow booksellers in surrounding towns also pop up in this short series of eight novels. The development of the relationship between Julia MacMunn and Theodore Terhune has a decidedly modern touch, something that few mystery writers ever bothered with in series mystery novels, no matter how long they carried on with their characters.

Graham Montague Jeffries (1900–82), better known as Bruce Graeme, was born in London on 23 May 1900. After serving at the age of eighteen in the Westminster Rifles Regiment during the First World War, Jeffries went on to work as a reporter at the *Middlesex County Times*, a position he held throughout the 1920s. He also worked as a film producer during the 1940s. According to a biographical blurb on the rear dust jacket panel of one of his later books, Graeme was "a persistent traveller, making frequent trips in Europe and to the U.S.A., and when in England [he] lives in an Elizabethan farmhouse in the Weald of Kent."

Jeffries also wrote under the pseudonyms David Graeme (claiming he was Bruce's cousin), Peter Bourne, Jeffrey Montague and Fielding Hope. He was astonishingly prolific in crime and adventure fiction, writing more than one hundred books over a period of more than sixty years. He also managed to pen a few non-fiction works on history and true crime. In addition to his bookseller/writer detective Theodore I. Terhune, he created five series characters: Superintendent William Stevens, Inspector Pierre Allain of the Sûreté, Detective Sergeant Robert Mather, Inspector Auguste Jantry and—the character he is probably best known for—Richard Verrell, alias "Blackshirt", a professional thief who becomes a successful crime novelist.

Blackshirt, and later his son, Anthony Verrell (aka Lord Blackshirt), appeared in fourteen books between 1926 and 1947. Thanks to Jeffries' son Roderic, also a mystery writer, Blackshirt was revived in 1952, beginning with *Concerning Blackshirt*. Writing as "Roderic Graeme", Jeffries' son wrote an additional twenty novels for the series. Eventually, Roderic Jeffries began writing crime and suspense fiction under his own name (as well as other pen names, like his pseudonym-loving father), creating three series detectives: Don Kerry, Brandy and Inspector Alvarez, the last of whom solved crimes in Majorca.

A recurring theme throughout the work of "Bruce Graeme" is the role of the mystery writer in the world of crime. Dozens of his books feature mystery writers, novelists or movie scriptwriters as the protagonists. The melding of crime fiction, creative writing and "real crime" makes up the plot of many of the Terhune books, as well as being featured in other Graeme novels, such as *The Coming of Carew* (1945), *No Clues for Dexter* (1948) and *The Undetective* (1962), in the first of which a fictional character comes to life and commits the crimes that previously existed only within the pages of novels. It should come as no surprise, that along with

John Creasey and Nigel Morland, Jeffries helped found the Crime Writers' Association in 1953.

Though he sold over four million books in his career (as stated frequently on the dust jackets of his Hutchinson novels in the 1950s), Jeffries has been unjustly forgotten as one of the most innovative and original writers of crime fiction among his contemporaries. These new editions of the "Bruce Graeme" mystery novels from Moonstone Press are long overdue and hopefully will introduce an imaginative, amusing and entertaining writer to the ever-growing audience who crave traditional detective fiction from the heyday of the Golden Age.

J. F. NORRIS
Chicago, IL
June 2020

The First Clue

Helena Armstrong peered through a damp, clinging blanket of fog, trying in vain to discover whether she was on the right-hand side of the road or on the left, or whether, indeed, she was even on the road to Willingham, and not in the middle of a bordering field—the car had just bumped over something which might have been a shallow ditch. At that moment, Helena's world was a very sane, ordinary world, just the identical kind of a world it had been for the past two hundred and ninety-six days, and was likely to be for the next sixty-nine. But suddenly Helena's world ceased to be sane and ordinary, for phantasmal shapes materialized from out of the wreathing bank of fog; she saw them silhouetted against the white background formed by the glare of her headlights; and they were vaguely and unreasonably menacing. She counted them—three, four, five—five nightmarish figures in shapeless mackintoshes, and soft hats crushed well down on their foreheads. She saw one of these mackintoshed, soft-hatted shadows flash an electric torch at the registration plate; she heard a grating, unpleasant voice call out: "It's the Armstrong girl all right, boys; go to it." Then her world became a world of clutching hands, hot breath—a world of evil and terror.

"Help! Help!" she screamed piercingly. One of the clutching hands was clamped over her mouth, stifling her cries; the hand was rough and calloused, and it hurt her because it squeezed her lower lip against the sharp edge of her teeth; she tasted blood, then swiftly realized that the harsh hand must have been in recent contact with raw onions. "Damn you!" a voice said viciously; a strangely soft, liquid voice. She thought that she must be nigh to fainting, for her head swam, and the menacing face made visible by the dashboard light began to revolve in fantastic gyrations. Resolutely she took a grip upon herself and mastered her hysteria in time to witness the continuation of the drama. A bicycle shot into the circle of light; it clanged against the rear mudguard as its rider jumped off. A voice demanded: "What is happening?"

Helena sobbed; the gagging hand could not prevent that bubbling gasp of disappointment. If only the newcomer had been a policeman, or at least a man with muscular limbs and burly shoulders. But no! She could just see, sideways through the corner of one eye, a slight figure in loose-fitting tweeds, a meek, ordinary face, horn-rimmed spectacles.

The soft, liquid voice spoke again—Helena realized that it belonged to the owner of the oniony hands. "Deal with him, Bert."

Helena saw one of the shadows move towards the tweed-suited man; she wanted to scream a warning because, with illogical disregard of her own plight, she felt desperately sorry for the poor rabbit; he could not stand a chance of defending himself, and would suffer on her account! But the oniony hand was there to prevent any warning, and she saw a mackintoshed arm lifted in the air and come down again with a vicious swipe in the direction of the rabbit's head. True, the rabbit moved his head with surprising swiftness, but even so the girl in the car heard a thud of flesh against flesh—or perhaps something harder than flesh against flesh. She heard the rabbit gasp, and her heart echoed the dismal sound, even though her mouth could not do so.

Probably the man with the torch flashed the light directly at the rabbit's face, for it was suddenly and very clearly illuminated, just as though a limelight were being played upon it. Helena saw quite distinctly the expression of reproach which flashed across the rabbit's eyes—she was unable to decide whether it was a young face—and again she thought: "Oh dear! Why did I scream?" Then she saw the face become strangely angry, and suddenly things began to happen.

Precisely what happened was something which Helena was never able to describe with any accuracy. In the first place, Oniony Hands obstructed her view, for he still stood by the side of the car with his arm thrust through the window, clasping her in such a manner that she could neither move nor make a noise; the only way she could see what was happening was by peering over his shoulder out of the corner of her right eye. Then again, the characters in the drama seemed to move in and out of the enveloping shadows like wooden puppets, suspended by strings from above. Nothing was distinct; first the flailing arms had no bodies, then the bodies lacked arms and legs; it was not even possible to see whether there were two, three or four shadows taking part in the mêlée—she thought four must be the maximum number, for Oniony Hands took no part, nor did another man, who had opened the near-side door and was rummaging about the car. Nor were her ears of much assistance; she heard thuds, bangs, groans, and other extraordinary noises, but the episode remained in her memory as formless and terrifying an adventure as any genuine nightmare. The last act of the melodrama was far more real: the arrival of another bicycle, and another person, this time in the longed-for blue, a real burly-shouldered individual.

"What's going on here?" he asked unoriginally.

"The cops!" somebody shouted—it was not Soft Voice, "Beat it!"

The five vicious shadows dissolved into the blanket of fog; Helena was left with her blue-uniformed rescuer and her rabbit. But Rabbit lay on the road, motionless.

II

When Rabbit came to, he found himself in surroundings strange to him: a symphony of lavender, deep violet and a soft green to harmonize. Symphony, harmonize! Dreamily he corrected himself; symphony was related to music, not to colour. He was using the wrong word. Then, what was the right? Symposium? He started to shake his head, but quickly ceased, for the movement made his senses reel. He closed his eyes. Symphony, symposium! Symposium, symphony! Or sympathy? Sympathy for his poor head! Synchronism! What was he trying to work out?

Presently his thoughts clarified. Lavenders, violets, greens. They made a room charming; utterly, beautifully charming. Fresh, spring-like, feminine. Of course, feminine! A feminine bedroom! That explained the haunting fragrance of lavender. What other perfume was better associated with lavenders, violets and greens than sweet, lingering lavender? Even the pillow-cases smelled of lavender, and were tinted a delicate mauve. If ever a room were truly and completely feminine…

Consciousness returned with a rush. What was he doing in a woman's bed-sitting-room? His own room was ultra-masculine; untidy, bleak, reeking in hair-oil, and tobacco-smoke which no amount of fresh air could dispel. He blinked his eyes once or twice as he made an effort to focus the lavenders and the violets into something more tangible than an impressionist blur of matching colours. The composite picture became clearer: two pictures on the wall, landscapes both of them, one of lilac bushes, the other of a bank of violets. Naturally! A fireplace, with a flaming, crackling log fire. A lattice window, with drawn dimity curtains. Kate Greenaway! How many times had he seen the spit of this window in a Kate Greenaway picture? A dressing-table, with an alarming array of toilet flagons and pots. And, of course, a bottle of lavender water. A large bottle.

A reading-lamp beside the bed. A chair, upholstered with glazed chintz. And somebody sitting in it! A woman!

"Are you feeling better?"

Rabbit travelled the long, long distance from dreamland to reality. He couldn't see her too clearly; the mist in his eyes had not entirely dispersed; but what he could see embarrassed him. She belonged so essentially to the room he was in; dainty, fresh, spring-like, feminine. If she had not spoken he would have taken her to be an angel. But she had spoken, and her voice had been far too lovely to belong to a dream.

"Yes, thank you."

What he was doing lying on a bed, crumpling its fragile dainti-ness, he could not think, but obviously he had no right to be where he was. He tried to struggle to a sitting position.

"Please do not move," a distressed voice insisted. He felt a cool hand on his forehead, gently pressing his head back on to the pillow. He relaxed, but felt terrifically better; the hand seemed to have charmed away all the aches and pains in his head. And the mist in his eyes. And the intangible barrier obstructing his memory.

He felt particularly pleased about the disappearance of the mist in his eyes, for she was lovely to look at.

"Are you all right?" he croaked anxiously. "Did those men hurt you?"

"Thanks to you they did not."

He laughed, not because of what she had replied, but from an exuberant and irrepressible desire to laugh; he always laughed when he was happiest; it acted like a safety-valve, and thus he was enabled to retain a sense of proportion.

"You mustn't thank me, but Mrs. Taylor."

"Mrs. Taylor?"

"She lives at Wickford."

"Oh!" Wickford was half-a-mile distant from the scene of the attack, and two miles from Willingham. But Helena was unable to understand what connection Mrs. Taylor could have had with her rescue.

"She is a cripple. I visit her every Wednesday night to leave her some books——" He had a sudden, alarming thought.

"My bicycle——"

She smiled gratefully. "Is quite safe."

"And the books?"

"Were there only three?" He nodded. "They are still in your saddle-bag."

He was relieved; he couldn't afford to lose those three books; they were recent publications, and barely read. "I was on my way home after my visit to her," he continued. "Usually I return almost immediately, but it was her birthday, so she begged me to stay for a while and have a glass of port with her. I did. So you see, if Mrs. Taylor had not had a birthday today I should not have been cycling home at the time I was. I live at Bray-in-the-Marsh."

He was about to continue, but hastily checked himself, and grinned sheepishly. He had a nervous habit of chattering to cover his embarrassment.

"Then I am grateful to Mrs. Taylor for having a birthday today, but that does not lessen my gratitude to you, Mr.—Mr.——"

"Terhune," he supplied. For the second time he grinned nervously. "More commonly known among my friends as Tommy Terhune, but I was christened Theodore."

"Then why are you known as Tommy?"

"It's a long story."

"Please tell me."

He talked on: "You see, Mother and Father had been married for more than six years before there was any sign of their having a kiddie. They were both very disappointed, for they loved children and badly wanted some of their own. At last, however, Mother was able to give Father some good news. He was so overjoyed, he immediately announced that if the child should be a boy his name was to be Theodore. Theodore means 'the Gift of God'," he explained awkwardly.

Helena repressed a smile as she studied the man on the bed. In appearance he was less a Gift of God than any man she had met. In many ways he resembled an overgrown schoolboy—but a very studious schoolboy—for his hair was a light chestnut, and very tousled, while his expression was preoccupied, as though he were habitually engaged upon some abstruse problem. The intense seriousness of his face when in repose was relieved by his mouth, for its lines suggested that laughter was never far away from his lips. She was sure that he must possess a sense of humour. She was equally certain that he was of a retiring disposition. What she could not decide, to her own satisfaction, was his age. With one expression he looked in the early twenties; with the next, in the middle thirties.

"I still do not understand how Theodore has become Tommy."

"I told you it was a long story," he explained apologetically. "When the nurse showed me to Father she said: 'Here is Theodore, Mr. Terhune.' Father took one look at me and said grimly: 'His second name is to be Ichabod'."

Helena was startled. "Ichabod!"

"It means 'the Glory has Departed'," he told her ruefully. "I must have been an ugly, unromantic little devil."

She laughed, though she had tried not to. She laughed until the tears streamed from her eyes, and she was compelled to dab them away with her tiny handkerchief. Presently she realized whence her rabbit's sense of humour had come—from his father. She decided that she would like to meet his father; she was sure he would prove to be very nice.

"But still—Tommy——" she gasped.

"Father kept his word; he christened me Theodore Ichabod Terhune. Of course, for the first twenty years of my life I never let on to anyone what the 'I' stood for, but at school the boys quickly spotted the significance of my initials T.I.T. In other words, Tit, which immediately became Tom-Tit, because I was on the small side. From Tom-Tit to Tommy was, in schoolboy imagination, a mere stepping-stone, so Tommy I became, and Tommy I have been ever since. I must say I prefer Tommy to Theo." He coughed nervously. "I must get up. I am spoiling your—your lovely divan."

"Are you feeling better?"

"I think so."

"Then let me help you over to the chair near the fire."

His head began to swim again directly he stood upon his feet, but the sensation quickly passed, and his legs felt stronger than he had anticipated. He reached the chair without difficulty, and sat down. She pushed another chair to the other side of the fireplace and followed his example.

"I haven't thanked you for coming to my help, Mr. Terhune," she began.

He looked embarrassed. "Please do not thank me," he interrupted hastily. "I—I did nothing. In—in fact, I am not sure that I know what really happened. I remember hearing a cry for help, and seeing one or two men clustered round a car. Then I remember somebody aiming a blow at my head, but hitting my shoulder instead. After that everything is obscure, for the next thing that is clear to me was finding myself here."

Her voice was suspiciously choky. "The brutes! One of them must have knocked you unconscious when you were not looking. A policeman came along—we found you lying in the road——"

"Oh!" His expression became bleak. "Then I didn't do much to help?" he said flatly.

A quick gasp of reproach. "You must not say that. You fought gallantly, and kept the men at bay long enough for the policeman to arrive. Directly they saw his uniform they ran. But it was you who saved me in the first case." Her eyes shone. "You were splendid. You fought three of them at once. I saw you knock two of them over, one with your fists, the other by throwing yourself at his feet."

"I used to play Rugger for the first fifteen," he explained diffidently. "I have also done a spot of boxing in my time—as a lightweight!" he added, as if that fact were of consequence.

A puzzled light gathered in her eyes. Her rabbit did not look as though he had played for a school fifteen—though it was true that he had the figure of a speedy wing three-quarter. But, she thought, he looked far too meek to be an aggressive player, or a successful boxer—until she remembered the expression which the torchlight had revealed, just before he had leaped into action. There had been little in his face then to remind her of a rabbit.

"Why did the men attack you?" he continued, as if anxious to direct the conversation along a different course. He looked round the room. "Were they after money?"

She read his thoughts and smiled demurely. "I am the last person in the world they could have hoped to rob. I am only a secretary-companion—to Lady Kylstone. This is her house, and my name is Helena Armstrong," she added, suddenly realizing that probably he knew neither her name nor where he was.

"But your bedroom?" She nodded. "I knew it must be."

"Why?" she asked curiously.

"Because it breathes the same personality as yourself: it is you all over again. You were responsible for decorating and furnishing this room, weren't you?"

She flushed. "Yes. Lady Kylstone gave me *carte blanche*," she admitted unsteadily, thinking that her rabbit was really the most extraordinary man she had ever met; it seemed difficult to forecast what he was likely to say or do next.

"I knew it," he stated, with a self-satisfied nod of his head. "But returning to this attack upon you, if they were not after money, what were they after?"

"I don't know. I have been puzzled by the attack ever since it took place."

"How many men were there?"

"I counted five."

"Five! The—the cowards! Had you any goods in the car?"

"There was nothing whatever in the car."

He frowned in perplexity. "It seems pointless for five men to attack a lonely woman in a car unless they were after something or other. They must have known they were taking risks, fog or no fog, for the road to Willingham is quite a busy one as a general rule."

"They all wore blue mackintoshes and soft hats crushed down over their foreheads."

"Obviously they hoped to remain unrecognized. I know!" he exclaimed unexpectedly. "They must have mistaken you for some-body else, perhaps some woman whom they had reason to believe was wearing jewellery, or who had a lot of money in her bag. I suppose they could not have mistaken you for Lady Kylstone?"

She became excited. "They might have done; I was driving one of Lady Kylstone's cars, and they flashed a torch at the registration plate to make sure of the number." Then enthusiasm faded from her expression; she shook her head. "That theory does not hold water; in the first place Lady Kylstone has very little jewellery, because she is not fond of it; also she is noted for never carrying much money about with her; she never moves without her cheque-book, and gives cheques for almost everything she buys, even if it costs only ten shillings. As a girl she was robbed; ever since then she has been careful to see that she should not suffer twice. Besides," she continued, "I have just remembered something. When one of the men looked at the registration number he called out: 'It's the Armstrong girl all right, boys; go to it.'"

"Had the man seen your face before he said that?"

"No."

"He knew you were in the car just by recognizing the registration number?"

"Yes."

"Does Lady Kylstone use the same car?"

"Sometimes, but mostly she travels in her Daimler. Gibbons— her chauffeur—drives. But I use the small car quite often."

"Then the men could not have been certain that Lady Kylstone was not in the car—unless they had been tipped off, quite recently, that you were driving?"

"I suppose not," she agreed doubtfully.

"If they were so sure that you, and not Lady Kylstone, were driving the car, it was very definitely something of yours they wanted."

"But they could not have wanted anything of mine, Mr. Terhune," she denied in a perplexed voice. "I am sure that I possess nothing which five men would be willing to risk imprisonment to obtain. If I had, it certainly was not in the car. But I have not: I know I have not. I possess nothing, beyond some nice clothes, in the world."

He wanted to add, "and a face and figure for which most women would give a fortune". But he hadn't the courage. Besides, the circumstances scarcely warranted such a trite remark.

"Was there anything of Lady Kylstone's in the car?"

"I do not think so. Indeed, I am sure there was not."

He stroked the crown of his head, which was beginning to throb painfully. "How did they make you stop the car? Did one of them jump up on the running-board?"

"No. I was crawling along the road, with the spotlight fixed on the grass verge, when I was startled by a loud shout. Then I saw what I believed to be a light immediately in front of me. I was so startled that I jammed my foot on the brake harder than I ought to have done considering the greasy state of the road. I skidded in consequence. It was while I was trying to find out whereabouts I was after correcting the skid that the men closed in upon the car."

"And then?" he questioned eagerly.

"I screamed for help. One of them thrust his arms through the window and placed his beastly hand over my mouth. The brute! He had one of those horrible, oily voices, and his hands reeked with onions."

Terhune started. "Onions or garlic?"

"Garlic!" Helena reflected. "I believe you are right, but why do you ask?"

"Because I associate oily voices with garlic, and the two, in combination, with foreigners. Did the voice sound foreign?"

"Yes. Yes, it was a foreign voice," she admitted excitedly. "Why didn't I realize that before?"

"You have not yet had an opportunity of remembering your adventure very clearly."

"If he were a foreigner, then the attack upon me is all the more inexplicable. I have lived in England all my life."

"So have I."

A wistful expression clouded her eyes. For the time being she chose to forget about her adventure in the fog. "I have always wanted to travel. Have you?"

"No."

"Why not? Wouldn't you like to see other countries, and find out for yourself how other people live?"

"I have never given the matter thought."

She saw that the large blue eyes behind the horn-rimmed spectacles were intensely serious. "I am surprised to hear you say that; you gave me the impression of being a dreamer."

"So I am," he answered promptly. "But I am a very practical dreamer. I only allow myself one dream at a time, and concentrate upon trying to make it come true."

She leaned forward. "What is your present dream? Tell me about yourself."

He reddened. "I am a—a very ordinary person. I—I live at Bray-in-the-Marsh, as I have already told you. I have lived there for—for many years."

She had previously observed that he stammered very slightly whenever he was embarrassed. "Please do go on," she encouraged. "I am often in Bray, but I don't remember having seen you there."

"I—I keep the bookshop on the corner of Market Square and Station Road. I love books," he added enthusiastically, and there was a dignity in his voice which robbed his explanation of any suspicion of being a snobbish excuse.

"So do I."

"Do you?" His voice became warmer. "My bookshop is divided into three sections; a lending library, the sale of modern publications, and, best of all, the sale of antique and valuable books and first editions. That part of my business gives me both pleasure and sorrow."

"I know," she interrupted quickly. "Pleasure when handling beautiful books, sorrow when having to sell them again."

"You really do love books," he stated confidently. Then he continued: "I think that, on the whole, I get more pleasure than sorrow from the books. I would not change my job for any other in the world," he stated defiantly.

"Why should you?" Yet she wondered if lack of ambition was responsible for his obvious contentment. Even if he were in the middle thirties he was still too young to be satisfied with settling down for the remainder of his life as a bookseller in a small, quiet, out-of-the-way market town. If he were double her age that would be another matter… "What is your present dream?" she demanded abruptly.

She could see by his face that the question embarrassed him: what an open countenance her funny little rabbit had, she reflected; it mirrored his every emotion.

"Writing," he admitted at last.

She felt absurdly pleased with his reply. "Books, of course?"

"Yes."

"What kind? Poetry, history, a philosophical treatise?"

He shook his head, laughed shyly. "You rate my accomplishments too highly. I don't aspire to anything more ambitious than—than detective stories."

She giggled. Her rabbit writing detective stories! Really, he was incomprehensible; he was always being something different from what one expected. If he had told her he was engaged on *The Golden Age of Roman Literature*, *The Evolution of Bookbinding*, *The Travels of Burckhardt*, or even *Thoughts and Reflections of a Rustic Bookseller*, he would not have surprised her; his studious features prompted one to believe that he probably could speak at length upon any subject from Algebraic Equations to *Zittel's Palaeontology*. But to think of his writing stories which dealt with crime, violent death, and hazardous adventure was too fantastic…

"What do you know of crime and detection?"

"Almost everything—at second hand," he replied simply. "I have read practically every book published which deals with one or another aspect of crime: all Captain Arthur Griffiths' works, Hargrave Adam's *Police Encyclopaedia*, Moylan's *Scotland Yard*, H. B. Irving's *Studies in Criminology*, all the books in the Notable British Trials series, and hundreds of other books dealing with crime, punishment, and law. To say nothing of fiction," he continued boyishly. "I know my Sherlock Holmes by heart, and my Doctor Thorndyke, my Lord Peter Wimsey, and a host of others."

"Have you published any stories?"

"I have had three published in the *Saturday Evening Post*," he whispered reverently.

"So now you dream of writing a novel?"

"I have already started one. As soon as I am an established writer I shall permit myself to dream of other things—perhaps of travelling abroad—but not before."

The quiet determination and unassuming confidence in his voice impressed her. Apparently there was no possibility in his mind that he might not become established. Before she could make any comment he rose to his feet.

"I must go," he murmured apologetically. "I have already kept you too long. Can you—you tell me where my bicycle is, Miss Armstrong?"

"The policeman tied it on to the luggage grid; it is still there. But you are certainly not going to cycle home. I am going to take you there in the car."

"Please, no! I am very, very grateful to you for your offer, but I could not permit of your being out in this fog."

"But your injury——"

"Is nothing," he lied cheerfully. "It is not safe for any car to be out in such a thick fog. I shall walk home. I am very fond of walking, and the exercise will loosen up my muscles. They are flabbier than I thought."

There was reason in his argument, but she protested vigorously. He remained adamant, so presently, surprised by his obstinacy, she acknowledged defeat. They exchanged mutual thanks, and said good-bye at the door of the garage. But as he stood ready to leave he said hesitatingly: "If you find out anything more about the attack upon you tonight, Miss Armstrong, I should be very grateful if you could have me informed; the mystery has excited my curiosity."

"I will let you know," she promised.

III

Terhune's home was the four rooms and small kitchen which comprised the upper floor above the bookshop. Here he lived a bachelor existence, attended during the day by Mrs. Mann. Mrs. Mann was a large woman; she had a large family, and a small husband who had a small income. This income she augmented by looking after Terhune. He used one room as a bedroom, one as a private library-sitting room, the third for receiving guests—this was rarely used, and was the only tidy room in the building. The fourth room was a small dining-room.

It was the library to which he carried his bread, cheese and beer supper upon returning from Willingham. Although the dining-room adjoined the kitchen, most cold meals he ate in his sitting-room, for there, surrounded by his beloved books, he was happiest. All four walls were lined with books; he had a desk there, littered with papers, a battered old armchair not to be matched for comfort, a collapsible table for his typewriter (or his meals), a radio, and a fireplace. What more could any bachelor want? There was deep abiding peace in that room; there, inside it, one could escape from the outside world and its problems, and live in another world of books, or a world of dreams, whichever one chose. So, on most nights, as soon as the premises downstairs had been closed, Terhune retired to his library, and there read or wrote until bedtime, with an interval for supper, which he carried in on a tray, and ate, still reading, his book propped up in front of him, usually against the beer bottle.

This routine he attempted to follow after his unusual adventure in the fog. To a point he succeeded. He lighted the fire in the study, prepared his supper on a tray, carried it in, sat down, propped up a novel before him, and began his meal. He ate heartily, for the walk home had given his appetite a sharp edge, but it was not long before he found his attention wandering from the book. The previous evening he had found the story particularly interesting—even tantalizing, for it was a problem of detection—but now the plot had lost its savour; it paled into insignificance when compared with the mystery of the attack upon Helena Armstrong.

He gazed into the heart of the fire, which was burning cheerfully, and reflected upon the possible and probable causes of the attack upon Lady Kylstone's attractive young secretary. In view of Helena's reiterated denials that the car contained anything of value, or, indeed, anything which might tempt five men to risk imprisonment, the likeliest explanation of the attack was that the men had stopped the wrong car by mistake. Unfortunately, Helena's evidence failed to substantiate this theory. Unless excitement had made her imagination run riot, not only had the attackers taken the precaution of verifying the car's registration number, but they had even mentioned her by name. "It's the Armstrong girl all right, boys; go to it." What could be plainer evidence than that Helena was the intended victim? Had the men referred to her as the Armstrong *woman* one might have suspected a confusion of identities. But no! They had (if Helena were to be believed—and he did believe her) entitled her the Armstrong *girl*; proof enough, to his mind, that the hold-up had been carefully planned, and that Helena had been kept under surveillance.

He frowned his perplexity. If it were admitted that care had been taken in the preliminary stages, it was difficult to believe that the men would have risked wasting all their spadework by mis-timing the hold-up. On the assumption that no mistake had been made, what was their object in holding up Helena's car? Was it Helena herself, the men wanted? If Helena had been Lady Kylstone then the answer might well have been that the attack was staged for the purpose of kidnapping Lady Kylstone, for Sir Piers Kylstone's widow was a rich woman: not only had she inherited more than a million pounds sterling from her late husband, but also twice that amount, in dollars, from her father, John Stillman Cruickshank, of Chicago, U.S.A. At least, so said the social columns of the daily press. But Helena was not Lady Kylstone: Helena was just Helena, private secretary with a salary. Nobody could truthfully say that she would make a good subject for ransom.

Another possibility occurred to him. Perhaps the car was what the men had been after. Perhaps the attack on Helena was not the principal crime but merely an accessory, as it were. Being Lady Kylstone's car, and therefore known to others as her car, it might be required as a necessary adjunct for a more important plan than the mere holding-up of a very nice, but rather unimportant, person. The theory was a fascinating one, and appealed to him as a good frame around which to build the skeleton of a fiction plot. But though Terhune dreamed of writing readable detective fiction, he possessed an extremely practical outlook; he believed in rendering unto fiction the extravagant fancies which belonged to fiction, and to everyday life the dull, uninteresting facts of life.

Lady Kylstone's car was a very ordinary car; Lady Kylstone was an ordinary person (so he had been told), while the neighbourhood which surrounded Willingham, Wickford and Bray-in-the-Marsh was ordinary, prosaic Kent countryside, where births, marriages and deaths were matters of importance to everyone living within the radius of the neighbourhood. To associate such rural surroundings with a complicated sequence of criminal activities was a fancy to be rendered unto the realm of fiction, so he bothered no more with it because he was dealing with facts.

What were the plain, unvarnished facts? he asked himself. Helena Armstrong had been travelling home to Willingham from a visit to Ashford (why had she visited Ashford?). The car had been stopped by five men (adequately disguised by mackintoshes with upturned collars, and hats crushed well down over the forehead) for some obviously specific, but unknown, purpose. Helena had testified that there had been nothing whatever in the car to justify the hold-up—no goods, no money, no papers (but surely she must have had some sort of handbag with her?). Available evidence seemed to prove that the men had not held up the wrong car, and that they must have had some very good (or bad!) reason for their actions. There had been something in the car. But what?

These were the facts, and they set a pretty problem for some policeman to solve. Whither would investigations lead? It was annoying to think that probably he would never hear. Unless he dared, later, to get into communication with Helena. Having been in at the beginning it would be interesting to follow the affair through to the end, he thought.

One reflection prompted another. He knew that there was fascination in unravelling imaginary crime—how, otherwise, was one to account for the millions of armchair detectives? Perhaps there was also some fascination in trying to solve a real crime, even if it were a case of five per cent fascination to ninety-five per cent hard work. There must be, he decided, for now that he was faced with a series of trifling but unexplainable facts, he realized that he would give much for the opportunity of following up the strange business to see whither it led. To make a complete picture from pieces of a jig-saw puzzle was fascinating; to work out the correct answer to a complicated arithmetical sum was fascinating (except to young students, perhaps!); to invent a new substance was fascinating; to complete a crossword puzzle was fascinating. To make sense out of nonsense was fascinating. Was it not natural, therefore, to wish for the opportunity of discovering why—and what…

He shrugged his shoulders regretfully. He had played his part in the drama. Now it was the turn of somebody else to hold the stage. What was the use of repining about what could not be? So thinking, he returned to his novel.

I V

Just after nine-thirty the following morning Terhune was overjoyed to see—of all people!—Helena Armstrong enter his shop. He hastily advanced to meet her, and was rewarded by a dazzling smile.

"Good morning, Mr. Terhune. I had to come in to Bray to buy some bulbs in the market—bulbs are Lady Kylstone's hobby—so I thought I would take the opportunity of calling in to learn whether you arrived home safely last night, and how your head is." She spoke breathlessly, as though embarrassed. "Does it ache?"

"Not in the slightest. I feel fine; all the better for a slice of adventure. And you, Miss Armstrong?"

"I, too, am all right except for being somewhat tired. I did not sleep for some time after going to bed. I am afraid I was too busy thinking."

"Of the attack?"

"Yes. I tried to imagine what reason there could be to account for those men stopping my car, but I failed utterly. The more I reflected the more senseless everything became. I am beginning to think they must have escaped from a lunatic asylum."

He shook his head. "If there had been only one or two men I might agree with you. But not five. I don't know much about lunatics, but I very much doubt whether you would get five lunatics to agree upon any one course of action. Besides, the papers would be full of such an escape, had there been one."

"Then what on earth did they want from me?"

"You have remembered nothing new?"

"Nothing."

"When you entered the car this morning did you find anything in it which the men might have wanted to obtain?"

"No. As a matter of fact I made a special search in case I had overlooked or forgotten something, but all that I found were a set of tools, a pump, and a jack."

He remembered a thought of the night before. "By the way, there was something I wanted to ask you. Did you have a handbag in the car with you?"

"Can you imagine a woman going anywhere without a hand-bag?" She pointed to a bag which she had tucked under her left arm, "Here it is——"

Her abrupt pause made him glance quickly at her face; he saw by her expression that something had startled her.

"What is the matter?"

"I have just remembered something. While Soft Voice was grabbing me in his horrible oniony hands, and you were fighting three of the other men, the fifth was groping about on the seat next to me, and on the floor by my feet."

Terhune's serious eyes gleamed with interest. "Does a woman normally keep her handbag on the seat next to her when she is driving?"

"I think so, but I never do. I have a habit of keeping it behind me in the small of my back—I like the feel of something solid there. But they couldn't have wanted my bag; the idea is really too ridiculous."

"Why?"

"There is positively nothing in it to interest anyone but myself." Her eyes laughed as she offered the bag to him. "You can see for yourself, Mr. Detective. I haven't opened it since I left Ashford to return to Willingham."

He refused to accept the bag from her. "I would rather not."

"Silly! Why not? There is nothing in it which I have reason to hide. Please take it: remember, I am just as interested as you in discovering the reason for last night's queer happening."

This time he took the bag from her, and having cleared a convenient space for its contents, he began to extract them. First, a dainty lace-bordered square of cambric, smelling faintly of lavender. Next, a purse. He hesitated.

"Open it," she ordered. "A detective must be thorough to be efficient."

There was no sting in her words, so he opened the purse. Inside were fourteen coins: a half-a-crown, two florins, three sixpenny pieces, four pennies, one halfpenny, and three farthings. Nothing else.

Her eyes twinkled. "Not a great fortune when divided among five men," she pointed out.

He continued his examination: a small fountain pen—propelling pencil combination, cigarette-case, packet of book matches, compact, lipstick, driving licence.

He was disappointed. "There is nothing here," he muttered.

"What did you expect to find in a handbag likely to tempt five men to hold up a defenceless woman?"

"I don't know," he confessed. "I suppose that, at the back of my mind, was the thought that perhaps you carried a paper which they were after."

"A paper?"

He grinned foolishly. "I have been reading too many of Dennis Wheatley's books lately. But what I should like to know is this: was it a coincidence that fog enabled the men to hold you up, or did they take advantage of the fog to carry out a previously prepared plan?"

"Why would you like to know that?"

"For this reason: if it were merely coincidence that fog helped them, if they had made their plans to hold you up last night particularly, then they must have reason for believing that only last night would you have had in your possession whatever it was they were after. But if they had been awaiting a convenient opportunity, such as a foggy, or an extra dark, night, then one may assume that you always have with you the object they wanted."

"But I neither had, nor have, any object, as you call it, which anyone else could possibly want," she denied with exasperation.

"I still think they were all lunatics, so don't let us talk any more about the silly business." She glanced pointedly at the book-shelves which surrounded them. "I was hoping you would show me some of your books."

The suggestion met with his entire approval. "Give me a moment to replace these things in your bag." He picked up the cigarette-case from the table on which he had spread the contents of her bag, and let it slide into the large pocket from which he had taken it. He heard a slight clinking noise, which surprised him, for presumably the bag was empty. He picked out the case again and looked inside. There was nothing to be seen.

She saw him frown with perplexity. "What is the matter?" When he told her she laughed. "The case must have fallen on a key that has worked its way beneath the lining. For weeks now I have been meaning to free it and mend the hole, but every time I have picked up my needle for other work I have forgotten the bag."

"A key of what?" he questioned sharply.

"I do not know. It belongs to Lady Kylstone. She asked me to take care of it for her."

"Tell me what she said."

The glance which she bestowed upon him was quizzical; she was not at all sure that she appreciated his barking at her in the manner of counsel examining a witness. But when she scrutinized his face she relented; he appeared to be awaiting her reply with such intense eagerness that she became infected with his excitement.

"Some time ago Lady Kylstone asked me if I were a careful young woman with my personal belongings, and whether I was in the habit of losing things, or leaving them about where they might get lost. I told her that I was usually very careful not to lose anything, whereupon she passed over a key to me and said: 'Will you keep this key for me, my dear? I want you to take very great care of it. Keep it until I ask for its return, unless anything should happen to me. If that should happen, take the key to Ashford and give it personally to Mr. Howard.'"

"Mr. Howard?"

"The principal partner in the firm of solicitors who look after Lady Kylstone's affairs."

"Is that all you know about the key?"

She nodded. "That is all I was told. I decided to keep the key in my handbag for safety. One day I discovered that it had worked its way through a hole in the lining. There it has been ever since. As a matter of fact, at first I was more careless about mending the hole than I might otherwise have been because it seemed to me the key was even safer under the lining than above. Then I forgot about it until you mentioned the clinking noise." Her voice became husky with excitement. "Do you think those men were after the key?"

Before he could reply to her question he was interrupted by the arrival of a smartly dressed woman. "Excuse me," he murmured to Helena. He turned to the newcomer. "Good morning, Mrs. Lawrence," he welcomed. "Did you enjoy *I Bought a Mountain*?"

"So much so that I felt quite sad about reaching the last page. But there, I enjoy *all* the books that *you* recommend, Mr. Terhune. I tell everybody that you have the best taste in books of anyone I have met."

"It is nice of you to say so."

"What have you put aside for me today?"

"The latest Philip Gibbs."

"Oh! That is *sweet* of you," Mrs. Lawrence gushed, as he passed the book to her. "I love his books. But I must try not to read this one too quickly, otherwise I shall be compelled to pay a second visit to Bray today, just to borrow another book." She glanced sourly at Helena. "I must not keep you now, must I, Mr. Terhune? I know how busy you always are on market days. But you will probably see me tomorrow."

Helena watched Mrs. Lawrence sailing out of the shop. "A widow?" she questioned shortly.

"Yes. Do you know her?"

"I do not, and I do not want to, particularly."

"Then how did you guess that she was a widow?"

"You are not the only amateur detective, Mr. Terhune." Her voice became warm again. "Do you think it was the key?" she asked again, eagerly.

The interruption had restored him to a more balanced state of mind; contact with the normal routine of a day's work had forced him to realize that he had been on the verge of allowing his imagination, and his passion for dramatic fiction, to affect normal, prosaic reasoning. It was easy to base a thrilling story on the episode of the key—but probably very foolish to do so. No doubt there was an entirely commonplace explanation of Lady Kylstone's request.

"I should not have thought it necessary for five men to stage a hold-up just to obtain a key from your bag," he replied cautiously. "A pickpocket could have robbed you of it far more easily, and certainly less openly."

"I suppose so," she agreed dubiously.

"Have you mentioned the attack upon you to Lady Kylstone?"

"No."

"I think you should do so, in case it had something to do with the key."

She nodded her head in agreement. "I will do so at luncheon." She saw two more people entering the shop, books under their arms. "I must go now," she added hastily, holding out her hand. "Good-bye, Mr. Terhune, and thank you."

V

Some hours later, when he was about to close the shop for the luncheon hour, the telephone bell rang. He lifted the receiver. "Hullo?"

"Is that Mr. Terhune?" The voice was rich, musical, American.

"Yes."

"This is Lady Kylstone speaking, Mr. Terhune. Helena has just told me of the extraordinary affair which took place last night when you rescued her from five hold-up men."

"I did very little——"

"Don't interrupt, young man. I dislike false modesty. I believe Helena's version of what happened, so I am not anxious to hear another."

"Very well, Lady Kylstone."

"Now, listen to me, young man. Helena has described you to me as a bright, intelligent person—stop pulling my sleeve, you are distracting my attention—those words were not addressed to you, Mr. Terhune, but to Helena, as you may have guessed. To continue: I distrust the opinion of young women where men are concerned, and should like an opportunity of meeting you, to judge your character for myself. If you are not otherwise engaged, would you care to dine with two lonely women tonight?"

The request confused him in its unexpectedness; he found himself at a loss for words.

"Well, well, young man, have you a tongue in your head, or haven't you?"

"Yes, Lady Kylstone."

"Then why don't you answer? If the prospect dismays you——"

"I shall gladly come," he interrupted hastily.

"That is better. I like quick decisions. We shall expect you at seven o'clock promptly, for sherry. Do you prefer dry or sweet wines?"

"Dry."

"As I expected. It is only silly women like Helena and myself who prefer sweet wines. You will come in your ordinary clothes——"

He chuckled.

"Why are you laughing?"

He raised his eyebrows. Evidently Lady Kylstone had sharp ears. "I have no evening clothes, Lady Kylstone."

"Why should you?" she snapped. "Evening clothes make all men look alike. I like to meet individuals, not tailors' dummies. One more thing, Mr. Terhune. Is it true that you are a judge of a readable book?"

"I believe so."

"Then bring me one that I shall enjoy. If your choice is a bad one I shall never ask you to my house again."

"What type of book shall I select, Lady Kylstone?"

It was her turn to chuckle. "Let that be a test of the intelligence Helena swears you possess, Mr. Terhune. You have heard me talk to you over the telephone; now see if you guess, from my manner, my taste in literature. Seven o'clock sharp, Mr. Terhune. I dislike unpunctuality. Good morning."

VI

Terhune replaced the receiver in a daze, then went upstairs to eat the lunch which Mrs. Mann had prepared for him, feeling that the world had become, suddenly, a most extraordinary place. Twenty-four hours ago he would have scoffed at the suggestion that so many strange things could have happened to him in so short a time. Even now he found it difficult to believe that he was not a character from an E. Phillips Oppenheim novel. But the fact remained that within eighteen hours he had been involved in a peculiar holdup, met a charming girl, been exceedingly tantalized by the singular details of what appeared to be an unusual mystery, and lastly, had been invited to dine with Lady Kylstone, one of the recognized (though passive) leaders of local society. And all these things had happened to one Theodore Ichabod Terhune, a very ordinary member of a rustic community!

For years he had lived at Bray-in-the-Marsh. In that time nothing more exciting than the annual visit of Sanger's Circus had happened, either to Bray or to him personally; the only two pretty girls he had met had quickly become engaged to local bloods; his sole contact with 'Society' had been in selling books to Sir George Brereton (he had a standing order to buy on Sir George's behalf every published book on fly-fishing, old or new), the Hon. Mrs. MacMunn (all first editions of Michael Arlen and Ethel Mannin) and Mr. Justice Pemberton (four detective novels per week—these, of course, from the lending library). For years—nothing! And now, within eighteen hours—everything! At least, enough to go on with.

For once, Terhune did not read while he ate: he was too preoccupied with the reason for Lady Kylstone's invitation. That it was connected with the attack upon Helena Armstrong was apparent. It seemed as though she wanted to discuss the affair with him. But why? Had he, by accident, stumbled upon a domestic secret? Was the key, in fact, that which unlocked the cupboard containing the family skeleton? And would Lady Kylstone, in consequence, ask him to maintain a discreet silence, or request him to forget all that had happened? This was a likely theory, yet, he believed, improbable. Lady Kylstone's voice had sounded pleasantly warm; the voice of an individualist whom one might grow to like. It had been nice of her to ascertain his taste in wines, for instance.

What kind of book would she appreciate? was his next thought. A light romance? Possibly. Her warm voice suggested a warm nature; a nature to whom deep, affectionate love would be normal and natural. But the romance would need to be neither syrupy nor sexual. He had a feeling that she would be contemptuous and intolerant of a romance based upon the complex emotions of the so-called 'smart set'. From the little he had heard of her, simplicity was the keynote of her character. At the same time the romance would have to be well-written, a sound piece of literature. Would she like a Priestley title? He nodded his head in answer to his own question. She would surely like Priestley's books. But had she read them all? In all probability she had. What of C. S. Forester?

Then Terhune had a brilliant idea. A few days previously he had purchased a small library from a man who was sailing for India. Among the volumes taken over had been a copy of Housman's *A Shropshire Lad*, bound exquisitely in tooled calf. That, he believed, might appeal to her, both for its contents and its binding. He had many times seen her house when passing by; though not large, it was architecturally handsome, and beautifully kept; the home, in fact, of a person of taste. The longer he considered the suggestion the more he felt encouraged to take her Housman's book. And—an afterthought!—the latest C. S. Forester.

Having made his decision, his thoughts reverted to the key. The suggestion that the key had been the object of the hold-up was incredible, for the reasons he had already given to Helena. Five men to secure one little key! Fantastic! Yet it was strange, Lady Kylstone's wanting to meet him, unless the key had some connection with the affair. His conviction that the key was of significance grew, and would not be dislodged.

Having estimated that it would take him forty minutes to reach 'Timberlands', as Lady Kylstone's home was picturesquely and justifiably named (there were twenty acres of woodland behind it), Terhune left Market Square precisely at six-twenty. To his surprise, he reached his destination ten minutes before time, and came to the conclusion that eagerness had made him pedal faster than usual.

In view of his hostess's regard for punctuality he decided to ride on as far as the cross-roads and return. This he did. As he rang the bell a clock on the far side of the door melodiously struck the hour of seven. He grinned, and hoped that Lady Kylstone had noted the fact.

Briggs opened the door. Terhune knew Briggs well; the old man was a cracksman-adventurer fan; he had read every 'Saint' book not once but several times; Bulldog Drummond also; with *The Lone Wolf*, *The Grey Seal*, and *Lemmy Caution* in close rivalry for third place.

"Good evening, sir. Her ladyship is waiting for you in the drawing-room."

"My bicycle, Briggs———"

A wisp of a smile disturbed Briggs's austere face as he took Terhune's coat and hat. "I will put it in the garage, sir." The smile faded as he opened the door of the drawing-room. "Mr. Terhune," he announced quietly.

As Terhune crossed towards the fireplace, where Lady Kylstone and Helena sat, one on each side, he was surprised to see that his hostess was utterly different from his mental portrait of her. That picture featured an elderly lady, white-haired, sharp-featured but kindly-eyed, dressed in unostentatious clothes of good quality. In not one respect did his likeness hold good. Lady Kylstone was moderately tall; she had an enviably straight back, her hair was only sprinkled with grey, and was beautifully dressed. Her clothes were fashionable and expensive, but in keeping with her age, which he now placed at fifty (thus under-estimating by more than four years). Her face was expressive, alert, and full of character.

While he shyly greeted her she frankly inspected him.

"Humph! You are not so young as Helena said, are you? I put your age at twenty-nine. Am I right?"

"You flatter me by two years, Lady Kylstone."

"Do I? Then I cannot grumble at a young girl for not knowing better."

"I said that I could not guess Mr. Terhune's age," Helena protested.

"I know you did, my girl, but the manner in which you spoke about him convinced me that you thought him to be about twenty-five. Am I right?"

Helena nodded.

"I thought so. Now, Mr. Terhune, make yourself useful. I dislike being interrupted by servants coming in and out of the room, so you can serve Helena and me to a glass of Solera, and yourself to the Manzanilla."

This he did, whereupon Lady Kylstone continued: "Now draw up a chair between us—no, no, not that one. That is a woman's chair. I like to see a man in a big chair, into which he can disappear and be comfortable."

When he was settled, Lady Kylstone raised her glass. "Welcome to Timberlands, Mr. Terhune." The three people sipped their sherry. "Before we talk, show me the book you have brought me."

"I have brought two."

Her eyes twinkled. "You were hedging, in case your first choice misfired?" she accused.

"I am afraid so."

"There is no need to be afraid of hedging," she snapped. "Every intelligent person hedges. Where is your first choice?"

He passed *A Shropshire Lad* to his hostess. Her eyes warmed as her fingers caressed the rich scarlet leather; she opened the pages at random and read out:

> "And since to look at things in bloom
> Fifty springs are little room,
> About the woodlands I will go
> To see the cherry hung with snow."

She gently closed the book and laid it down upon an occasional table beside her.

"Young man, what prompted your choice of books?"

He told her of his reasoning. When he stopped speaking she nodded her head, pleased.

"Well thought out. You have brains. Some people would reprove you for wasting them by keeping that bookshop of yours in a small, backward country town, but I do not. You are happy, are you not?"

"Very."

"To be happy and contented is the principal recompense in life. Remember that, and do not allow yourself to be weaned away from any course of action which keeps you happy—unless, by so doing, you are causing unhappiness to others. I am like you. I live where I am happiest. I am a rich woman. I could travel to any part of the world I might wish to visit; live in any other country I might prefer. I could reside in a huge mansion, or in a fashionable town house or in both; I could surround myself with a score of servants if I desired. But the things in life which make me happiest are the simple, the good and the beautiful, as you cleverly guessed. That is why I continue to live here in Timberlands. I wouldn't change places with any other woman in the world." She changed the conversation abruptly. "As a man capable of intelligent reasoning, what do you make of the attack on Helena?"

"I can make no reason out of it."

"Why not?"

He repeated the gist of his deductions, which he had discussed with Helena.

"Then you think those men were really after that key of mine?"

"It is the only article in the car which could account for Miss Armstrong's being held up, but as I have explained to you, Lady Kylstone, why five men should have taken the trouble and risk of holding up a car to secure a key when one man might have done so with far more success is a question to which it is not easy to supply the answer." He paused. "May I ask you a question, Lady Kylstone?"

"That is why I asked you here tonight," she replied enigmatically.

"Are there any other people, besides yourself and Miss Armstrong, who knew that Miss Armstrong was carrying that key around with her?"

"For goodness' sake do not keep on calling her Miss Armstrong. Her name is Helena; as you may soon be seeing her quite often you might as well get on friendly terms with her as soon as possible. Are you really as old-fashioned as you look?"

Terhune grinned in embarrassment; what his hostess meant by her reference to his seeing Helena quite often was beyond his understanding, but in the meantime he had a feeling that Helena herself should be consulted on such a personal matter. He turned to her.

"With your permission——"

She nodded. He noticed that her cheeks were pinker than their proximity to the fire warranted.

"Tsch!" Lady Kylstone exclaimed testily. "What were you asking? Whether anyone else knew that Helena had that key? Yes. Howard—my solicitor—knew. Why do you ask?"

"It might be interesting to know how, if the key were what those five men wanted, they knew that Miss—that Helena—carried it about with her."

"I have told nobody save Howard; and that old wind-bag is like Caesar's wife, above suspicion. Have you told anyone, Helena?"

"Not a soul."

"Then there is your answer, young man. In the meantime you have not yet ascertained what door that key unlocks, nor my reason for asking Helena to take charge of it. No doubt you have built up a pretty little mystery story of that request of mine."

"I—I did think it was—was strange."

"Whereas it was really nothing of the sort, young man. The key which Helena has been carrying about in her bag unlocks nothing more romantic than the door of the Kylstone family burial vault in the Willingham church cemetery." She laughed upon seeing the expression on his face. "Do you find that news disappointing? If so, you will find the explanation as to why I gave it to her equally depressing. Among my many dislikes is that of anything suggesting the macabre. Guarding the key of the vault in which my remains may one day be kept has always, to me, seemed gruesome. I refused to keep the keys in my possession—originally there were two—so I gave one to my sister-in-law to keep for me, the other to my brother, who lived on the other side of Ashford.

"I should have known better than to have given anything to my sister-in-law for safe keeping. She is thoroughly careless and completely irresponsible. She lost the first key within three months of my having given it to her. I had a second key cut. Twelve months ago she lost that, too, so I refused to give her a third, Fortunately, my brother is a more careful person. He kept the key safely for many years, he, like the rest of my family, having settled in your country. A few months ago he developed a sudden desire to visit his own country again, so back he went, and there is no knowing how long he may remain there. He may return to England next week, he may never come back. He is like that, and I love him because he is.

"Before he left, Wesley—my brother—visited Timberlands and returned the key of the vault to me. I refused positively to keep it in my possession even overnight. As soon as Wesley had left for London I passed the key on to Helena, and asked her to take charge of it. And that, young man, is the story of the key."

"Does your brother know that Helena has the key?"

Lady Kylstone glanced sharply at her guest. "Your brain works quickly. He does: I realized that fact as I spoke. But Wesley is in the States."

"Why did you not send the key to Mr. Howard, Lady Kylstone?"

She laughed drily. "So! You are becoming an amateur detective?"

He reddened. "I——I apologize, Lady Kylstone. In my interest I was forgetting——"

"Nonsense! I have already said that I welcome your questions. Why did I not send the key to Howard? Because of your funny English traditions. Generations ago the first Kirtlyngton was knighted on the field of battle, at Agincourt, on the twenty-fifth of October, fourteen-fifteen. On returning to this country, Sir Piers Kirtlyngton purchased lands here with his share of the booty—the ransom money of a French noble—and settled down in this country for the rest of his life. On his deathbed, Sir Piers charged that a vault should be built in the churchyard for his remains and those of his descendants. He further instructed his heir, and all future heirs of the family, that, on every anniversary of the battle which had brought fortune and nobility to the family, the vault should be opened and garlands of flowers hung within. To ensure the fulfilment of his instructions Sir Piers laid a dire and dreadful curse upon any descendant who failed to carry out this obligation.

"If family records are to be believed, the four generations following Sir Piers faithfully decorated the vault on each twenty-fifth of October. The sixth Piers defied the curse. In consequence, he lost his head on the scaffold. This summary fate quickly brought the family to heel. For the next seventy-five years the ceremony of decorating the vault was faithfully carried out, and the family flourished and prospered. Then a second daring descendant chose to disregard the instructions of the old martinet. Another Piers Kyrlston (as the family name had, by then, become) died a particularly unpleasant death at the hands of the Spanish Inquisitors. Since then the twenty-fifth of October has been strictly observed according to tradition. You will understand why I chose to have somebody local take care of the key for me. If I had sent the key to Howard each year I should have had to write at least six letters, and fill in a dozen receipts and whatnots to obtain temporary possession of the key. You are lucky, young man, not to have dealings with that fusspot firm."

"Why haven't you changed your solicitors?"

Lady Kylstone's eyes twinkled. "About two hundred years ago the then Sir Piers appointed the then Mr. Howard to be his attorney. One would be asking too much of the Kylstone family in suggesting a break with tradition by changing their legal advisers."

For some minutes there was complete silence in the room. Fascinated by the story he had just heard, Terhune stared at the fire; and a series of pictures passed quickly through his mind; he saw the first Sir Piers kneeling before Henry V, to receive the cherished accolade of knighthood; the sixth Sir Piers, also kneeling, to receive not honour but oblivion; not the flat blade of the steel, but the sharp edge; another Sir Piers twisting in agony as the hooded Inquisitors slowly turned the wheel of the rack...

Colourful pictures, but what bearing had they on the strange event which had brought him to Timberlands? The sharp flame of interest in his eyes died away. One fact seemed to stand out clearly; whatever it was the five men wanted of Helena, the key of the Kylstone family vault could not be it.

He said as much to his hostess, but to his surprise she shook her head.

"But for something which happened some days back I should have agreed with you. Now I am not so sure. Five days ago Briggs came to me with an extraordinary story. The previous afternoon— his afternoon off—he had cycled over to Ditchley to visit his daughter. On his way home, about ten-thirty p.m., as he was passing the church, he thought he heard the sound of voices. Instead of cycling on as quickly as he could, which I know I should have done, he stopped his bicycle and listened. For a time he heard nothing more, so he was on the point of continuing his journey, thinking his imagination had tricked him, when he again heard a voice. He got off his bicycle and crept along the side of the hedge to investigate.

"The night was very dark, and he neither saw nor heard anything further until he had reached a point at the back of the church, overlooking the graveyard. There, through a gap in the hedge, he saw a small round light moving up and down. This time he would have run away but for the fact that he heard somebody mutter a particularly rude swear word. Being convinced that ghosts do not swear, he remained where he was, to realize, the next moment, that the light he had seen was that of an electric torch, and the voices those of men examining the door of the Kylstone family vault!"

In his excitement Terhune very nearly knocked over his glass of sherry. "Were they—were they trying to open it?" he stammered, and nervously drank what remained of the Manzanilla.

"It is impossible to say. Briggs was so startled by what he saw that he stepped back a pace, and tripped over a dead branch. Naturally, he made enough noise to awaken the dead. As he picked himself up he heard the noise of running feet, followed by that of an automobile engine being started up. Then he heard the car disappearing in the distance. He had startled the intruders into flight.

"The story Briggs told me naturally aroused my curiosity, but I instructed him to say nothing to anyone about what had happened. Later on I drove to the church and examined the door of the vault. I found nothing of any consequence."

"You did not tell me," Helena remonstrated.

"I did not tell anyone, child. I did not treat the affair seriously— until you told me what had happened to you last night."

"What can it mean, Lady Kylstone?"

"That is what I am beginning to wonder."

"Had any attempt been made to force open the vault door?" Terhune asked.

"I saw no marks, but it is quite possible that Briggs arrived in time to prevent any attempt. In any event, I imagine that the vault door is capable of withstanding any brute force other than a charge of high explosive. I might add that the upper part of the vault, and the door, are recent—as your English history goes," Lady Kylstone added drily. "That is to say, about one hundred years old. In those days builders used good materials and good workmanship."

"Then the men were after the vault key?"

She nodded. "It would seem so. Examination had shown them that the door could not be forced, so they—whoever *they* may be—made plans for robbing Helena of the key."

"Why should anyone wish to enter the vault?"

"Ah! Now you are indeed piloting your craft through uncharted waters. I can think of no reason why anyone should wish voluntarily to enter the vault. It is an extremely depressing place. If it were not for the sake of tradition I should refuse positively to go down there until I have to be carried."

Helena shivered. "Please don't talk like that, Lady Kylstone."

"Do I make you feel sad, child? Ah, well! The older one becomes the less frightening is the prospect of death. Particularly when one has led a happy life."

"Lady Kylstone," Terhune asked abruptly, "are you going to inform the police of the attempt to break into the vault, and the attack on Helena?"

"What proof have I that they were trying to break into the vault? Or that the vault key was the object of the attack?"

"The two episodes correlate too perfectly for that solution not to be the most probable."

"To us, maybe, because the three of us here are romantics—yes, young man, behind that serious face and that unambitious nature of yours I detect the romantic: as for me, I am incurably so. It is easy for us to dramatize what has happened, but what is the first question which the police would put? The one you have already asked: why should anyone wish to enter the vault? What would be their reaction upon learning that the only things to be found in the vault are old bones, a rheumatics-provoking chill, and tradition? They would deride the idea of anyone's wanting to break into such a dismal place."

"They would investigate the attack upon Helena," he maintained defensively, for he had a great respect for the police.

"They are already doing so. Jelks, the local sergeant, arrived here just after lunch, to take down particulars of the affair which Constable Brown had reported to him. But I wonder what result their investigations are likely to have. Those five men may have travelled to this district in two separate cars, from two distant towns, in a different county, probably Sussex. They might even have come from London."

"Not in last night's fog."

"True, but the fog did not become really thick until nightfall. What clues could Helena give the police to help them identify the five men? None. She was not able to give the number of their car; she did not see a face which she can describe; she did not hear a name mentioned. I shall be a very surprised woman if police investigations lead to an arrest."

There was no denying the force of Lady Kylstone's reasoned argument, but he detected a flaw. "They might tackle the problem from the other end—who informed the men that Helena was in the habit of carrying the key about with her? You told nobody of the fact, Helena was equally silent, Howard is above suspicion, your brother is in New York. The obvious answer is that the men could not have been after the key, because they knew neither of its existence nor that Helena had charge of it."

"I thought you were quite convinced that the men were after the key."

"So I was and so I am still, Lady Kylstone, especially in view of what Briggs reported to you."

"Are you inferring that there must be a spy in this house who passed the information on to the men?"

"Either here, or in Mr. Howard's office," he corrected tactfully. "Indeed, the leakage is more likely to have come from the office than from here."

"Why?"

"It would have been just as easy for a spy here to pass on the actual key as the information of its whereabouts."

"That is quite true," Helena interrupted eagerly. "It would have been a simple matter for Biddy to have taken the key out of my bag without my knowing."

"Biddy! Nonsense! Biddy has been with me ever since my marriage," Lady Kylstone denied crossly. "Neither Biddy nor Agnes would dream of doing anything so despicable. As for Briggs, I am sure he would rather harm his own daughter than me. Gibbons, the chauffeur, is equally reliable."

"Neither Helena nor I was trying to make one of your servants out to be guilty, Lady Kylstone," Terhune interposed. "We were, indeed, exculpating them by pointing out how easily one of them could have saved the five men the risk and trouble of holding up Helena's car last night. It would not even have been necessary for the key to have been taken away from the bag; a wax impression could have been made from which a duplicate key might be cut. That is, if the key is not of a complicated pattern." He glanced inquiringly at his hostess.

"I think one would probably call it complicated." She looked at the clock on the mantelpiece, and then at Helena. "There is just time for Mr. Terhune to examine the key before the meal is served. Where is it, my child?"

"Still in my bag, which is in my bedroom. Shall I fetch it?"

"If you please."

Terhune opened the door for Helena. As he closed it behind her and returned to his seat, he asked: "Is it known to many people in the neighbourhood that you are in the habit of hanging garlands in the family vault on each anniversary of the Battle of Agincourt?"

Her eyes twinkled. "You must live in a world of your own if you cannot answer that question yourself. I believed the ceremony was a matter of common knowledge. On that day each year the vault is visited by a number of people. It is a recognized trip; if the day is a fine one they come from miles around."

"Is the vault open to the public?"

"On that one day of the year. Perhaps I should have added that the throwing open of the vault to the public was proclaimed in sixteen hundred and sixty by the Piers Kylstone (by that time the *R* had been dropped from the name, and the *E* added) who was created a baronet in that year by a grateful Charles the Second, as a sign of family loyalty to the Crown. From that year onwards the Kylstones spent a considerable sum on beautifying the vault, making it resemble, on the anniversary day, a hot-house more than a burial vault." She sighed. "A truly macabre proceeding, but there—you English——We Americans cannot help loving you, but we shall never understand you and your traditions. The flowers would do so much more good at the cottage hospital."

The door opened abruptly. Helena entered. Her face was white; her eyes alarmed.

"Lady Kylstone——Lady Kylstone——"

"What is wrong, child?" she asked sharply.

"The key—it is not there—it is gone——"

"Helena! Surely you haven't lost it today of all days?" Helena shook her head dumbly as she attempted to recover her breath. "Not lost..." she gasped. "Not lost—but stolen. The window is wide open... there is a ladder outside, resting against the window-sill..." Unexpectedly she sat down on a convenient chair and burst into tears.

VII

Lady Kylstone rose swiftly to her feet and crossed the floor towards Helena; Terhune appreciated what a graceful figure she possessed when she moved; meanwhile he remained standing by his chair, awkward and embarrassed, not knowing what, if anything, he should do.

She laid her hand affectionately on Helena's shoulder. "My dear child, you must not take the matter to heart like this. If the key has been stolen the blame is not yours."

"After what happened last night I should have brought the key down with me. You asked me to take great care of it."

"Good heavens! I did not mean that you were never to let it out of your sight. Besides, you were not to know that anyone was daring enough to burgle a house that was full of people. Now dry those eyes of yours; they are too pretty to be red and puffy."

Helena did as she was told. As soon as she had recovered her composure Lady Kylstone continued: "Tell me what happened, Helena?"

"When I entered the bedroom my bag was still on the dressing-table, where I had left it. I opened it, but could not find the key, so I turned everything out on to the bed. I still could not see it, and was just about to look on the floor under the dressing-table when I noticed that the curtains were billowing into the room, and that the lower half of the window was open. As the cold air was rushing into the room I went to close the window. It was then that I noticed the ladder against the window-sill. I guessed what had happened, so I hurried straight down here."

Lady Kylstone glanced at Terhune. "Those men must want the key very desperately."

"How could they have discovered so quickly that the key was under the lining?" he asked Helena.

"But they didn't," she admitted miserably. "This afternoon I carefully rescued the key from beneath the lining, and sewed up the hole through which it had slipped. If I had not done so the key might not have been found."

"Then it is my fault for having searched the bag," he pointed out glumly.

"No. I should have done the same even if I had not visited you this morning; Lady Kylstone wants the key for tomorrow."

"Tomorrow?" he questioned curiously.

"Tomorrow is the twenty-fifth of October, the anniversary of Agincourt," Lady Kylstone supplied for herself.

"What!"

"Is there anything strange in that, young man?"

"Perhaps everything," he stuttered excitedly. "Then the vault will be open to the public all day tomorrow?"

"From ten a.m. onwards, after the flowers have been arranged. Why?"

"If the man who stole the key of the vault from Helena's bedroom had cared to wait a few more hours he could have entered the vault without having to take the risk and trouble of breaking into this house?"

"Yes," Lady Kylstone admitted wonderingly. "That is so." Then she added: "Unless he was not aware that the vault was to be opened tomorrow."

Terhune's eyes flamed. "I don't believe in that theory, Lady Kylstone. I am convinced that whoever revealed the information about Helena's possessing the key would have been equally informative about the vault's being open on every twenty-fifth of October."

"Then why should he, or they, have stolen the key tonight?"

"I—I have an idea, Lady Kylstone, to explain a lot of what is mystifying us at the moment, but it—it is almost too fantastic——" He paused.

"The entire affair is beginning to be fantastic," she snapped. "What is your idea, young man?"

"A Mr. X wants to enter the vault—Heaven alone knows why——"

"I agree," she murmured drily.

"By waiting until tomorrow he can enter the vault without any trouble at all. But he was not satisfied to wait until tomorrow. First, with the help of others, he visited the vault a few nights ago, perhaps in the hope of breaking into it there and then. He was interrupted by Briggs, but not before he discovered that only the key or a charge of T.N.T. could open the door. He decided to rob Helena of the key. Time made him desperate. Instead of taking the wiser course of trying to steal the key by employing a pickpocket he made plans for holding up Helena as soon as possible. I think he may have had a secondary reason for proposing this step; the hope of using the key immediately after obtaining possession of it. The attack failed. Upon realizing that only one chance remained of carrying out his scheme, he risked discovery by breaking into this house and stealing the key from Helena's bedroom."

"How did he know the key was in the bedroom?" Helena asked.

"Where else does a woman usually keep her bag when she is not carrying it around with her?"

Lady Kylstone nodded her head understanding. "I follow your reasoning; it sounds credible—up to a point. But why must Mr. X have the key tonight rather than tomorrow, or the next night?"

"Because he wants to enter the vault before anyone else does so," he explained excitedly.

Lady Kylstone gave thought to his suggestion before committing herself, but presently she nodded. "Your theory sounds plausible, because it makes clear many factors which otherwise are unintelligible," she agreed briskly. "I am glad I followed my impulse to ask you here tonight; it pleases me to know that you are as intelligent as your eyes—and Helena—made you out to be. Nevertheless, your theory still does not solve the very important problem of why anyone should desire to enter that gloomy vault, yesterday, today, or to-morrow. I can assure you———"

He fidgeted impatiently. At last he burst out: "Forgive my interrupting, Lady Kylstone, but I believe that the time for discussion has passed. If my theory is right, then the men who stole the key are already on their way to the vault. If they are to be prevented from entering something should be done at once."

This time she did not pause before answering. "What do you suggest should be done?" she demanded crisply. "Telephone the police———"

"No!" she snapped. "Not unless we have to." Her eyes sparkled. "This is becoming a personal matter between myself and the men who are so anxious to desecrate my late husband's family tomb. Ring that bell, young man." She indicated the electric bell by the side of the fireplace; and continued: "The cottages farther along the road are occupied by tenants of mine; several husky men live there who should be glad of doing something for me for a change. If there is to be a fight in the churchyard..." She laughed; there was so much animation in her voice that he was convinced she was thoroughly enjoying the moment of excitement which had intruded itself so unexpectedly into her peaceful existence. "If there is to be a fight," she continued, "I think our mysterious friends in mackintoshes will find themselves roughly treated."

Briggs entered. "Dinner is served, your ladyship."

"Then tell Biddy and Agnes to unserve it, and keep it warm for later on."

Poor old Briggs's mouth opened wide in astonishment. He stared at his mistress, goggle-eyed. "Your ladyship———"

"And tell Gibbons to drive both cars into the road, facing Willingham, keep their engines running, and remain by the big one. Then get on your bicycle, Briggs, and hurry to Rockaway Cottages as quickly as you can. Ask Croker, Judd, Kelley and all the other men there if they can oblige me by coming here as soon as possible. Promise them a fight——"

"A fight, your ladyship!" Briggs stammered incoherently.

"A fight, Briggs—with fists and clubs. Now hurry, man, hurry! The matter is urgent. There is no time to be wasted——"

"Very good, your ladyship." Briggs shook his head in bewilderment as he hurried away.

Lady Kylstone turned towards Terhune; he saw that her face was vivacious, exhilarated. "Can you drive, young man?"

"I can, but I have no licence."

"Never mind about that; I will hold myself responsible for any trouble. You drive the smaller car; I will go in the big car with Gibbons."

Helena gasped. "You, Lady Kylstone!"

"Of course, child. This is my first real excitement in years. I only hope that Mr. Terhune's theory is right; if it isn't I am afraid we shall all of us look very foolish."

"If you are going, so am I."

"No, Helena. You must stay here. Remember, you had your share of the excitement last night; tonight it is my turn. Besides, all the spare room will be needed for the men. Now be a good child and fetch me my fur coat. And all the electric torches in the store cupboard. I am going to examine that vault tonight if it means pulling it down brick by brick."

VIII

Events moved swiftly. In a little more than fifteen minutes' time from the moment of Briggs's leaving the drawing-room to carry out his mistress's orders Terhune found himself at the wheel of Lady Kylstone's second car. With him in the car were three men from Rockaway Cottages: six in all had answered Lady Kylstone's call; the other three were in the car in front, whose tail light was Terhune's guide along narrow, winding roads which, familiar to him as a cyclist, seemed strangely different to him in the glare of the headlights as he drove at a steady forty miles an hour.

Although there was no sign of the previous night's fog, the night was dark with heaving, drifting patches of cloud which concealed all but a few stars. There was a strong wind blowing from the west which snatched the dying leaves from the trees and slapped them against the windscreen and the nearside windows. The surface of the road was still greasy from a sharp shower which had fallen during the afternoon. Driving, indeed, was far from easy, but he was a safe driver, and was not unduly worried by unfavourable conditions; he drove automatically, which was fortunate, for he could think of little else beyond the strangeness of the adventure which had overtaken him.

How many times in the last few years had he ridden these roads on his bicycle? So many times that he could have painted a true picture of the district from his memory. The row of a dozen low-roofed, quaint, but sound cottages known as Rockaway Cottages (even legend could not explain the name), each with its garden patch, large enough to grow about half the family's vegetable requirements for the year, its three or four fruit trees and soft fruit bushes (from which a year's supply of jam could be made), its stock of firewood, rambler-covered walls, tiny leaded windows, and oak doors for which collectors would have paid good prices if Lady Kylstone had permitted a sale.

Beyond Rockaway Cottages on the right two large grazing fields, each twenty acres or so. Opposite, woodlands, much of it belonging to Timberlands, the rest to the Hon. Mrs. Mac-Munn. Beyond the grazing fields, a rolling vista of ploughed land; Peartree Farm; with more woodland beyond rising to a fair height. Sir George Brereton's

Elizabethan home. Mrs. Townsend's apple orchard, which was steadily going to rack and ruin because nobody could persuade the old lady to spend money on giving the fruit trees the attention they needed in the way of manuring, grease-banding, pruning. George Barker's farm, with its acres and acres of hop-fields, and its two picturesque oast-houses.

Typical Kent countryside, with its air of complete detachment from the outside world, its sweet smells, its lovely orchards, its fields of cropping sheep, its old, old houses, its serenity, its peace. He knew it so well, and loved it; every mossy roof, every creaking well, every oak-beamed wayside inn. He loved its detachment, because it matched his own detachment from the world of cities and towns; he loved its peace and serenity, because his nature was serene, and he relished peace and quietness so that he could read his books, and nurse his dream of becoming a novelist.

It was this familiarity, this love for the country through which he was passing, which made the reason for what he was doing the more unreal—or whimsical, if you please. Even in city, or town, or suburb there would be something unusual in rushing a number of men to a churchyard for the purpose of fighting thieves who were proposing surreptitiously to enter a vault there, but here, in this world within a world, in this neighbourhood of farms, hop-fields, orchards and old-world residences, the adventure became startlingly absurd, and left him with the impression that he was acting a role in one of the local amateur society's melodramas.

As the car rounded an unusually sharp turn he smelled the sweet, cloying odour of newly turned earth from the field on his right. This smell, because it was symbolic of a countryside where the unusual never happens, caused a flurried feeling of panic to sweep over him. Doubts assailed him—he wondered if he were not making a fool, not only of himself, but of Lady Kylstone as well. After all, this present expedition was based on nothing more concrete than supposition on his part, but had he been making a fictional mountain out of an actual molehill? Twenty minutes ago his deductions had sounded reasonable enough, but now they seemed far-fetched. Had he allowed his common sense to become biassed by the hundreds of books on crime and kindred subjects which he had digested in the past few years?

That the crime of housebreaking and robbery had been committed was beyond doubt. Equally certain was it that the robbery had not been purposeless: the man who had stolen the key presumably wanted it for unlawful purposes. No imagination was needed to deduce those points, they were irrefutable—unless the thief were a lunatic! But the theory that the need for the key was urgent, that the thief or thieves were in desperate need to enter the vault before anyone else could do so—that was his, and his alone. There might be no more justification for such a wild flight of fancy than for declaring the moon to be square.

He began to regret his impulsiveness; his face flamed as he foresaw the possibility of the men from Rockaway Cottages waiting about at the churchyard, perhaps for hours, waiting, waiting, waiting for something that was never likely to take place. He could almost hear their surreptitious chuckles, their pointed asides to one another about "that bookseller man" from Bray. He could picture Lady Kylstone's face as the hours passed and nothing happened.

These thoughts were followed by another, scarcely less unpleasant. By now the key of the vault had been in the possession of the thief, for, at a minimum, three quarters of an hour, perhaps longer. It might be that his theory had been right but the thief might have already reached the vault, opened it, and left without leaving any trace of his visit. The men who were travelling to the churchyard to prevent the vault being entered might wait about the churchyard for hours without knowing that the precaution had been taken too late...

Despite the snap in the air, Terhune presently realized that he was sweating. He was more than relieved when he saw the red light ahead slow down and come to a stop. As he switched off the engine of the car he was driving he discovered that his hands were shaking.

Gibbons had stopped in a side road, some two hundred yards from the church, where the two cars were not likely to be seen by the thieves. By the time Terhune and the three men had walked along to the foremost car, Lady Kylstone, Gibbons and the other three men were waiting for them.

In a low whisper Terhune gave instructions to the men. They were to hide themselves, in pairs, behind convenient gravestones; they were not to smoke, or to make any sound which might betray their presence; above all, they were not to move until he gave the signal—he wanted to make sure that the thief should not escape with the key still in his possession. The men granted their ready assent to these instructions; they could make neither head nor tail of what the strange business was about, but her leddyship had asked for their help, and they didn't want to let her leddyship down—real kind she always was to her tenants about repairs and things, besides the Christmas present of a ton of coal and a parcel of groceries for each household—aye, they were right willing to give a hand to her leddyship, especially when that hand was to be a fist...

As quietly as possible the men made their way into the church-yard, going by way of a stile over the hedge that was farthest away from the main entrance to the churchyard. The going was not too easy, for the night remained dark, but the men were not worried by the lack of moonlight, they had lived in the country all their lives, and were used to moving around in darkness—especially Kelley, who had a name for a bit of poaching like, now and again. They reached the vicinity of the Kylstone vault, and seeing no sign of other men, they selected their own hiding-places. Gibbons accompanied

Terhune to a large spreading laurel on the right of the vault, where they crept in beneath the lower branches.

For Terhune the ensuing wait was agonizing and interminable. With every minute he became more depressed, thinking that the thieves must already have come and gone, or perhaps were not coming at all. Although he had resolved not to keep glancing at his luminous dialled watch, when the first hour had very nearly elapsed he could no longer resist the impulse to check up on the time—it was with a distinct shock that he saw that six minutes only had gone by.

The wind soughed through the trees which were dotted about the churchyard; the branches whipped against one another like old bones being rattled in a wooden tub, the shrivelled leaves rustled together like the sighing of souls in torment; some fell, and as they were whisked against the faces of the waiting men their touch was that of a skeleton finger.

Another fifteen minutes (in reality, four) passed. Then Gibbons touched him on the arm. "A car coming, sir."

Terhune listened, and heard the hum of an approaching car. Then he saw the reflection of the headlights dancing among the skeleton-like trees. He stiffened, glad that the time for action had arrived. Unfortunately, the car went past the church, the noise of the exhaust fading away in the far distance.

Three times this same thing happened, but the fourth car which approached came to a stop about a hundred yards from the church. Both engine and lights were switched off, warning enough to Terhune that his deductions were being justified, and that the men who had stolen the key were about to enter the churchyard.

Another minute passed, during which nothing happened. Because of the gusty wind, which had become stronger in the last few minutes, Terhune reflected that it might not be too easy to hear anyone approaching the churchyard. Nor was it likely to be easier to see them, for a bank of low, heavy clouds, extending some considerable distance, was being driven towards them, making the night darker than ever. There was a smell of rain in the wind, too; he hoped sincerely that it would hold off until later, conditions were already bad enough.

Yet one more minute went by; it seemed like many more than that. He began to fear that the alarm was a false one; perhaps the car had stopped farther off than he had believed, outside the rectory, perhaps. Visitors for the rector! Then all his fears were set at rest; a small, ghostly light danced towards him, seemingly without visible support.

The light picked its way towards the Kylstone vault: when it arrived within a few feet of the entrance he saw and counted the accompanying shadows. Four only. The fifth—if there were a fifth—had probably been left in charge of the car. Four only. Four against eight. The fight was not likely to be a heroic one for the men hidden in the churchyard, but he was not unduly worried on that score. He was not conscious of feeling heroic; the one thought which occupied him was—recover the key.

Gibbons stirred restlessly, and touched Terhune on the arm, questioningly. Terhune placed his hand firmly on the chauffeur's shoulder in restraint. The time was not ripe for attack. He hoped the other men were not equally impatient. Apparently they were not, or, if they were, they obeyed instructions and made no move.

The dancing light and the four shadows reached the vault. A voice mumbled words, of which only one or two were distinguishable. "... you... put... care..." The voice was cockney, and coarse; decidedly it was not Soft-Voice who had spoken.

He crouched closer to the ground so that he could obtain a better view of what was happening, for there was a branch in his way. The men seemed to be arguing—Heaven alone knew what about—the wind was too gusty to hear a word. Damn them! Were they never going to fit the key into the lock?

As if in answer to his plea one of the shadows directed the beam of the torchlight at the lock; another stretched out his arm in the same direction, and fumbled about. A squeaking noise followed; it sounded eerie. Terhune's spine tingled until he realized that the rusted hinges of the vault door had probably been the cause of the squeal. He saw the man with the torch disappearing into the vault.

"Go for them, lads!" he bellowed.

IX

The subsequent happenings were nightmarish in effect. Eight shadows appeared, more or less noisily, from behind tombstones or trees, and converged upon the three shadows which were on the point of following the torchlight down into the vault. All the shadows merged into a confusion of flailing arms and swaying bodies, of thumps, and blows and gasps. The wind raged; the trees bent before the gusts, and clapped their branches together in protest, or perhaps in joy; the fallen leaves swept along the ground in eddies. Then, through a small rift in the clouds, a watery moonlight threw a faint illumination on the scene which sketched the tombstones in relief; the rippling shadows of the fast-moving clouds made the stones appear to jump about in sympathy. To make the scene more bizarre, the deep, solemn bells of the clock in the church tower chimed the hour of eight.

Terhune made directly for the vault itself, lest the man who had entered might take advantage of the mêlée to fulfil the purpose of the nocturnal visit; although he was unaware of the fact, behind his horn-rimmed glasses his usually solemn eyes flamed with excitement. His blood tingled with the impulse to fight, to feel his clenched fists sinking into soft flesh. He reached the vault door, and saw that his reasoning was not at fault; the man with the torchlight was hurrying down the stone steps which led down to the tomb of the Kylstone family.

Terhune hurried down after the dancing light. Six steps or so down his feet slipped from under him; he pitched forward. He might have died there and then if his head had landed on the stone floor of the vault, but fortune was on his side. His outstretched hands wildly grasped at the man below him; somehow he managed to claw hold of the mackintosh, and this helped to break his fall. He landed heavily and pulled the other man over on top of him, but still—the fall did not kill him, nor did he suffer from any broken limbs: only from bruises, and of these he knew nothing until later.

Terhune's tumble knocked the torch from the other man's hand; it fell upon the floor, where it rolled over three and four times before coming to a stop, its light still shining, to cast a dispersed yellow-white radiance which faintly illuminated the eerie scene.

Before Terhune could clamber to his feet he found himself straddled by the other man, who took advantage of the situation by trying to choke his opponent into insensibility. Actuated by the spirit of self-defence, Terhune automatically grasped and struggled to upset his heavier and larger adversary. Meanwhile his thoughts registered a confused impression of a strong smell of onions—no, garlic!—and he realized that the man on his chest was Soft-Voice.

To feel a heavy man sitting on his chest was no new experience for Terhune—he had played Rugger too often—although to feel a pair of sinewy hands squeezing his throat came in a somewhat different category. He had no knowledge of the best method of combating the hold, but as something had to be done, and done quickly, he wriggled his body into a convenient position and kicked for goal. He had lost none of his old skill; the toe of his boot caught Soft-Voice squarely on the back of his head. With a grunt of pain, Soft-Voice lurched forward and fell on top of Terhune's face.

Once again Terhune gave a violent heave and wriggle; this time he managed to get clear of his opponent.

That moment should have been the beginning of a good scrap; Terhune, at any rate, was all worked up for one. But Gibbons chose that moment to bellow down from above: "They've all cleared off, Mr. Terhune: are you all right down there?"

Soft-Voice was quick-witted, and no hero. Realizing that he was heavily outnumbered, he made a dash up the steps for liberty. Upon seeing Gibbons outlined against the watery moon, he bent his head and charged. Poor Gibbons, thinking that the black shadow mounting the steps was Terhune, made no effort to defend himself; consequently it was as an innocent person that he received the full force of the butting head. He reeled heavily backwards, bumped against Croker and fell over Kelley's feet. By the time the three men had sorted themselves out Soft-Voice had disappeared into the darkness.

Terhune appeared at the vault door. Gibbons inquired warily: "Is that you, Mr. Terhune?"

Terhune said: "Yes." Before he could say more another shadow appeared from behind the laurel tree.

"Well, young man, so everything has happened as you believed it would. I congratulate you on your perspicacity."

"Lady Kylstone—I—I thought you were in the car."

"So you might, Mr. Terhune, but that proves that you know very little about women. I had no intention from the beginning of missing the fun. I am glad the moon came out at the right moment, I had a grandstand view. If the odds had been more equal the fight might have been a good one." She pressed the button of a torch which she held in her hand; its white beam revealed the open door of the vault.

"Come along, young man; we will not wait until the morning before finding out what those men wanted in the vault; my curiosity is far too strong."

Down in the vault Lady Kylstone and Terhune stood side by side and flashed their torches about. Looking about him Terhune saw a large stone chamber, about twenty feet square and twelve feet high. The walls were covered in bas-relief, executed in marble, representing scenes from a battle which he concluded to be the famous Battle of Agincourt. Otherwise the vault was bare, dismal, and empty. Empty, not only of the coffins or caskets which he had anticipated seeing, but also of anything to attract the unwelcome attention of the men who had sought to enter it.

Lady Kylstone was the first to speak. "There is nothing here," she said abruptly.

"Not even coffins," he mentioned.

"The tomb proper is in a second vault beneath our feet," she replied impatiently. "We are standing on the trapdoor, which is only opened for burials——"

"Not on anniversaries?"

"No. Besides, it is about twenty feet deep. The men would have needed a rope or a ladder to reach the floor. It would be absurd to imagine anyone wanting to go down—there could be positively nothing there."

"It is equally absurd to imagine anyone wanting to visit the upper part, for there is nothing here either."

"It is too ridiculous——" she began, exasperated. "I had begun to believe we were on the verge of making an extraordinary discovery."

For the second time she directed her torch about the vault. Terhune did the same. The two white splashes of light danced hither and thither. At last, when he was on the point of concluding that Soft-Voice and his friends were, after all, lunatics, he espied something on the floor in the right corner farthest from the door, something that bore a strong resemblance to gold.

That something was gold, as he quickly discovered when he picked it up.

Lady Kylstone quickly followed him to the corner. "What have you found?" she questioned eagerly.

"This!" He displayed the object on the palm of his hand. "A gold fountain pen."

"A fountain pen! How on earth did that come to be here?"

"It must have been dropped by one of the visitors to the vault——"

"Nobody has entered the vault since the last anniversary a year ago," she interrupted testily.

"Perhaps it has been lying here ever since." He broke off, startled. "Surely the pen cannot be what the men were after?"

"Nonsense! As if anyone would want to break into a vault for the purpose of recovering a lost fountain pen, even if it is gold. Besides, granted that fact, why should that person have waited until now before trying to get it back?"

"Heaven alone knows!"

"The owner could have obtained the pen at any time during the last twelve months by applying to me," she continued with relentless criticism. "Alternatively, supposing that the owner had no wish to apply to me for the key he could have waited until tomorrow, and have been the first visitor to enter the vault."

"The first *visitor*," he corrected. "But not the first *person*."

"Ah!" Lady Kylstone exclaimed crisply. "The owner may not have been willing to take the risk of the pen's being found by anyone else—myself, for instance?"

"That is the only explanation I can think of."

"In those circumstances, young man, I am compelled to ask once again: Why has the owner waited until now before breaking into the vault in the hope of finding it first?" She laughed softly. "And your answer, I suppose, is as before: Heaven alone knows!"

"I am afraid so," he agreed ruefully.

"I wonder why the owner was so afraid of my finding that pen. Is there anything special about it?"

With Lady Kylstone holding her torch close, Terhune examined the pen more carefully. At first glance it was no different from any other fountain pen, except that it was of gold, not ebonite, but upon turning it round he noticed a tiny device embossed upon the casing. He peered closely at the device, which appeared to be that of a mythological god—Mercury, he assumed—holding outstretched in his right arm an obvious automobile tyre.

"What is it? What is it?" Lady Kylstone asked impatiently. "What are you staring at?"

Upon being told, she shook her head, perplexed. "This is all very mystifying. Is the device familiar to you?"

"No."

"Nor is it to me." She shivered suddenly. "I am beginning to feel cold," she said abruptly. "There is no need for us to stay down here any longer if we are quite sure there is nothing more to be found."

"Shall we have one more look around?" he suggested.

She nodded. For the third time the light from the two torches circled the vault; this time without result. Lady Kylstone shrugged her shoulders and led the way up the stone stairway. He followed her closely, fearing lest she should do what he had done earlier on, slip on the mossy steps. Half way up he laughed. She halted instantly, and faced him.

"Why do you laugh?"

"I was thinking of the many stories I have read in which detectives find themselves investigating a crime which apparently has no clue."

"Well?"

"In this case, Lady Kylstone, the circumstances are precisely the opposite. We have found a clue without a crime."

"A very fortunate circumstance," she said tartly. "As a mere clue has led us into the chilly depths of a burial vault on a cold October night, where on earth—or under it—would a crime lead us? I am sure I should catch pneumonia or rheumatic fever. Come along, young man. Let us hurry back to Timberlands so that we may eat our postponed meal before it is irretrievably ruined."

Taken by and large, he thought, the suggestion was a good one.

The Second Clue

O nce every month Terhune went to London to buy new books for his lending library. Usually he selected the last Tuesday of each month for this visit. There was no particular significance in this day, but he was a man of regular habits, and having chosen a last Tuesday in the month for his first visit, thereafter he made a habit of keeping to that particular day. At the same time, this regular habit served a useful purpose because Miss Amelia reserved that day for attending the shop during his absence.

Miss Amelia was an extraordinary soul. She had reached that period in life when women begin to use the method of subtraction rather than addition to arrive at their age each birthday. Her straight black hair was already streaked with grey; she had pale blue eyes, usually hidden behind steel-rimmed spectacles, sharp features, thin lips, and a sallow complexion. In appearance she was typical of the bad-tempered, vinegary spinster as popular with the dramatists as she is unpopular with the dramatists' characters. But Miss Amelia, not being a histrionic puppet, belied her appearance. Her heart overflowed with kindness and generosity, and all Bray-in-the-Marsh loved her. So much, indeed, that the postman was among the few people to know that her surname was Tweedale. Ever since she had arrived in Bray as a young girl of twelve she had been known as Miss Amelia, and as Miss Amelia she would continue to be affectionately known until the day of her death—for the idea of her living anywhere else was unthinkable.

Miss Amelia lived on the far side of Market Square in rooms above Collis, the grocer's. She lived simply on a very small income inherited from her father, who was reported to have been headmaster of one of the lesser-known public schools. Her three rooms were as neat as a new pin, but she was rarely to be found there, except first thing in the morning and late at night, for few days in the month passed by without somebody or other needing her kindly services—as a companion to Mrs. Stewart Lawson whenever Mrs. Lawson's daughter went to Scotland, which happened frequently; as piano-player at the village school for musical drill (every Friday from two o'clock to three), as a member of the Hospital Helpers' Knitting Bee (each alternate Monday), and so on.

On Tuesday, the 29th of October, Miss Amelia entered the shop precisely at eight-thirty, which was precisely her usual time of arrival.

"Good morning, Mr. Terhune." Her thin lips parted in an insignificant smile; in the privacy of her own reflections she thought the world of Mr. Terhune, whom she considered quite as intelligent as her poor, dear father—she could have paid Terhune no greater compliment than that. "It is a lovely day for a visit to London; dry and sunny, and just cold enough to keep you on the move."

"Then I shall probably keep warm enough, Miss Amelia, for I have plenty to do there. Among other commissions I have to try and find an illustrated book on Tudor architecture for Mr. Belcher; he is thinking of adding a wing to his house."

She sighed. "Dear Mr. Gregory; it is so nice to know that he loves this neighbourhood as much as his dear uncle, Mr. Jasper, did. But why does he want to make his house larger? It is already too large for a single man. Now if he were thinking of marrying..." she hinted delicately.

Terhune shook his head. "Mr. Belcher is like me; not a marrying man, Miss Amelia. I believe he intends to make up for having no wife and family by entertaining."

"All his friends from South Africa, no doubt. But dear me! I must not keep you gossiping like this, Mr. Terhune; you will miss your train."

He chuckled. "I am not riding my bicycle into Ashford today; I am going by car for a change. Lady Kylstone is taking me."

"Lady Kylstone!" Miss Amelia arched her greying eyebrows. "I have heard that you dined there last Thursday."

His eyes twinkled. Of course she had heard. No doubt everyone in the small town of Bray-in-the-Marsh had heard. And all the inhabitants of Willingham and Wickford as well. No doubt everyone was equally well aware of what had happened in the churchyard. The account of that adventure would be much too choice a titbit of news to remain for long out of circulation. This conclusion was justified by her next words.

"I have heard that there were strange goings-on at Willingham churchyard that night," she continued. "When Mrs. Robinson told me of them I could not believe her—she has a marvellous imagination for such a quiet person——"

"For once, rumour is probably correct, Miss Amelia. Lady Kylstone heard that some men were proposing to try and break into the family vault, so she collected a few men together, including myself, and we went there to prevent them."

She was thrilled; he did not remember having ever seen her face so expressive. "Dear me! To think that her story was true after all. Whatever can the country be coming to, Mr. Terhune? Why, I have lived here"—she coughed drily—"a number of years now, but never has anything like that happened before."

She gazed at him with pleading eyes, but she was too late; through the glass-panelled door he saw a car draw up, and recognized Lady Kylstone and Helena inside.

"There is Lady Kylstone; I must hurry. Some other time, Miss Amelia, I will tell you what little there is to tell about last Thursday night." He snatched up his hat and gloves from a pile of books on which he had placed them. "Good-bye, Miss Amelia. I shall be back again about the usual time."

"Good-bye, Mr. Terhune. Enjoy yourself in London." She gazed at the rapidly disappearing back and sighed wistfully—many years had passed since last she had visited London; she wondered whether it had changed much—it would be nice to wander through Liberty's for a change—with Harrods and the Army and Navy Stores for good measure—and a matinée, perhaps...

"Good morning, young man," Lady Kylstone welcomed him as he stepped inside the car. "Did you make arrangements for today's weather? The last twice Helena and I went to town it rained nearly all day."

"I was just as unlucky myself last month." He sat down in front of Helena. "Good morning, Helena." He reflected that the wind must be keener than he had suspected, for her cheeks were flushed.

"Good morning, Mr. Terhune."

"Tommy," he suggested tentatively.

"Tommy," she obliged in a low voice.

Lady Kylstone chuckled. "If I didn't like you for yourself, young man, I think I should still like you on account of your father. I should have liked to have met him; I think we should have appreciated each other."

"I am sure you would."

"Ichabod! The glory has departed! I know just how he must have felt when he was permitted his first glimpse of the wizened, red little morsel of humanity which had just been born to him; I experienced much the same emotion when I looked at my eldest son. Nurse told me later that I cried because he was so ugly. Of course, the next morning I thought him the dearest angel in the world." She changed the conversation abruptly. "I suppose nearly everyone in Bray knows what happened at the church last Thursday?"

"Judging by the number of people who came into the shop to buy books yesterday, I should say that the word 'nearly' is superfluous. Even Sir George Brereton came in to inquire whether I had bought any new books on fly-fishing."

"And took advantage of the occasion to introduce the events of Thursday night, I suppose?"

"Yes."

"I hope you sent him away with a flea in his ear—or should I say 'fly' in his case?"

Terhune grimaced. "He went away rather annoyed with me."

"He will get over that mood; George is a good-hearted man except when he starts on the subject of fly-fishing. I have been very nearly as busy as you in answering inquiries; first it was Alicia MacMunn, then Gregory Belcher, then the judge's wife—I never can remember her Christian name, Helena——"

"Mildred."

"Of course. Mildred Pemberton! I should remember it; I have heard it often enough. Then the Rector called, and later, Dr. Harris—at one time I contemplated instructing Briggs to disconnect the telephone, and inform my friends that I was not at home. You have told nobody the real facts of the affair, young man?"

"No, Lady Kylstone. I merely said that you had been told that men were trying to break into the vault, and that you gathered some of your tenants together to prevent that happening—which you did, just in time."

"Good. Now tell me, young man, have you given further thought to that strange business?"

"I am afraid I have done nothing else."

"Nor have I. The more I consider it, the stranger it seems. Have you come to any fresh conclusions?"

"Yes," Terhune admitted wryly. "That we missed a wonderful opportunity possibly of learning the identity of the men who tried to break into the vault."

"How?" Lady Kylstone inquired sharply.

"Did anybody visit the vault the following day?"

"About thirty people, according to the verger. Why?"

"You should have had somebody on watch to take a note of everyone who entered the vault. It is possible that one of the men who were at the churchyard Thursday night might have entered the vault the following morning in the faint hope of our not having found the fountain pen."

Lady Kylstone exclaimed with annoyance. "How stupid of one of us not to have thought of taking such an elementary step as that. Come, come, young man; considering all the books on criminology which Helena tells me you have read, you should have thought of that plan sooner."

He nodded meekly. "I could have kicked myself when the idea occurred to me in bed Sunday morning."

She laughed softly. "Which goes to prove that writers of crime fiction are no better amateur detectives than ex-detectives are amateur writers."

II

The journey to town proved thoroughly enjoyable for the three people inside the car. Terhune found himself liking Lady Kylstone more and more. He found her both witty and intelligent. There were few subjects with which she did not have sound if slight knowledge; in many, that knowledge was comprehensive. Even in his own pet subject—literature—she was a worthy debater; in some respects her intimacy with European writers was more developed than his, for she could read both French and German.

At the same time, he was puzzled by her. She was undeniably American in her mental outlook, and in the way she dressed; now and again she would phrase a sentence in a manner that was more American than English (especially in the use of the word 'gotten'); very occasionally an inflexion that was decidedly American crept into her voice (this applied especially to the word 'figure', for she pronounced the *u* with unmistakable emphasis). Nevertheless, in spite of having been born and bred in the New World, and of having travelled extensively before marriage, she seemed thoroughly content to live a life as much English as that of the most fanatical member of county society. On the other hand, her obvious love for the quiet peace of rural life had not prevented her responding enthusiastically to the interest and excitement of the affair at the churchyard. In some ways, he decided eventually, she had a complex nature.

Although Lady Kylstone more or less monopolized the conversation, he was equally conscious of the presence of Helena. He thought she looked even more charming than ever, and concluded that the particular shade of blue she was wearing was responsible; it exactly matched her eyes, and toned with the blue lustre of her dark hair. He noticed that laughter was never long absent from her eyes and lips, but what he found particularly refreshing about her (being of a serious nature himself) was her freedom from self-consciousness, and an intelligence that, while not as brilliant as Lady Kylstone's, was unusually common-sensical. He had a feeling that she would make a very pleasant companion.

Time passed quickly. In what seemed to them all a remarkably short while, Gibbons brought the car to a stop in Leicester Square. Terhune alighted regretfully; he had never shopped in his life, but it occurred to him that he would have welcomed the opportunity of accompanying Helena through Dickens and Jones', where she intended buying some 'undies'...

Lady Kylstone's sharp eyes did not fail to note the flush which reddened his cheeks as he realized the trend of his thoughts. Her eyes twinkled mischievously, but she made no remark other than: "Don't forget, young man; four o'clock sharp at this same spot."

"I shall be here," he promised.

Hat in hand he watched the car swing into the stream of passing traffic—Helena glanced back, and seeing his hair ruffling in the wind, decided once and for all that her rabbit, for all his seriousness, was no more than an overgrown schoolboy.

From Leicester Square, Terhune proceeded to Haymarket, where he caught a bus for the Publishers' Book Centre, where he spent the next thirty minutes in their showrooms buying some of the latest fiction for his lending library, and also three recent books which clients had ordered from him. Thence to Charing Cross Road, where he hoped to pick up a book on Tudor architecture for Gregory Belcher. The search proved not only quick but successful. Having completed his business for the day he found the time to be twelve-thirty-one. Time for lunch, and afterwards, perhaps, a News Theatre for an hour. He turned into Old Compton Street, and made for the Restaurant Torremolinos.

For a man of regular habits he was unusually fond of ferreting out restaurants new to him. In the past few years he had rarely lunched at the same restaurant twice—French, Italian, Indian, Chinese, Japanese, Hungarian, he had tried them all in turn. During his previous visit to town, having lunched at an Indian restaurant, he had noticed the Restaurant Torremolinos, a restaurant not new to him alone, it seemed, for the paint was all fresh, and the work of alterations still proceeded. A notice:

RESTAURANT TORREMOLINOS

OPENING NEXT WEDNESDAY

SPANISH DISHES

Moderate Prices.   *Dry Sherry a Speciality.*

had been prominently displayed on the outside of a whitewashed window. There and then he had decided where to lunch upon his next visit to town.

Upon arrival opposite the Restaurant Torremolinos he saw that the whitewash had disappeared from the windows; in its place was close yellow net curtaining which effectively concealed the interior of the restaurant. Similar curtaining had been hung across the glass-panelled door, but a menu had been pasted up on the outside. Above the door was a model windmill to illustrate the name of the restaurant.

He read the menu; there was a long list of Spanish dishes, and a luncheon of the day consisting of:

> *Sopa de macarrones*
> *Lenguado frito*
> *Chuleta con legumbres*
> *Compota de manzanas,*

with all of which he was entirely unfamiliar. But the prices seemed reasonable, so he decided to investigate. He pushed the door open and entered.

The interior of the restaurant was garish, but colourful. It was not large, and as in most Soho restaurants, the best possible use had been made of the limited space by using small tables and small chairs, packed closely together. On each table was a small flower-stand, made in the shape of a windmill; the condiments, likewise, were housed in windmills. The tablecloths were brightly coloured; the cash-desk was draped in a magnificent-looking Spanish shawl. To add to the brightness of the scene, the walls had been painted to represent what Terhune imagined to be a typical Spanish scene: bleak mountains, a sea incredibly blue, a Spanish house, complete with patio, sloping roof, mosaic floors, tiled bricks, and iron-barred windows; and, of course, very prominent, a ruined windmill tower.

In one respect the restaurant was different from other Soho restaurants. Despite the lack of room, a small bar had been cleverly built into an otherwise inconvenient alcove. Complete with polished counter, high stools, large mirror, blazing light, a score of bottles containing different types of sherry, and a dark-haired girl, dressed in Spanish costume, to serve, the corner looked very attractive.

The restaurant was not full; only seven people were eating; they occupied three tables between them, while three men were seated at the bar. Doubtless the place was not yet known, he reflected, as a short, fat, smiling-faced *maître d'hôtel* advanced towards him.

"*Buenos dias, señor.* You are alone?"

Terhune nodded.

The man pointed to a small table near the window, laid for two. "The señor would like that table, perhaps?"

Terhune nodded again; as far as he could see, that table was as convenient as another.

"Then I will reserve it for you, señor, in case you should wish to have a sherry first at the bar."

The invitation to do so was too obvious to be misunderstood, but Terhune was not unwilling. He walked over to the bar and sat down on one of the high stools. The Spanish-looking girl at the other side of the bar interrupted her conversation with the three men already there and gave him a dazzling smile.

"Manzanilla, señor, I believe."

He was astonished. "How did you know?"

"By looking at you, señor. I can usually guess a señor's taste in sherry by his appearance."

She served him with the sherry, turning on her smile again as she did so. It was an exciting smile, and he thrilled to it, but directly he had passed over the money to her she returned eagerly to the three men, and continued the conversation apparently at the point where it had been broken off. Terhune grinned ruefully, and glanced at the people who were already eating.

Of the seven diners, four were at one table; all men, all foreigners; they spoke in a foreign language which he concluded to be Spanish. He regretted not being able to understand, for there was laughter both in the eyes and upon the lips of all four men. They spoke and shouted noisily, but the sound was not unpleasant, for they were so frankly enjoying themselves.

Another table was occupied by two people. He paid them little attention; they were obviously English, and obviously lovers; they spoke in low whispers, and were aware of no one but themselves. The man who sat at the third table came under a different category; noting that he could do so without being observed, Terhune inspected the other man with considerable interest. Was he a foreigner? Terhune could not decide—at first appearance, no! But a closer study made one doubtful. His hair was exceptionally black for a Briton's—and his brown eyes of an unusually dark shade. There was also a peculiarly saturnine cast to his profile, but presently Terhune appreciated the reason for this—the upper part of the left cheek was scored by a long white scar.

Unexpectedly the diner returned Terhune's stare, evidently becoming telepathically aware of his scrutiny. For a fractional part of a second the two glances met. Then Terhune turned away, embarrassed, with the reflection that he would not care to become an enemy of the man with the scarred face, because there was something ruthless, something frightening about the keen, suspicious black-brown eyes. As an unconscious measure of deception he proceeded to inspect the face of the man nearest to him at the bar; at the same time he drained his sherry with what he hoped was an air of complete detachment.

A chuckle of laughter passed along the line of three men and was echoed from the other side of the bar.

"I do not believe you, Tony; you are lying," the girl accused teasingly.

Tony—the man nearest to Terhune—shook his head. "I swear by Santa Maria that I have told you da trut', *cara mia*," he said, speaking with a strangely elusive accent, in a soft, smooth voice. "I have told you, word for word, what da dame said to her boy friend."

The voice was repulsive; it put Terhune in mind of a snake wriggling across a garment of stiff silk. Moreover, it matched the face of the speaker, for Tony had a round, plump face, a swarthy, greasy complexion, black sleek hair, and a slight moustache.

He went on: "Do you know what da boy friend's answer was, *cara mia*?" An anticipatory flash of white teeth. "He said to da dame: 'If I see you with dat son of a bitch again I shall...'" The rest of the sentence became a whisper, inaudible to Terhune. Not so to the rest of the group. They roared with renewed laughter; the girl behind the bar in particular; her shrill voice echoed round the restaurant. Tony waved his left hand in an expressive gesture. "Isn't dat da best ever, Dolores?"

Dolores wiped her eyes. "Fancy threatening Nicky with *that*—Tony, that's the peachiest story I've heard." She choked with bubbling laughter.

The conversation continued, but Terhune was not conscious of its purport. He gazed at Tony's stocky back, and told himself how absurd it was to allow one's imagination to run away with one—such an idea was fantastic, impossible. He turned, and thoughtfully studied his own reflection, which stared back at him from the ornate mirror which backed the rows of sherry bottles. The studious face appeared normal enough; the serene eyes behind the horn-rimmed spectacles quite sane; certainly it was not the face of a man given to indulging in wild theories.

"I suppose you are not off your chump, are you, Tommy, me lad?" he mentally asked the mirrored face. "It can't be that that little episode the other night has turned you screwy?"

If the face in the mirror were a reliable guide his suspicions were unjustified. Reassured, he again turned his head in Tony's direction. In doing so he smelled for the second time the pungent odour of garlic. It was unmistakable. Garlic! Garlic—and a soft voice...

"Steady, old lad, steady," he hurriedly warned himself. "Soho is another name for garlic; they eat it for breakfast, dinner and tea around here. Fancy a Soho restaurant without garlic! As for soft voices, there are plenty of those in the world. Remember young Dodds at school; all the kids called him Daisy because he had such a soft voice. So had that man who used to live at Folkestone. I always had a feeling I wanted to rub his tongue with a piece of sandpaper whenever I heard him speak."

This mental adjuration proved futile; the conviction deepened within him that Tony of the Restaurant Torremolinos and Soft-Voice of Helena's adventure were one and the same. To admit the possibility was to have faith in unbelievable coincidence—but if coincidences never occurred, doubtless the word would never have found itself in the dictionary. The chances of Tony's being the man with whom he had struggled in the Kylstone vault were a million to one against—no, forty million to one against (he believed that to be roughly the population of the United Kingdom), but it still remained strange that Tony had a soft voice and hands that reeked of garlic.

Terhune was astonished by the sheer excitement which was aroused within him by the possibility of Tony's being that other man. His was not an excitable nature; in company with others he had always believed himself to be more than normally stolid. Except when he was in the boxing ring or on the football field. Yet he was excited. Definitely. But why? That was a question for which he could find no ready answer. Granted that the incredible had happened; that both he and his adversary of last Thursday night had chanced to pick upon the same restaurant for luncheon—what of it? Was that any cause for excitement? There was nothing he could do. He could not have Tony arrested; what evidence had he to support such a wild charge? But supposing—supposing that Tony were Soft-Voice? Then Tony was one of five men who could supply an explanation of the mystery surrounding their attempts to recover a gold fountain pen from a burial vault—a pen which they could have had for the asking. Again—what of it? Tony might know the answer to several perplexing questions, but he was not likely to speak.

Terhune realized that his thoughts were becoming chaotic. He wondered if the sherry were responsible, though a single sherry had never before affected him to any extent. Perhaps food might help him to see the affair in its proper perspective! Besides, the girl Dolores was looking at him suspiciously. Evidently he was not supposed to sit at the bar with an empty glass in front of him. Yes, food, decidedly!

He left the bar and threaded a way through the chairs towards the small table reserved for him. In doing so he glanced in the direction of the scar-faced man. For the second time their glances crossed; again Terhune was impressed by the intensity of the other man's expression; it was vital, analytic, unpleasantly questioning. The brief encounter lasted no longer than before; Terhune passed on to his table, but he did so feeling that he was an object of keen interest to the man with the scar.

As he sat down a waiter approached him. "Good morning, señor," he greeted, handing over the menu.

Terhune glanced at the list; here and there similarities in language acquainted him with the nature of the dishes; it was not hard to guess that *Sardinas frescas* were probably fresh sardines, and *Un rosbif con patatas*, roast beef and potatoes. For the rest…

He took the easiest course. "The set lunch," he ordered.

"Very good, señor," the waiter muttered, with a hint of super-ciliousness in his voice to suggest that he was quite aware of why the señor had ordered the set lunch.

While he waited for the soup to be served, Terhune crumbled his roll of bread and absently began to eat; meanwhile he gazed at Tony, and meditated upon Tony's nationality, also upon the chances of Tony's being his adversary of the previous Thursday night. With regard to nationality, it seemed to him that Tony was probably an Italian American. That he was born an Italian was reasonably sure—the dark complexion, sleek black hair, tubby figure, soft voice, and the occasional Italian word, all went to prove this. At the same time, the use of American slang, and the American inflexion, suggested that he had spent many years in the United States. True, there were a number of Londoners, habitués of the cinema, whose habit it was to ape the American gangster of the screen, yet, having inspected them, and heard them speak (there were always many to be found in the Soho district), Terhune had always decided they were not the real thing. In Tony's case he did not suspect a sham. He was convinced that Tony had lived in the United States.

A puzzled frown settled on Terhune's high forehead. For the first time he realized that a link connected fact with theory. It was a slender, fragile link, liable to snap asunder at the first hint of critical analysis; still, it was a link. Lady Kylstone was an American. So, perhaps, was this man Tony. It was impossible to say what signif-icance there could be in this association of nationality, but it made Terhune regret that he could not know more of Tony, that he could not 'investigate' the American, as it were.

The waiter placed the soup on the table. Terhune thanked the man, and began automatically to eat. It was good soup, as one might expect of a new restaurant, but he was not aware of the fact; he was too preoccupied with the man at the bar. For instance, supposing that one were to learn that Tony had a bad record. Would such information not serve to add a second link to the first? In any event, it would be interesting to know just what kind of a man this Tony was; to obtain such information should be an easy matter to a firm of inquiry agents. Lady Kylstone, he was sure, would readily agree to pay the necessary fees. If only he knew Tony's name and address...

Excitement transformed his face as one reflection crowded in upon another. Why not try to learn that name and address? It might not prove a difficult matter. Dolores seemed on familiar terms with the man, but even if she could not supply Tony's address, she might be more helpful in respect of Tony's friends, one of whom might become the source of information.

Abruptly the spark of enthusiasm vanished from his face as he realized that he was trying to run before he could walk. He had assured himself that obtaining Tony's address should be easy. But it might prove a complicated and difficult matter. If Tony had a police record, for instance—*if*—then his friends (probably criminals, like himself) were not likely to disclose his address for the mere asking. Birds of a feather, they were more likely to put any inquirer on the wrong track. In fact, the two men at the bar with Tony might even be two of the men who had helped to break into the vault.

Fried sole replaced the empty soup plate. He picked at the fish, which was tasteless to his palate. In doing this he was unjust to the chef, for the sole was exquisite. Despondency, not the chef, made the food tasteless; he was like a prisoner staring through bars at green fields which he cannot reach. It seemed too bad that a possible clue to the mystery surrounding the fountain pen was within his reach, yet he dared not stretch forth an arm to grasp it.

The man with the scarred face paid his bill and walked out of the restaurant. Terhune saw him go, but paid no attention; he was interested only in Tony—Tony of the soft voice and garlic-impregnated hands. A mulish expression was settling on Terhune's face; there were occasions when he could become extremely obstinate, and this was one of them. Fate had guided him to the Restaurant Torremolinos; perhaps—who knows?—for the specific purpose of following up the affair of the gold fountain pen: it would be poor thanks for so generous a gesture tamely to leave the restaurant without making some effort to learn more of Tony. The point was—what could he do? What?

Tony himself supplied the answer. Sherry after sherry had disappeared down his throat; in the past five minutes his voice had become surprisingly louder.

"Betcha me life da dame wrote da letter to me," he shouted. "Betcha ten shilling, *beniamina.*"

"*Si?*" Dolores shook her black hair. "I would rather bet ten shillings; that's worth more than your life, Tony darling. But I won't bet a penny: no woman would have written like that to a man."

"You t'ink not?" He waved his arms about, nearly knocking over a sherry glass. "I will prove it to you—see? I have da letter at home. I will fetch it, and you shall apologize to me."

He slid off the stool, but she quickly held out a restraining arm. "Don't worry, my pet. The letter will keep. You can show it to me the next time you come in."

"You don't believe me, no? I'll show you. I am going home in ten minute time. I'll bring da letter wit' me tonight. I'll show you. Then you give me a kiss, no, instead of a ten-shilling note?"

"No," she asserted firmly. "I would sooner give you ten shillings than kiss a man who would make a woman write that kind of a letter. Keep your silly old letter. I don't want to see it."

He laughed boastfully. "I'll show you. Now give me another sherry, *cara mia.*"

Terhune's eyes glowed, for Tony's intention of returning home had given him an idea. He glanced at his wrist-watch. One-fifteen! By one-thirty he could finish his meal. That would leave two and a half hours to spare before the appointment with Lady Kylstone and Helena. In the meantime he would follow Tony home, to learn the address at first hand.

Flushed with eagerness to carry out his plan, he hurried through the rest of his meal in case Tony should leave earlier than intended. Tony, however, revealed no intention of leaving hurriedly, so Terhune ordered coffee and liqueur. When these arrived he asked for his bill, and paid it, so that he could be free to stay or leave as circumstances demanded.

For another thirty minutes Tony remained with his friends at the bar, but just as Terhune was beginning to despair of the Italian's intention to leave the restaurant, or, for that matter, that he would be able to leave it if and when the intention was transformed into action, Tony got off the high stool and announced in a loud voice that he was going home.

"About time, too, if you ask me," Dolores said pointedly. "I have never seen a man drink so many sherries at one session."

"You should worry! My dollars are good. Come along, boys."

To Terhune's dismay the two friends accompanied the Italian out of the restaurant—it had not occurred to him that they might leave as well. Further reflection reassured him; it should prove no more difficult to follow three men at once than one—perhaps easier, in fact. He hastily drained the remains of the liqueur, gathered his outer clothes, and followed the three men into the street.

They were not far away; they were parting company. As he slipped on his overcoat Tony went off to the right; the other two men went to the left, and disappeared into Charing Cross Road. Of this Terhune was not aware, for by then he was already occupied on the task of shadowing Tony.

It did not occur to him that the chase might be a long one; this was, perhaps, because the Italian had spoken so lightly of fetching the letter and returning there and then to the restaurant; it was scarcely likely that he would have journeyed any considerable distance just to prove his boastful words. No, Terhune's principal thought, as he carefully sauntered along Old Compton Street, was of astonishment at his own sensations.

He could not, indeed, comprehend the reason for the buoyancy of his feelings. He felt elated, gay; never more so. He was thrilled, excited; he could not remember ever having been more excited, even in his boyhood days. He felt utterly unlike Tommy Terhune of Bray-in-the-Marsh, he might have been a completely different person.

The Italian proceeded, slowly and not too steadily, for half the length of Old Compton Street. Presently he turned right, then left, then right again—before long Terhune found himself in streets which he recognized neither by sight nor name. They were far from being salubrious; not one face in a dozen looked British. He was not surprised; subconsciously he had imagined Tony's living in such a neighbourhood. Even as the reflection occurred to him the chase came to an end. The Italian turned into the doorway of a large block of tenement flats. Terhune was elated. Unless all his deductions and intuitions were at fault he had achieved something, however little, towards discovering the reason for robbing a family vault of a gold fountain pen.

III

Terhune found no difficulty in learning the name of the building which Tony had entered; it was carved in stone, above the main entrance, for all the world to see:

BLACKAMORE BUILDINGS
Anno Domini, 1890.

The name of the road he had already noted: Haymeadow Road.

Tony (Somebody or Other), Blackamore Buildings, Haymeadow Road—surely enough information for inquiry agents to work on. He glanced at his watch. Two-fourteen! Good going! he thought. There was still time to visit a news theatre before meeting his travelling companions. He turned away from Blackamore Buildings; though not without a feeling of reluctance. To leave the neighbourhood was an anti-climax. Having done so much, it seemed a pity to leave it to somebody else to carry on—after all, if an inquiry agent could ask a few questions, so could he, Theodore Ichabod Terhune, otherwise known as Tommy.

Probably the wish was father to the thought, but he had proceeded no more than a dozen paces on his return journey when he remembered Lady Kylstone's reluctance to give the police authorities any more information than she could possibly help with reference to the strange doings at Willingham. In the circumstances she might be just as unwilling to entrust a firm of inquiry agents with the investigation of Tony's identity.

He did not dare to consider this argument dispassionately, for he knew how intensely interested Lady Kylstone had since become in learning more of the gold fountain pen. Instead, acting on wilful impulse, he retraced his steps towards Blackamore Buildings, and mounted the four stone steps which led up to the door by which the Italian had entered the building.

Already he had invented a pat story: "Can you tell me which room Tony occupies? A ten-shilling note dropped out of his pocket while he was having a drink, I want to return it to him. What is his other name? I don't know; I only heard him called Tony; he has a small black moustache, black hair, dresses well" (the occupants of Blackamore Buildings might consider the flashy clothes modish), "and has a short, plump figure. Tony Balzani!" (Or Cesaresco! or Pasolini!) "That is probably the man I want. Where does he hang out? Third floor, fifth door on the right! Thanks, old man" (or missus! or sonny!).

Terhune congratulated himself as he passed into the cold, stone hall: there was more than one advantage to be gained by having a writer's brain; one could invent stories of that nature on the spur of the moment! If necessary, it could be embroidered——

A man brushed by him, outward bound. Terhune grimaced. His pat story was still-born, for it was none other than Tony who had bumped against his shoulder, and three people near by, a man and two women, had witnessed the slight collision. He couldn't spin the story to any of them…

For all that, his brain did work remarkably quickly.

"Was that Tony Cesaresco who just went out?" he asked the group of them collectively. "I wanted to speak to him."

"You mean Tony Malatesta, don't you?" the man grunted.

"That might be the name; most foreign names sound alike to me. The man I am after was named Tony something, and had a small black moustache. Are there any more Tonys in this building?"

"Tozens," replied one of the women with a disparaging sniff—she had the appearance of a Slav. "Te place is full of Tonys, Giuseppes and Pietros." She spat, with the aim and force of an artist in expectoration.

"Does Tony live on the second floor?" Terhune jerked his head doorwards, to indicate which Tony he meant. "That is where my Tony hangs out."

The same woman shook her head. "Tony Malatesta, he live on te first floor, number twenty-tree. Maybe, you mean Tony Cellini; he look like Tony Malatesta? He live on te secont floor, number tirty-eight."

"Maybe," Terhune agreed. He turned to leave.

"You want Tony Cellini, no? He is up tere in his room just now. I saw him go up tere not ten minutes ago."

Terhune silently cursed the woman, whose eyes, he noticed, were sharp with suspicion. He reflected quickly that it might be as well for him to go up to the second floor; he could always descend again later, pretending that Tony Cellini had turned out to be the wrong Tony after all.

"Thanks," he muttered, proceeding towards the circular stone staircase which led to the upper floors.

His shoes echoed hollowly on the stone floor; the atmosphere of the hall chilled him. Everything seemed of stone, cheap white tiles, or dirty concrete; floors, stairs, walls. Even the ceiling was of concrete, colour-washed a dirty lemon. He proceeded up the stairs, watched by the frankly staring eyes of the three people on the ground floor. Presently he ascended beyond their gaze, but though he was not a heavy walker, his progress remained noisy, for the concreted walls acted as a sounding-board.

He paused upon reaching the first floor, and listened to noises from below. He heard nothing; the hall was unpleasantly quiet. Unpleasantly, because there had been no sound of the three people going about their business. He was convinced that they were still staring upwards, listening to the sound of his movements. If they did not hear him continue his journey to the second floor they would become actively suspicious. He might find himself in a nasty situation. Blackamore Buildings might not be occupied by desperate criminals; at the same time, from the little he had seen of the people of the neighbourhood, he judged them to be peculiarly 'insular', and liable to resent uninvited guests.

Because he had no desire to become the centre of a rough-house he carried on to the upper floor. This he did, noisily, so as to leave the people below in no doubt about his movements. The ruse was successful; as he reached the second landing he heard the sound of their conversation, which gave him reason to hope that he had lulled any suspicions of him they might have had.

Perhaps now they will move on, he thought, as he leaned over the iron banisters. Unfortunately, they apparently had contrary intentions. The hollow echo of their voices travelled up the staircase well; the sibilant voice of the Slav woman indicated that she was continuing a long story of some woman who had been stupid enough to fall for a sailor...

He looked at his wrist-watch. Less than fifteen minutes had elapsed since last he had glanced at it. The matter of time was not yet urgent, but he felt very foolish, hanging over banisters waiting for the story of the stupid woman to reach its climax.

He heard a door bang. He turned swiftly, and saw a woman emerge into the stone corridor behind him; she carried a slop pail in one hand. She looked casually at him and proceeded to her destination, but he did not doubt that she would soon return to her room. It would be better, he believed, if she did not see him there when she came back. As noiselessly as possible he descended to the first-floor landing.

This, fortunately, was unoccupied. Meanwhile, the monotonous voice below continued. Like King Charles, the stupid woman was an unconscionable time a-dying (apparently the news of the sailor's marriage to a Glasgow girl had brought about a resolution to commit suicide), so Terhune decided to wait five minutes more, and then to take the risk of the Slav woman and her companions not believing the weak excuse he had prepared.

To his relief, some two minutes later he heard a burst of laughter from the three people below, followed by the sound of footsteps vanishing in the distance, and finally the bang of a closing door. Then silence. Cautiously he descended to the hall, which he found empty.

Once in the street he turned right, in the direction from which he had approached Blackamore Buildings. He was not sure that he would be able to find his way back to Shaftesbury Avenue, for Tony Malatesta's route had been as erratic as his unsteady gait. However, he believed that by going to the end of the road and there turning left he would find himself proceeding more or less in the right direction.

This he did. At the far end of the second road he found himself at a junction of several roads which, at first, he did not recognize. He eyed the various passers-by dubiously as he realized that he had wandered into a doubtful neighbourhood. He was not uneasy; the bad old days when only policemen in pairs or a doctor dared to walk about without fear of molestation were no more. For all that, he recollected that he had several pound notes in his wallet, and the expression of cunning and rapacity which seemed common to the foreign-looking faces which surrounded him was far from reassuring.

"Lost yourself, mister?"

He turned quickly. Two men were leering at him; stocky-shouldered men, with cloth caps and jerseys; typical looking toughs, the pair of them.

"Which way is Shaftesbury Avenue?" he asked curtly.

The feeling of uneasiness, caused in the first case by the furtive disreputableness of the neighbourhood, was not lessened by the reaction of the two men to his question. The taller of the two (he had a cauliflower ear) grinned broadly, and exposed his uneven, blackened teeth.

"Do we know the way to Shaftesbury Avenue, me old cock-sparrer?"

The second man (he had a cast in his left eye) puckered up his low forehead. "Shaftesbury Avenue! Why, ain't it the way the gent 'as just come from?"

"Come orf it, Bill. You ain't got no sense of direction whatever. Shaftesbury Avenue's that way." The first man pointed in an entirely different direction.

"Shurrup! Yore barmy. It's where I said; bet yer two to one in tanners."

"That's a bet. Let's ask them other two chaps there. Here, mates, what's the way to Shaftesbury Avenue?" They appealed to another two men who seemed to have appeared from nowhere. These two men slouched toward the group.

"What do you want to know for?" one of them asked.

"This gentleman here wants to find out."

"You do, eh?" The newcomer had a crooked nose; he, like the man with a cauliflower ear, looked like an ex-pugilist. "What do you want to go to Shaftesbury Avenue for, mister?"

"That's my business."

"Cocky, aren't you? Nice bit of stuff that coat's made of." He stretched out a gangling arm and rubbed his thumb and forefinger up and down the lapel of Terhune's overcoat.

There was unholy mischief in the faces of all four men; with a sinking feeling Terhune realized that he was in for a rough-house.

"Take your hand off my coat."

"Or what?" the other man mocked. "Looking for a scrap?" He squared up in a fighting attitude, but unexpectedly gave a violent push which threw Terhune into the arms of the man with the cauliflower ear. This second man pushed Terhune upright again, giving a loud oath as he did so.

Terhune glanced swiftly about in the hope of seeing one friendly face which might offer the prospect of assistance, but the ring of vicious thugs around him prevented his seeing beyond. Then the ring closed in; arms pushed him hither and thither, hands grabbed at him and ripped off the buttons of his overcoat, knocked off his hat. A pair of arms hung on to him from behind, a hand slithered into his inside breast pocket…

Suddenly the ring dissolved; one man alone remained behind. Terhune glimpsed a scarred face, startlingly familiar, and below, in the man's grasp, the precious wallet. He acted swiftly. He lashed out with a straight left, which caught the scarred face squarely on the chin; at the same time he grabbed at the pocket-book with his right. The tactics succeeded. As the other man rocked with the force of the blow, his grip on the wallet relaxed. Terhune did not wait to continue the combat, which could only end one way if the rest of the gang joined in again. He ran, ingloriously, as fast as he could, making for the most respectable-looking of the roads opposite.

There was a shout from behind; the sound of pounding feet. Terhune spurted. Though not quite so fast as the spurts which, in the past, had often scored a snap try, it carried him away from his long-legged pursuer. By threading in and out of the astonished bystanders he covered half the length of the street without losing his lead; ahead of him he saw a broader road, with a welcome stream of traffic flowing in both directions. The sight empowered his wind—he had only to reach the main road to be safe from molestation. He spurted again, but this time Nemesis overtook him. A man approaching from the opposite direction thrust out a leg; Terhune tripped over it, staggered about in a crazy pattern as he tried to recover his balance. Just as he became steady again, a pair of strong arms wrapped themselves round him, then a second pair. His own arms were twisted behind him in a threatening lock...

"We'll take him along, Jim." The scar-faced man picked up the wallet, which had fallen to the ground, and thrust it into his pocket. Then, to Terhune: "Unless you want a broken arm you'll keep quiet, me lad. Get a move on."

Helpless, there was nothing else Terhune could do. He moved forward, gazing despairingly at the faces of the people in the street, who stared at him with incurious eyes without making any attempt to rescue him, or even to remonstrate with his captors—he supposed they were all part of a criminal world into which he had strayed by accident.

So, through dismal streets unknown to him, the while he wondered whether some fantastic time machine could have wafted him back into London of a century ago. It couldn't be true that a twentieth-century London could be the scene of such an outrageous and blatant abduction. Where in the name of Heaven were the police? But there were no police to be seen, nor people with courage enough to assist him, although on three occasions he called out for help. The men to whom his appeal was addressed glanced at his captors, and laughed with wry embarrassment, as though they would have liked to assist, but dared not.

Unexpectedly, as they turned a corner, he caught a welcome glimpse of a blue uniform.

"Help, officer, help!"

The shout caused the policeman to whirl round. With startled eyes he stared at the approaching group of three men. Then, to Terhune's utter amazement, a broad grin spread across the constable's face.

Terhune wondered if the world had become a madhouse overnight. "Help!" he called out again. "Help!" Before he could add more he was forced by the compelling arms of his captors to turn to his right and mount a short flight of stone steps. It was then he recognized the familiar blue lamp of a police station!

I V

Terhune was marched before the desk sergeant, and his arms were released. The sergeant looked inquiringly at the scar-faced man.

"Picking pockets," the scarred man replied succinctly.

Terhune laughed. He couldn't stop himself.

"Stow that racket," the sergeant growled as he scratched something down in the book before him. "What's your name?"

Terhune succeeded in choking back his laughter. "Look inside there." He pointed to the wallet, which was now lying on the desk before the sergeant.

The desk sergeant scowled. "None of your lip, me lad. It won't do you any good. Now, what's your name?"

"Terhune."

The sergeant laboriously wrote down 'Terhune'. "Christian names?"

"T. I."

"I said names, not initials."

Terhune reddened. "Theodore Ichabod."

The desk sergeant slammed the pen down on the desk. "Look here, me boy, I don't know whether you're drunk or mad, but don't you serve up any of that funny business here. Theodore Ichabod!" he muttered angrily. "What do you think this place is, a ruddy Sunday-school?" He picked up the pen. "Now tell me your real names."

"Theodore Ichabod."

The sergeant's cheeks turned a brick-red. He glared at the man with the scarred face. The other man laughed. "Write it down; he may be telling the truth. I know a poor devil named Henry Mons Kitchener Wipers Brown."

"Wipers Brown! Ichabod Terhune!" The sergeant muttered something unintelligible as he scratched away. "Address?"

"One, Market Square, Bray-in-the-Marsh."

The sergeant thrust away his stool and stood up. He looked apoplectic. "If I hadn't got this uniform on——" he began thickly.

The man with the scar chuckled. "Keep your shirt on," he interrupted. "There is a Bray-in-the-Marsh in Kent, not far from Ashford."

"There is?" The sergeant glowered at Terhune and climbed back on to his stool. "Well, maybe he comes from there, maybe he doesn't, but there are too many funny names about this customer to please me." Nevertheless, he began writing.

"Now, may I ask a question for a change?" Terhune asked drily.

"What question do you want to ask?"

"Are you trying to charge me with an offence of some sort?"

"There isn't any trying about it. You are being charged."

"With what offence?"

"You know as well as I do. With stealing a money wallet."

"That is strange."

"What is?"

"I seem to remember reading in a text book on criminal law that *animus furandi*, or the criminal intent, must exist at the time of taking possession, and that the goods must be taken fraudulently and without a claim of right made in good faith—with intent, at the time of such taking, permanently to deprive the owner thereof."

"Think yourself a blooming lawyer, do you? If you go spouting all that stuff to the beak he'll give it to you hot and strong." The sergeant chuckled maliciously. "I hope he blooming well does, too."

Terhune continued drily. "To continue my argument. As the goods must be taken fraudulently and without a claim of right it follows that there is no larceny if goods are taken under a *bona fide* claim of right. Do you agree?"

"Thank the Lord, I don't have to. What are you getting at?"

"This, my dear sergeant! I possess a claim of right to that wallet for the simple reason that it happens to be my personal property. Therefore, under the wise and just laws of this country I cannot be charged with the larceny thereof, for a man cannot steal whatever belongs to him."

The sergeant gazed beseechingly at the scar-faced man, who picked up the wallet, opened it and began to examine its contents. There was a strained silence.

"He seems to be right," the man with the scar agreed in a toneless voice. "He has his name and address inside."

"Have I got to scratch all this Ichabod business out again?" the sergeant appealed.

"I am afraid so."

The sergeant glared at Terhune as if he particularly regretted scratching the name off the charge sheet. Meanwhile Terhune swung round to face the man who was responsible for his predicament.

"Perhaps you will give me a good reason for my not charging you with false arrest?" he demanded angrily.

The other man smiled mirthlessly. "I don't think I should try that if I were you, Mr. Terhune. Amateur lawyers should beware of going beyond their depth. False arrest is a ticklish subject. Besides, now that I am beginning to understand matters more clearly, I think you should thank me for saving you from being roughly handled by Tony Malatesta and his roughnecks."

"Tony Malatesta! Were those men friends of his?"

"I take it so, as Tony Malatesta was among them."

"I didn't see him."

"He was behind you. I believed that you were trying to steal the wallet from him; I apologize for the mistake. But why did you snatch the wallet from me and run like a hare?"

Terhune began to feel confused. "I—I thought you were—one of the gang."

"I! What made you think that?"

"Because of the way you were inspecting me at the Restaurant Torremolinos."

"While I was suspicious of you because of the way you were inspecting Tony Malatesta. I think you and I had better talk this matter over. But first"—he turned to the desk sergeant—"would you mind telling Mr. Terhune who I am?"

"With the greatest pleasure," the other man agreed, with unconcealed malice. "Detective-Inspector Octavius Ptolemy Maximilian Sampson, of the C.I.D."

The inspector chuckled. "The Sampson is right, Mr. Terhune. For the rest I am just plain John Henry. On your right is Detective-Sergeant Groves of the division. Would you mind accompanying me?"

The two men entered a small room and sat down at a table. "Now, Mr. Terhune, would you please tell me why you were so interested in Tony Malatesta?"

"Something made me suspect him of being a criminal."

"What was that something?" Sampson asked sharply.

"His soft voice, and the garlic on his hands."

"I don't understand."

Terhune realized that he was floundering in deep water. Lady Kylstone had stated expressly that she did not wish to inform the police of the queer events of the past Wednesday and Thursday nights; on the other hand, satisfying the sharp-eyed Inspector was likely to prove a very awkward matter if he did not reveal the true circumstances.

"It is not a matter entirely personal to myself..." he began hesitatingly.

"Please understand that I cannot compel you to make a statement," the inspector said with asperity.

"May I speak to you unofficially?"

Sampson reflected. "I cannot promise that, but if you care to trust to my discretion——"

Terhune decided to do so. "Last Wednesday night a Miss Helena Armstrong was motoring along a quiet country road in thick fog when her car was stopped, and she was attacked by five men who apparently wanted to steal something from the car. She cried out for help, and fortunately I rode into the picture almost at once. I—I—well, there was a rough-house in which I got the worst of it, but the village bobby came along just then, so the five men vanished as quickly as they could. Later, Miss Armstrong told me that one of the men, who had spoken in a soft, silky kind of a voice, had hands reeking with garlic."

"Ah!" Sampson's eyes glowed. "So when you smelled Tony Malatesta's hands you put two and two together?"

"Yes."

"What were the men after?"

"That is the point. After a series of deductions——" Terhune coughed. "I mean, after talking matters over we arrived at a conclusion that the only possible thing in the car which the men could have wanted to steal was the key of a family burial vault in Willingham churchyard."

"A burial vault! Whose vault was it?"

"The Kylstone family's," Terhune replied hesitatingly. "The Kylstone family have lived in the same neighbourhood for the past five hundred years."

"Had they buried the family treasure with the family bones?"

"Not to Lady Kylstone's knowledge."

"If they were desperate enough to hold up a private car in order to secure the key there must have been something of value in the vault which they were after."

"You might say the same thing of my wallet which Malatesta tried to steal, but I can assure you that the haul would have been worth less than five pounds."

"It was not the money Malatesta was after, it was your name and address."

"What on earth for?"

"I think I can answer that question. You followed Malatesta back to Blackamore Buildings, didn't you?"

"How did you know that?"

Sampson's grim face creased into a dry smile. "Because I followed you, Mr. Terhune."

"You followed me! Why?"

"Because I was interested in trying to find out why you were so interested in Tony Malatesta—I also was anxious to learn who you were, and where you lived. The only difference was that I had planned to satisfy my curiosity in a more legal manner."

"I—I didn't know you were trailing me."

"No?" Once again the inspector smiled. "But Malatesta knew you were trailing him."

"He couldn't have known that," Terhune protested. "I was extremely careful."

"In the manner of our best fiction writers, no doubt. Please do not think me critical, but we cannot all be specialists in the other man's business, and you are, shall we say, no specialist in the operation of shadowing people. I don't doubt but that Malatesta knew of your interest in him long before he left the restaurant. Probably he saw your reflection in the mirror staring at his back."

Terhune reddened. "Was I as obvious as that?"

"I am afraid you were. But to return to the vault—what did you say was the name of the family?"

"Kylstone."

"The Kylstone family vault. Have you any idea what Malatesta wanted from the vault?"

"I—have an—an idea," Terhune stammered.

"You have?" the Inspector ejaculated sharply.

"A gold fountain pen."

"A what?"

"A gold fountain pen."

"Was it also studded with precious jewels?" Sampson asked ironically.

"Of course, I—I may be mistaken. As you say, I am no specialist in—in amateur detection. Perhaps I had better give you the full story."

"It might be a good idea," the inspector agreed drily.

The story did not take long to tell, but by the time it ended Sampson was frowning.

"I congratulate you on some first-class deduction, Mr. Terhune. But although, for the moment, I must agree with you that it was the fountain pen which Malatesta was after, the story does not make sense to me."

"Nor to me."

"Of course not, but I venture to say that the business is the more incomprehensible to me because of my knowledge of Malatesta."

"Why?"

It was Sampson's turn to hesitate, but he did not do so for long. "You have trusted me with your confidence, Mr. Terhune, so I shall reciprocate. But anything I tell you must be in the strictest confidence, because the information is official..." He glanced inquiringly at Terhune.

"I shall not pass a word on to a soul," Terhune promised simply.

"Not even to Lady Kylstone—or—Helena?" Sampson stressed shrewdly, his vulturine eyes quite changed by the twinkle in their depths.

Terhune reddened. "No," he growled.

"Then read this cablegram." Sampson pulled a wallet from his pocket, from which he extracted a dirty, torn piece of paper, which he handed to his companion. "But don't ask me how it came into the possession of the police, for that is something which I may not tell you."

Terhune read the cabled message, which was comparatively short:

Malatesta, 145 Worthington Street, New York City. Come to London by next Clipper stop Expenses and reward guaranteed stop Have important job for you.

Blondie.

"So Malatesta is an American. I thought he was. Who is Blondie?"

"That is something else I cannot tell you—for the simple-reason that we do not know—as yet. I wish we did. It was in the hope of finding out the identity of Blondie that I was detailed to keep an eye on Malatesta."

"But why is this cablegram of such interest to the police?"

"Because Tony Malatesta is a criminal, Mr. Terhune. He is not what the Americans call a 'big shot', but, at the same time, he is not a man to go after small money. You called that gold fountain pen a clue to an unknown crime. You may or may not be right in assuming the fountain pen to be a clue. But that cablegram is, and for this reason: we know enough of Malatesta to be quite certain that he would not leave New York unless the promised reward was substantial. In other words, whatever crime is to be committed, you may take it from me that it is no petty crime but something of considerable importance to somebody."

"Would the stealing of a fountain pen from a family vault come under that category?"

"That is what I should now like to find out," Sampson admitted in his metallic, expressionless voice.

The Third Clue

Thursday was market-day at Bray-in-the-Marsh. On this day Bray roused itself from its lethargy. It was not an important market, as markets go, but it made a welcome break in a week of inactivity, and an equally welcome excuse for all the inhabitants from miles around to forgather. They came, ostensibly, for the purpose of buying their groceries at the cut-rate and multiple stores, but the real attraction lay in the pleasure of meeting friends and acquaintances, and of exchanging the latest gossip over a glass of mild-and-bitter, or a gin and 'It', according to one's taste and purse.

The people of Bray would have angrily refuted any charge of snobbishness, but would have admitted, proudly, that Bray was 'conservative'. This conservatism did not stop short at Bray's almost solid vote for the election of a Conservative member to the House of Commons, for Bray had more unwritten rules and customs of local procedure, to which townspeople and visitors alike were expected to conform, than Fred Botts, the local scapegrace, had children—and they were more numerous than the eleven officially accounted for by Somerset House, if local gossip could be relied upon.

Among such customs was the selection of the right bar at which to call for one's drinks on market-day. There were three bars in Bray. The first, and most important, was the saloon bar of the 'Almond Tree'. This bar was superior, for the 'Almond Tree' was by way of being an hotel. True, guests were few and far between, especially during the winter months, but nevertheless there were three bedrooms available (there had actually been three occasions in the present century when all three had been occupied simultaneously). Therefore the 'Almond Tree' justifiably called itself a hotel, though it steadfastly, and conservatively, refused to be starred in the motorists' handbooks published annually by the A.A. and the R.A.C. Here, in the saloon bar of the 'Almond Tree', one would find the county folk every Thursday morning: Sir George Brereton, Gregory Belcher, Jeffrey Pemberton (the judge's youngest son—a rip of a lad, predestined by fate to come to a bad end while indulging in some mad escapade, but immensely popular with all), Julia MacMunn (only, and headstrong, daughter of the Hon. Alicia) and her cousin Mary MacMunn Meredith, Major Blye, Colonel Hamblin (a distant relative of Lady Kylstone), Dr. Harris (patients permitting), Edward Pryce, the artist (he was establishing a reputation for sunsets), Isabel Shelley, the actress (engagements permitting), and, of course, Winstanley. Winstanley was poor, possessed a dubious reputation, had a habit of purchasing his wardrobe at the annual Church Fund jumble sale, and drank excessively, without becoming drunk. But Winstanley was Winstanley: a Winstanley had dug his roots into the local soil generations before Piers Kirtlyngton had won his knighthood at the Battle of Agincourt, and though the family tree had long since been blasted by the storms of adversity, Winstanley remained an honoured name in that part of Kent, and the last Winstanley occupied a favoured niche in local society. Nobody ever dreamed of calling him anything else but Stan.

The 'Almond Tree' faced Market Square from the north; that is, not fifty yards from Terhune's bookshop. Across the other side of the square was the 'Wheatsheaf'. The 'Wheatsheaf', an inn pure and simple, was the assembling place for the second strata of society; the more prosperous farmers: George Barker, of Oak Forest Farm; Bram Hocking, of Peartree Farm; George Moore, of Three Ways Farm; and the others; and the retired folk: Mr.

Mortimer, who had been a big London contractor, and was perhaps the wealthiest person between Ashford and the coast (he
would probably have taken his drink at the 'Almond Tree' had
his aspirates been more clearly defined); Evan Forrest, owner of
Forrest and Son, the big Ashford stores; Thomas Pain, veterinary
surgeon, and Dai Lluellyn, bank manager (occasionally to be seen
in the 'Almond Tree' when there was a question relating to an
overdraft to be discussed). The 'Wheatsheaf' possessed by far the
cosier of the two bars, but north was north, and south was south,
and never must the twain meet over a glass (except in the case of
Lluellyn, look you!). Market Square was No-Man's Land, the right
and proper place for Sir George to congratulate Bram Hocking
on his prize sow's latest litter, or Major Blye to ask Pain whether
he could possibly run over and take a look at Ladybird, who was
coughing rather badly.

Lastly, the 'Three Tuns'. This public-house was the resort of the
drovers, the shepherds, the smallholders, and the local tradespeople.
As might be expected, the 'Three Tuns' was tucked away down a side
street. Lomax, the lessee of the 'Almond Tree', did not recognize
Adams of the 'Three Tuns', but Dai Lluellyn knew which of the two
banking accounts was the healthier, and it was not Lomax's. Perhaps
that was because the 'Three Tuns' was always filled with customers,
whereas the 'Almond Tree' and the 'Wheatsheaf' had to rely upon
Thursday and Sunday mornings for their profits.

On the Thursday morning following his visit to London,
Terhune found himself besieged as never before. He was not long
in doubt as to the reason—overnight he had become a Person of
Importance, and a Near Hero. Who had started tongues wagging
it was impossible to discover, but Terhune had a shrewd suspicion
that Briggs was the guilty person. No sooner was the curtain of the
door raised to indicate that the shop was open than Sims barged in
breezily.

"Good morning, guv." He looked around with an admiring air. "Got a few books here on the quiet, ain't you, guv? Have you read them all yourself, guv?"

Sims was himself a Character. He had appeared in Market Square for the first time fifteen years previously. There he had set up a small trestle table, upon which he had heaped large piles of intimate clothing: cotton shirts, woollen socks, pants and vests, cotton stockings, woollen bloomers, stocking-ette petticoats, and fearsome-looking corsets.

"Roll up, me lucky lads and lasses, roll up, me lucky mums and dads," he had bellowed in a fruity, cockney voice. "Pay a visit to Slick Sims if you want to buy West End falderals at knock-me-down bargain prices. Slick Sims, that's me, me lucky lads and lasses. Slick's the name, see, because I buys cheaply, not because I does me clients. No blooming fear. On the word of a man wot has never told the word of a lie, I sells me goods so cheap I loses money on every blooming thing I sells yer. Straight I do. Don't you laugh, mum. I'll prove it to you." He picked up a pair of voluminous, brilliant red bloomers. "See this pair of what-yer-never-mentions-in-public? What d'yer think of this garment? Ain't it fine and handsome? Take it from yer new friend, Slick Sims, who hopes soon to be yer old friend, that you wouldn't buy a pair of thingamybobs like this in London's largest shop." The expected laugh was easily evoked from the circle of interested spectators who had begun to assemble. "Now then, mum, what would yer reckon ter pay for them in a first-class stores?" Naturally there was no reply. "All right, mum, if yer too shy to tell me, I'll tell you. Two and eleven-three. Yes, mum, two and eleven-three. Now listen to what I sell at. Five shillings! That's me price. Five shillings!"

Of course, everyone laughed. "Five shillings, mum. A ten-shilling article going for half price. Who'll offer me five shillings? All right, then, four and a tanner. Four and a tanner, four and a tanner. Four bob, four bob, four bob. Three bob, three bob, going for three bob; best bargain you've ever seen; three bob. Half a crown, half a crown, half a dollar, half a dollar, two bob, two bob, one and eleven, one and ten, one and nine, one and eight, one and seven, one and six—going for one and a tanner—gone! There you are, mum; didn't I say I lost money on everything I sold? Two and eleven they cost me to buy, and you buy 'em for one and a tanner. If that ain't losing money I don't know what is. And here's another pair. Going for three shillings, half a crown, two bob..."

From that day Slick Sims had never failed to set up his trestle table in Market Square every Thursday morning. He did a thriving business, for he was a great favourite. He had an inexhaustible fund of bawdy stories which could just about be told in public; and could give moderately good impersonations of the ruling favourites on the radio, stage, and screen.

In reply to Sims's question, Terhune laughed. "I've read a goodish number of them."

"Lord luv-a-duck! You musta learned a thing or two from them books, mustn't you, guv?"

"Why?"

"I wus just thinking, guv. Just thinking." He became confidential. "You can give a man a tip or two about the law, can't you, guv, if you wants to?"

"Who said so?"

"That's what I've heard this morning. A man says to me, he says: 'That there Mr. Terhune knows more about things than what you might think—about crooks, and 'tecs, and law, and what-not.' Well, guv, if that's true, and you'd like to give a man a hint on somethink what's worrying him, well, Slick Sims is the man wot thinks a nod's as good as a wink to a blind horse."

"Somebody has been telling you fairy stories, Sims. I am no lawyer."

"But you does know a thing or two about the law, don't you, guv? Isn't it true you gave the sergeant at a London police station a bit of lip?" Sims gave a ripe chuckle.

"Who told you that?" Terhune asked sharply.

Sims winked his eye and tapped his nose. "Never you mind, guv. No names, no pack-drill; that's me motto! Then it is true?" he queried eagerly. Before Terhune could make any denial, he hurried on: "Look, guv, supposing a man came up to you and offered ter sell yer a hundred pairs of boys' socks at two D. a pair wot you've never been able to buy at less than five D., what would you think?"

"I should think that I was being offered stolen property."

"And would you buy 'em, guv?"

"I certainly should not, because, quite apart from not wishing to have anything to do with stolen goods, I should know that I was chancing imprisonment by buying them."

"That's wot I thought, guv. Thanks fer the tip, guv. I wouldn't touch them socks with a ruddy barge-pole."

Sims breezed out, but almost immediately somebody else entered; Terhune recognized Jeffrey Pemberton. This was the first time Jeffrey Pemberton had visited the shop, for Jeffrey shared neither his father's preference for a legal career nor his partiality for reading as a recreation.

"Good morning. You are Terhune, aren't you?"

Terhune nodded.

"I should appreciate your advice. My old aunt celebrates a birthday next Sunday; she's as rich as Croesus, and has everything she can possibly want, so I thought I would buy her a book for a change. Have you anything you could recommend for a dear old soul of seventy odd?"

"That depends on her taste. Would she prefer fiction? If so, modern or classical? Or a travel book, a book on art, or one on animals——"

Young Pemberton gestured vaguely. "Something with big type and plenty of illustrations—her eyes are none too good in these days."

"Would she appreciate illustrated history, and reproductions of old furniture and pictures?"

"Have you something in mind?"

"I have a copy, as new, of Clifford Smith's *History of Buckingham Palace*. It would make a very handsome gift."

"The very thing," Pemberton agreed enthusiastically. "Aunt Matilda is a die-hard royalist—she was presented at Court, so she is sure to like anything to do with any of the royal palaces." As Terhune turned away to obtain the book from the shelves, he continued: "I say, Terhune, you've been having a gay old time lately if all I have heard is true. Is it true?" he concluded naïvely.

"That depends upon what you have been told."

"That you had a scrap with a gang of damned hold-up men, that you saved Lady Kylstone from being murdered by a burglar who had knocked down old Briggs and forced his way into the house, that you dug up some buried treasure from the Kylstone vault, and, to add to all that lot, you trailed a gang of pickpockets to their hide-out in London, and helped Scotland Yard to arrest them."

"Not ten per cent of that story is true," Terhune pointed out drily.

"Even ten per cent is pretty good. You are a lucky devil, Terhune. D'you know, I have wanted to run into adventure ever since I was a kid and read *Treasure Island*, but the only thing I have run into was an old man on a bicycle, which cost me a ruddy fine lecture from my old man, and my insurance company the best part of a hundred pounds. Is it true that you are an amateur detective in your spare time?"

"Most certainly it is not."

The younger man looked disappointed. "That is what somebody told me—I forget who. I am rather sorry you are not."

"Why?"

"I thought I might have given you a helping hand some time or other. I say, what about coming along to the 'Almond Tree' about eleven o'clock and having a drink?"

Terhune's eyes twinkled as he shook his head. "I am sorry, Mr. Pemberton, but I am much too busy to leave the shop on a market-day."

"Some other day, then?"

"Gladly," Terhune assured his visitor.

Two women entered the shop soon afterwards; they were apparently strangers to each other, and possibly because of this fact, neither of them spoke much to him except in connection with their business. He was painfully aware, however, that their eyes glowed with avid curiosity and he suspected that, had either of them had the opportunity of being alone with him for a minute or so, that curiosity would have been quickly translated into a series of questions. As it was, one of them—a Mrs. Doyle—was left behind, but even as she opened her mouth to speak, somebody else entered, a man this time, so she closed her mouth and left, stamping rather heavily in her disappointment at being deprived of a few minutes' gossip.

The newcomer, bent almost double with rheumatic age, handed two books to Terhune. "The old woman says as will 'e please not give her any more of them books about ghosteses. She never could stand for ghosteses, not never since I met her, which is nigh on fifty year gone."

As he turned away to select two more books for old Mrs. Hobby, the old man said, with a throaty chuckle: "It is lucky some of we don't mind ghosteses, mister. I ain't never seen 'un yet, though I've spent night after night at lambing time in the field next the churchyard at Willingham. Aye, and in fields close by other charches too, long afore I came to live in these parts. And you ain't afeared of they, neither, from what I heard just now in the tap-room of the 'Three Tuns'."

"Don't you believe everything you hear at the 'Three Tuns', Hobby."

The lined old face puckered into a crafty leer. "Us knows what to believe and what not to believe, mister," he mumbled. "Us shepherds hasn't lived nigh on seventy-three year of age without knowing which way the wind blows from watching the straw. Seventy-three come next Christmas Day, mister; and there ain't many men as can boast of being as healthy as me..."

Terhune had heard the story often enough to close his ears to it. Presently Hobby stumped out of the shop, but immediately afterwards Gregory Belcher entered.

"Morning, Terhune."

"Good morning, Mr. Belcher."

"Did you succeed in finding me a book on Tudor architecture when you went to town on Tuesday?"

Terhune handed over his purchase. "I think you will find this is on the lines of what you want."

Belcher took the book closer to the door, where the light was clearer. He was among the tallest of Terhune's clients, for he stood six feet two inches in his stockinged feet. Fortunately for him his shoulders were proportionately broad; they, together with a slight thickening of his waistline, saved his figure from being lanky. He had a fine head of hair, completely white, though this whiteness was obviously caused by lack of pigment rather than age, for his face, permanently tanned by South African sun, was that of a vigorous man in his prime. With no hat he looked fifty, with a hat he looked at least ten years younger. In actual fact—said gossip—Belcher was forty-four years of age.

For several good reasons Belcher was a favourite subject of local gossip. He was blatantly handsome—as almost any tall man with white hair and a weathered complexion is bound to be—he was invariably tailored to perfection (more often than not in tweeds), he was rich, occupied a beautiful estate, he had led an adventurous life in Africa, north and south, and, most important point of all, he was a bachelor, as fine a catch as any woman could hope for.

"The very book," he announced presently in a satisfied voice. "How much do I owe you?"

"I had to give more for it than I had expected," Terhune explained. "Apparently it is a rare book besides being an authority on the period. I am afraid I cannot let it go for less than thirty-five shillings."

"It is worth every penny of that to me." From a well-filled wallet he produced two one-pound notes, which he handed over. "By the way, I hear that you had quite an adventure while you were in town."

"Whatever you have been told is probably a gross exaggeration," Terhune assured the other man as he pushed two half-crowns across the table. "From what I have heard this morning, somebody has been spreading around a most fantastic story which, if it continues, will finish by making me out to be the Commissioner of Police himself, in disguise."

Belcher laughed. "You do not need to tell me anything about rumour, Terhune. Don't forget, I am one of the chief victims around here of the dear old ladies who add two and two together, and make the total eight and a half. What really happened?"

"Nothing much. I suppose you have heard what happened last week?"

"To Miss Armstrong?"

"Yes."

"I have been told some vague story or other about some men holding up Miss Armstrong's car on Wednesday night, of your rescuing her just in time to save her life. I am afraid I did not pay much heed to it; that sort of thing just doesn't happen in rural England—except in gangster films."

"Well, it did happen, Mr. Belcher—I mean, about Miss Armstrong's being held up. The rest of it is all nonsense, of course. At any rate, Miss Armstrong told me later that she had heard one of the men speaking in a peculiarly soft, oily sort of a voice; she also said that the same man's hands had reeked of garlic."

"Garlic!" Belcher interrupted sharply. "The man must have been a foreigner."

"That is what I suggested. Well, on Tuesday I went to lunch at a new restaurant in Soho. There I sat next to a foreigner who spoke in the soft manner Miss Armstrong had described, and whose hands smelled very strongly of garlic. An absurd idea occurred to me that he might be the man Miss Armstrong had described; on the spur of the moment I decided to follow him home in the hope of learning his name and address."

"What did you want with the name and address?"

"I thought Lady Kylstone might be interested in hiring the services of an inquiry agent to investigate the man."

"Lady Kylstone! Ah! You mean, because of that business at Willingham churchyard on the Thursday night? Then that story is also true? You did prevent some men from breaking into the Kylstone vault?"

"Yes."

"This time last week I should have refused to believe that this neighbourhood could be the scene of so many strange happenings. Well! Well! Well! But surely you were placing great faith in the proverbial long arm of coincidence?" Belcher added drily. "Evidently you are a young man with a strongly developed imagination. I take it, then, that you tried to follow this soft-voiced foreigner back to his home?"

"I did more than try. I succeeded."

The other man looked astonished. "You mean that you actually discovered his name and address?"

"Yes."

"Humph! Please do not think me sceptical, Terhune, but surely if the man with the soft voice had been a genuine criminal you would not have achieved success quite as easily as that? After all, you are not a professional detective, are you?" Terhune grimaced. "I am not, as I found to my cost. He must have known that I was following him because, a little later, he turned the tables upon me, and shadowed me."

"Of course you shook him off your trail, as I believe the saying goes?"

Terhune reddened; it seemed to him there was a note of raillery in the older man's voice. "No," he replied shortly.

"You do not mean to say that he attacked you?"

"Only to the extent of trying to pick my pocket."

"Why should he want to do that?"

"Presumably to discover my identity, and the reason for my following him."

"I see. Then did he not get your wallet?"

"Fortunately, no. The rumpus was interrupted just at the right moment. By a detective, as luck would have it."

"Well! Well! A most remarkable series of episodes, Terhune. As I have said previously, before it happened I should have hesitated to believe it, but apparently truth is stranger than fiction after all." Belcher frowned, perplexed. "Do you know why the men tried to break into the Kylstone vault?"

The question left Terhune in a quandary; he was not prepared to lie, nor did he wish to be rude to his visitor by making any allusion to the indiscreetness of the question. On the other hand, Lady Kylstone might not want any knowledge of the gold fountain pen to be circulated.

He decided to prevaricate. "As far as I know, there is nothing in the vault that anyone could possibly want." Which was true in its way, for the fountain pen was safe in Lady Kylstone's safe.

"An extraordinary story!" Belcher commented. "Well, thanks for buying that book for me, Terhune." With that he approached the door. Before he could open it, Mrs. MacMunn entered.

"Hullo, Gregory! What are you doing here? I thought you were with Julia. Ten minutes ago she coolly informed me that she must leave me to my own devices until further notice as she had a date with you at the 'Almond Tree'. What indelicate manners the younger generation have! In my youth I should not have dared to leave my mother without permission, and most certainly such permission would not have been granted for the purpose of meeting a man in a public-house——"

"Hotel, my dear Alicia," Belcher corrected drily.

"To me there is no difference between an hotel saloon bar and a public-house," she said with asperity. "I had been married for five years before any alcohol passed my lips, and ten years before I even saw what a saloon bar was like. I still enter one with a feeling of distaste——"

"But you do so on occasions, Alicia."

"Of course I do; if I did not I should never see my daughter except at breakfast. But what was I saying——" she gestured vaguely.

"You were asking me what I was doing here."

"That is right; I was," she confirmed with a quick nod of her head. "What are you doing here, Gregory?"

"Buying a pair of ice skates, Alicia," Belcher replied drily. "Now I must go; Julia does not like being kept waiting. See you tonight." With an exaggerated sweep of his hat Belcher went out into the street.

Mrs. MacMunn turned a confused face towards Terhune. "Do you sell ice skates as well as books, Mr. Terhune?"

"I—no—I—I am afraid Mr. Belcher was—was pulling your—I mean, making fun..." Terhune came to an embarrassed stop. "I—I mean——"

"I know what you mean," Mrs. MacMunn said severely. "Tonight I shall tell Gregory Belcher what I think of his rudeness." Her manner changed; she became confidential. "Would you forgive my asking you a personal question, Mr. Terhune?"

He suppressed a sigh, for he believed he knew what the question would be.

"Certainly, Mrs. MacMunn."

Her voice sank to a whisper. "This morning I was told that you were a private detective. There is something which I must really tell you, although you will think me a stupid woman——"

"Please, please!" he pleaded hastily.

"What is it, what is it?" she asked, her expression confused, as if finding it no easy matter to readjust her interrupted train of thought.

"It is not true that I am a private detective. I never have been, and am never likely to be."

"But you saved Helena Armstrong from those terrible men last week?"

"I—I happened——"

"And you stopped somebody from robbing Kathleen Kylstone's vault?"

"Yes, but——"

"And you followed a celebrated London criminal back to his home?"

"I—I——"

She allowed him no time to finish his sentence—Alicia MacMunn rarely allowed anyone to finish a sentence. "Well, then, that makes you a detective," she claimed triumphantly. "That is what I want to speak to you about. What you did for Kathleen Kylstone, you can do for me. Will you, Mr. Terhune? Will you, for my sake?"

"Will I do what, Mrs. MacMunn?" he asked helplessly.

"Solve the mystery that has been haunting my life for the past twelve months," she replied surprisingly.

11

The morning continued as it had begun; the stream of people in and out of the shop was almost continuous. It was amazing how many residents had suddenly developed an interest in books; the names of many of them he knew only by hearsay, their faces he but vaguely recognized from having seen them at various local entertainments and celebrations—the Easter Monday Point-to-Point, the Rector's Annual Garden Party, the annual theatrical all-star matinée organized by Isabel Shelley and held at the local cinema, the Cottage Hospital whist drives, and so on. Although he knew only a small proportion of these people, he was surprised to learn how many of them knew him.

"Good morning, Mr. Terhune. It is so long since I last saw you—wasn't it at the dear Rector's last party? I have often said to myself: 'I must call in at Mr. Terhune's sh——er—library, to see whether he has any second-hand books on Spain. I love Spain—I was there for five days once, I feel I know it so well…"

Or: "Morning, Terhune. Thought I would take advantage of being in Bray today to speak to you on the matter of a good book on golf. Pickering—you know Pickering, of Puckhill Top?—is an obstinate old fool; his golf is becoming atrocious, but he won't employ the pro to put him straight. Says the pro would upset his style, and all that nonsense. But, between ourselves, I think he wouldn't be averse to picking up a few wrinkles from a book…"

Or: "Good morning, Mr. Terhune. My little Elizabeth is just becoming interested in dolls. Has there ever been a book published on dolls of all nationalities?"

The variety of books asked for by his visitors was legion, but one desire was shared in common—the desire to hear something from his own lips of the strange adventures with which rumour was crediting him. Long before the morning was half way through he was heartily sick of the subject and almost wishing he had never met

Helena Armstrong in the fog, even though the morning's turnover was three times greater than it had ever been. He lost count of the number of times he denied that he was either an amateur detective or a hero; upon each occasion his denial became shorter, and the tone of his voice more curt.

After noon, however, the pressure slackened, and at twelve fifteen he was gladdened by the appearance of Helena.

"Hullo, Tommy." She gazed at his serious face. "Why so worried? Haven't you done any business this morning?"

"Business! I haven't had a minute to breathe from the moment I raised the blinds until about ten minutes ago."

"Why the sudden interest in books?"

"The interest isn't in books but in me."

"You!"

"Yes," he told her, disgusted. "I have become a local hero. Everybody living within fifty miles of Bray has dropped in this morning to hear a personal account of my exploits."

She giggled. "That should teach you not to boast."

"Boast!" He choked with indignation. "Tell me, Helena, have you and Lady Kylstone discussed that little adventure of mine in town on Tuesday?"

"Naturally; it has been our chief topic of conversation ever since. After all, it isn't everyone who has the privilege of being friendly with a man who has thrice defeated the machinations of a band of desperate criminals."

He reddened. "Don't you pile it on too. Was Briggs about at the time of some of these discussions?"

"Very probably. Lady Kylstone is always talkative at meal times."

"I'll bet he is guilty of beginning the rumours. You wait until he comes in here for the latest Lawrence Meynell."

"Before I forget, Tommy, I have a message for you from Lady Kylstone. She says would you care to join us for dinner tonight?"

"Tonight! I should love——" He paused, then muttered an explosive "Damn!"

"What is the matter?"

"I have a previous engagement. With Mrs. MacMunn."

"With Mrs. MacMunn?"

"Yes. It is all a result of this stupid rumour that I am clever at amateur detecting. I tell you, I could wring old Briggs's neck for him, the silly old ass. I'll bet he was responsible in the first case. At any rate, apparently she has been haunted for the past year by some stupid mystery or other, so she has insisted upon my visiting her tonight so that she can tell me all about what happened. I tried to wriggle out of accepting, but you know what Mrs. MacMunn is—she is rather overpowering."

The happy twinkle faded from Helena's eyes, "Is—is Julia going to be there too?" she asked tonelessly.

"I suppose so. Why?"

"Oh, nothing! I just wondered."

"You must have had some reason for asking."

She shrugged her shoulders. "I know Julia MacMunn. She and her mother dine with Lady Kylstone every now and again. If I were a mother I should not risk leaving a five-year-old son of mine in the same house with her. She is a born vamp."

"I must admit that she looks one," he conceded. "For myself, I do not like that slinky, black-haired, sloe-eyed type of wench."

"That makes the danger the more acute. If Julia senses that you do not like her she will pick on you from sheer devilment."

"No woman would make me like her if I did not want to," he boasted.

She sighed. "You men!"

"Besides, I believe Gregory Belcher is to be there, too."

"Worse and worse," she muttered with a catch in her voice. "She has been angling after Gregory Belcher ever since he arrived here nine months ago. She is sure to encourage you if only to try and make him jealous."

"Thank you for the compliment," he said drily. "And do you really think of me as a puppet to dance according to how Miss Julia pulls the strings?"

Helena shrugged her shoulders. "I think it is time we changed the conversation, Tommy. After all, it is no business of mine if you are made a fool of."

III

Mrs. MacMunn had not Lady Kylstone's virtue of punctuality, as Terhune found to his disadvantage. Upon arrival at Willingham Manor he was shown by Phillips, the butler, into a long, narrow drawing-room, drearily overburdened by the cumbersome furniture of the early Victorian period. In summer the room was pleasant enough, for it had twin bay windows flanking tall glass-panelled doors, and a charming vista of immaculate lawns, extensive flower-beds, and beyond, the woods which separated the property from Lady Kylstone's. In winter, however, even the large fire which roared in the grate could not keep at bay the numerous draughts which were drawn towards the chimney from every window and door in the room.

"I will tell Madame of your arrival," Phillips said as he withdrew.

Terhune sat down on a chair which was situated at a polite distance from the fire, but it was not long before he became acutely conscious that a particularly virulent draught was whistling round the back of his neck from one of the bay windows. He endured it for several minutes, but as there was no evidence of an immediate appearance on Mrs. MacMunn's part he moved nearer to the fire, and sank into a cosy chair there. Soon a fierce heat was beating against his face and chest, but his ankles and feet remained chilled from a draught which flowed along the ground, Presently, in sheer desperation, he thrust them stiffly out before him so that they, also, might benefit from the fire.

More minutes passed. Outside, the wind howled dismally and a stray branch beat against the window with infuriating monotony. At first he was aggravated by this tapping noise, but soon he grew beyond caring, for he became drowsy with the heat of the fire. Just as he was about to fall asleep he heard the sound of a thump outside the door, and Mrs. MacMunn's high-pitched voice saying: "Dear me! Phillips, you really must move that table to some other place. I am always knocking it over." He jumped hastily to his feet.

Mrs. MacMunn swept into the room, her hand outstretched. "Good evening, Mr. Terhune. It was good of you to come. On such a windy night, too. Upstairs the noise of it is quite alarming; at one moment I felt sure that something really had to blow down. I hope you have put your car away safely in the garage."

"I have no car, Mrs. MacMunn. I came here on my bicycle."

"No car! Dear me! Dear me! I thought everybody had a car in these days. Then, of course, you prefer cycling to motoring?"

"As a matter of fact I do, for short distances."

"Ah! Then you share that preference with my dear father. It was always with difficulty that we could persuade him to go anywhere in the brougham if his destination was within walking distance. When bicycles were invented he was even worse, my poor mother told me. As for motor-cars, to the day of his death he refused to enter one. He thought they were an abomination." She sighed. "Sometimes, when Julia is driving my car, I agree with him. She is such a reckless driver. But there, I did not ask you here tonight to talk to you of my family, but to tell you of The Mystery. Please sit down, Mr. Terhune. We cannot dine yet—Julia is not yet home. I haven't seen her since my visit to you this morning; she sent me a message to say that she was going for the day with Gregory Belcher, but that she would be back in time for the meal——"

Julia gave the lie to her mother's statement by entering at that moment, with Gregory Belcher close behind.

"Hullo, Mother! Is dinner ready? I am famishing——" She paused abruptly, seeing Terhune.

"Julia, my dear, this is Mr. Terhune; I have asked him to dine with us tonight. Mr. Terhune, this is my wilful daughter Julia."

Julia held out a cool hand to Terhune. "Surely we have met before? You face is familiar."

"Of course you have; Mr. Terhune keeps the bookshop at Bray."

"Indeed!" Julia's sharply pencilled eyebrows expressed her astonishment.

Mrs. MacMunn indicated Belcher. "And this is Mr. Belcher." She laughed shrilly. "But, of course, you two know each other. I saw you in Mr. Terhune's shop this morning. Which reminds me, Gregory; you were very rude to me this morning. You pulled my arm—no, I mean my leg——"

"No difficult feat with you, Mother," Julia interrupted sharply. She inspected Terhune with supercilious eyes. "You said nothing to me this morning of any intention to have visitors tonight?"

"I had no intention then. It was not until I heard from Colonel Hamblin that Mr. Terhune was a very clever detective——"

"A detective!" Julia's dark eyes rested scornfully upon the insignificant figure of the embarrassed Terhune. "Are you a detective, Mr. Terhune? If you will forgive my saying so, you do not look like one."

"I—I—it is all a result of a misunderstanding——"

"My dear Julie," Belcher interrupted, "surely you must have heard of Terhune's exploit in rescuing Helena Armstrong from a gang of cut-throats—to say nothing of Kathleen Kylstone's family vault—I thought everybody in the neighbourhood knew of the story. It has caused quite a sensation."

"Is that what Jeffrey and Mary were talking about at the 'Almond Tree'?"

"And Blye, and Stan and Pryce and Uncle Tom Cobbley——"

A flicker of interest glowed in Julia's eyes. "Did you really do all those things people are saying you did?"

"The entire affair has been grossly exaggerated," Terhune assured her, unhappily.

"That is just his modesty, Julia. Do not believe his denials. I *know* what excellent work he performed. Hamblin told me everything, and he should know, being Kathleen's first cousin once removed, or uncle by marriage, or something. Anyway, that doesn't matter. In the circumstances I have decided to ask Mr. Terhune to investigate my Mystery."

"Mother!"

"Don't glare at me like that, Julia. It has worried me too long already."

"That stupid affair!"

"It was not stupid. For all we know, we might all have been murdered in our beds."

Julia turned away with a gesture of impatience. "I hope you are not proposing to tell Mr. Terhune the story before dinner. I have a ravaging hunger."

"If you had arrived home on time you could have satisfied it by now."

Julia laughed lightly. "I am sure you would not have been ready even if we had been on time." She turned to Terhune. "I call you as witness, Mr. Terhune. How long has Mother been downstairs?"

Belcher gave Terhune no chance of replying. "For Heaven's sake, Julie, have pity on Terhune. It isn't fair on him, to be drawn into one of the interminable arguments between your mother and yourself on his first visit here. It is bad enough when you treat your *old* friends to them. Don't you agree, Terhune?"

"I—I——"

"You see, Gregory," Mrs. MacMunn interrupted triumphantly, "Mr. Terhune will be no party to your rudeness. But as you want the meal in a hurry you shall have it." She rang the bell. "Though, speaking for myself, I do not feel in the mood for eating."

"That probably means that you had tea with Mrs. Harris," Julia scoffed.

"How did you know that?" her mother asked ingenuously.

"Because I know how that woman eats. It has always amazed me that her husband allows her to eat so much. Being a doctor, he should know better."

"She doesn't get any fatter in consequence," Belcher commented, as he hastened to open the door to Julia and her mother.

Terhune seldom enjoyed a meal less than the one he ate that evening. In the first place, Mrs. MacMunn revealed the extent of the tea she had shared with Mrs. Harris by trifling with her dinner, and the less she ate the more she talked. Her tongue rarely ceased, and what made her chatter the more aggravating was the fact that she never exhausted one topic of conversation, but, like a butterfly fluttering from flower to flower, she skimmed from subject to subject, often with so little reason that her audience were left at a loss to know what possible train of thought had led her to switch from the latest Academy success to the golf course at Westward Ho!, or from her losses at contract bridge to news of a cousin who lived in New Zealand. Upon rare occasions she addressed direct questions to one or another of the other three people who sat round the table, but in nearly every case she interrupted the answer before it was completed.

Yet this one-sided conversation was not without one advantage where Terhune was concerned. Finding it unnecessary to pay strict attention to his hostess, he interested himself in Julia. It was not long before he found himself acknowledging that she was extraordinarily attractive in appearance, if not particularly so in manner. There was a suggestion of gypsy in Julia, for her hair was blue-black, and so lustrous that it reflected all the high-lights, and created the impression of being burnished. There were depths, too, in her eyes, which were sometimes sleepy, but more often mocking, as though she harboured a private grudge against the rest of the world. Her complexion was wind-coppered; her lips vividly scarlet. Unexpectedly the reflection occurred to him that if reincarnation were a commonplace of existence, then Cleopatra lived again in Julia MacMunn—but a Cleopatra in whom the torch of passion had not yet been lighted.

As though intuitively aware of this inspection, during a rare moment of silence on the part of her mother, Julia directly faced him.

"Why do you live at Bray, Mr. Terhune?"

The question confused him. "I—I must live somewhere, Miss MacMunn."

"But why at Bray?" she persisted.

"Why not, Julia?" her mother interrupted. "Why do you live at Willingham?"

"Because I have the misfortune to have a mother who lives at Willingham," she replied scornfully. "If I had freedom of choice I should not live in a stupid little country village."

"Bray is not a village; it is a town."

"A town! Mother, how can you call Bray-in-the-Marsh a *town?*"

"It has a population of more than a thousand, and also a market, my dear, which is more than Willingham has."

Julia shrugged her shoulders petulantly. "If I were a man—a young man like Mr. Terhune—I should not waste my life living in a place like Bray."

"Surely it is Mr. Terhune's private business where he wishes to live, Julia?" Mrs. MacMunn said sharply.

"Of course it is; that is why I am so curious to learn his reasons. If he had to live there I could sympathize with him. As it is…"

"As it is, Miss MacMunn?"

"I despise a man without ambition, especially an intelligent man. And I give you credit for possessing more than a fair share of intelligence."

For once Terhune was stung to asperity. "Thank you," he murmured ironically.

Her eyes twinkled, as if she were pleased by his annoyance. "I am quite sure that Bray offers nobody any prospects of advancement; I am surprised that anyone can make a bare living from it."

Belcher chuckled. "Except the publicans, Julia."

"And especially the 'Almond Tree'," Mrs. MacMunn added sharply. "I am sure you and Gregory alone spend enough at the 'Almond Tree' to keep Lomax in comfort. Really, Julia, I cannot make you out. Your rudeness is inexcusable."

"Do you think I am rude, Mr. Terhune?" Julia challenged.

He felt strangely bold. "If you will forgive my saying so, I do, Miss MacMunn."

Belcher laughed cynically; Miss MacMunn beamed approvingly at her guest. But Julia's eyes sparkled angrily.

Feeling that he was master of the situation, and revelling in the sensation, Terhune continued easily: "But I have no objection to satisfying your curiosity. I live in Bray because I love the countryside and dislike city life, because I appreciate peace and quietness, and lastly, because I have no ambition above books."

"Now are you satisfied?" Mrs. MacMunn asked her daughter. "Personally, I endorse everything Mr. Terhune says. I am sure I would prefer to live on one pound a week in the country to existing on five in a city."

Julia's lips drooped sullenly. "I have no doubt Mr. Terhune has told us the truth about himself," she snapped. "But has he told us the whole truth?" She turned pointedly to Belcher, as though to put an end to the subject. This she did, thanks to her mother, for Mrs. MacMunn said lightly:

"Speaking of a pound a week, my dear, do you know that Mrs. Stubbs has not received any money from her husband again this week?..."

At last the meal ended, and the four people returned to the long, draughty drawing-room. There Phillips served coffee and brandy. As soon as he withdrew, Mrs. MacMunn turned excitedly to her guest.

"I am not going to wait another minute before telling you of the Mystery," she began. "To begin with, it took place last October."

"September," Julia interrupted drily.

"Nonsense, Julia, it was last October. I remember distinctly——"

"September."

"You are most annoying. I know it was October because I had just come back from the funeral of your dear uncle. Gregory——" She appealed to Belcher.

"I have always understood that Uncle Jasper died some time during the third week in October, Julie."

"Of course he did," Julia confirmed contemptuously. "But it was Mark Brereton's funeral Mother had attended."

"Was it poor Mark's funeral? Well, I knew it was the funeral of somebody with a name beginning with B. Then it was last September... but there, I suppose I ought to tell you first about my dear father. Do you remember Father, Mr. Terhune? He died about five years ago, the poor soul."

"I remember him quite well, Mrs. MacMunn; he bought quite a number of books from me."

"Of course he did. How silly of me to forget that. Then you know how fond he was of books, especially during the last ten years of his life, when he came to live with us after the death of my husband..."

"A number of people seemed to have died lately in this neighbourhood," Belcher commented cynically. "So far, this story of yours, Alicia, is a catalogue of deaths."

"Didn't you know that Mother revels in deaths and funerals, Gregory?"

"Be quiet, the pair of you," Mrs. MacMunn snapped. "I am telling the story to Mr. Terhune, not to you, Gregory."

"But I haven't heard it before, have I?"

"Haven't you? Then listen more carefully, and do not keep interrupting. Now I have forgotten what I was saying."

"About your father's love for books," Terhune prompted.

"Yes, of course. If you sold books to him then you probably know that his pet subjects were genealogy and heraldry?"

"I do. Was he not engaged on a genealogical and heraldic history of the principal families living round about Bray and Willingham?"

Mrs. MacMunn nodded her head violently. "Yes. He had got as far as the T's when he died."

"Then he cannot have left much unwritten," Belcher interrupted again. "Offhand, I cannot think of any U's, V's, or W's. Nor X's, Y's, and Z's," he added, with a chuckle.

"The Unwins and the Williamsons," Julia pointed out.

"No great loss to any genealogical history."

"That is just where you are wrong," Mrs. MacMunn contradicted triumphantly. "The Williamsons can boast of a murderer among their ancestors. Of course, the crime was political."

Terhune gazed despairingly at his hostess, wondering whether it was possible for her ever to maintain one train of thought for more than thirty consecutive seconds. From her he glanced at Belcher's cynical face. Perhaps if only he would control his caustic tongue her story might ramble less; it was a great pity he had to be present in the house on this one evening. Then Terhune's face reddened, for he looked into Julia's mocking eyes, and realized that she had divined his thoughts and was laughing at him.

"Don't forget that Mr. Terhune has to return home *some* time *tonight*," she reminded her mother.

"I am telling the story just as quickly as I can," Mrs. MacMunn retorted indignantly. She faced Terhune. "I do hope you are not feeling the draught. This is such a draughty room, especially when the wind is from the southeast."

His feet were chilled by a piercing draught of which Mrs. MacMunn seemed totally unaware, but he dared not say so; as Julia had said, he wanted to return home at a respectable hour.

"I am quite warm, thank you," he lied desperately.

"Julia wants me to instal central heating, but I am one of those old-fashioned women——"

"Mother dear! For heaven's sake finish your story before Mr. Terhune forgets the beginning of it."

"If he has heard the beginning of it," Belcher remarked.

"Of course he has; Father's history forms part of my Mystery. I should explain that he wrote the history entirely for his own amusement. He had a thick volume of lined parchment specially bound for the purpose. In it he wrote, in tiny longhand, the gene-alogy of all the local families, annotated by personal anecdotes of past and present members, and illustrated by coloured drawings of their armorial bearings. Father was meticulous in his work; I do not believe that he overlooked any interesting facts, which he obtained from many sources, like the British Museum, the Records Office, Somerset House——" She paused abruptly and turned to Belcher. Terhune groaned inwardly.

"You have reason to be grateful to that history, Gregory——"

"I know, I know, my dear Alicia. You have told me that a dozen times already, so tonight I will say it for you. Because of what your father learned of my family tree, when my uncle died you were enabled to advise the solicitors to the estate that I was the only heir. Would you like me to thank you for the thirteenth time?"

"You are intolerably rude tonight, Gregory. You have probably had too much to drink." She faced Terhune again. "Well, dear

Father had written this history of his as far as the T's when the poor dear soul died, leaving the work uncompleted. After his death it was suggested to me that I should offer the volume to the British Museum, but I felt that I just could not bear to part with it so long as I was alive. I decided to keep the precious volume in the library, and to will it to the Museum at my death—knowing that Julia was far too soulless for it to appeal to her."

Julia blew a smoke-ring into the air. "You are so sweet to me, Mother dear!"

Mother dear let the remark pass unchallenged—at last she seemed really to have applied her mind to the story.

"Well, I gave the precious volume a place of honour in the library, and there it remained for the next five years. And then came the day of the Mystery, the day of Mark Brereton's funeral last October——"

"September," Julia murmured.

"September then! Well, Julia and I were comforting the widow at her home while the remains of her husband were proceeding to the church, when suddenly I felt so ill that I could not wait for the funeral to be over before returning home. I left, leaving Julia to comfort Nan Brereton. Upon arriving home, Phillips said to me: 'It is fortunate you are home early, madame. The gentleman said that he did not think he would be able to stay for more than twenty to thirty minutes. I told him that I did not think you would be returning for at least two hours.'

"'What gentleman?' I asked Phillips.

"'The gentleman from Messrs. Foyles, the London booksellers,' he replied.

"'Gentleman from Foyles! I have not the slightest idea what you are talking about, Phillips.'

"'But, madame, I understood from the gentleman that you had requested his presence here.'

"'How absurd! Why should I be wanting a bookseller to visit me? There are enough books in this house already, without my wanting to buy any more.'

"'He led me to believe, madame, that you wanted to *sell* some books, not buy them. That is why he asked to be shown into the library, so that he could be making use of his time in assessing the value of the books.'"

Mrs. MacMunn came to a breathless pause. Belcher applauded.

"A very creditable performance, Alicia. You must have been taking lessons in histrionics from Isabel Shelley."

"Shut up, Gregory!" Julia ordered shortly. "Don't be so damned condescending; when you are, you become completely detestable."

Mrs. MacMunn ignored the asides. "You can imagine my bewilderment, Mr. Terhune, when Phillips told me about the man from Foyles, for it had never occurred to me to sell my dear father's books. Naturally I went immediately to the library——"

"I thought you were feeling ill, Alicia?"

Mrs. MacMunn bestowed a withering glance upon her tormentor. "Julia used too mild a word when she called you detestable!" To Terhune, again: "As I opened the library door I noticed the man fold some long sheets of paper into four and thrust them into his pocket. Directly he saw me he said: 'Good morning, madame. I am from Messrs. Foyles——'

"'What are you doing here?' I demanded.

"He looked surprised. 'I was instructed to come here for the purpose of valuing your library, so that we might make you an offer for it. I have just completed the task.' He touched his pocket, so I concluded that the papers he had just placed there were his notes.

"'I have no wish to receive any offer for my books,' I told him. 'I have no intention of selling them.'

"'But, Mrs. Mortimer——'

"'I am Mrs. MacMunn, not Mrs. Mortimer. Mrs. Mortimer lives at Wickford Manor.'

"He appeared terribly distressed. 'Then I must apologize most humbly, madame. My firm distinctly informed me that I was to call upon Mrs. Mortimer at Willingham Manor'——

"Well, to shorten a long story, Mr. Terhune, the man departed after many apologies for having troubled me, and I gave the matter no further thought until some days afterwards, when I met Mrs. Mortimer at—at—where did I meet her, Julia?"

"Does it matter, Mother?" Julia asked wearily.

"No, I suppose it does not," Mrs. MacMunn admitted vaguely. "During the course of conversation I expressed the hope that her husband was not too hard hit by the Stock Exchange slump, and that Messrs. Foyles had been able to make a satisfactory offer for her library——"

"Me-ow! Me-ow!" Belcher taunted.

"If you knew the airs that woman puts on because her husband is wretchedly rich——"

"I do. I avoid her like the plague."

"Well, then. Anyway, Mr. Terhune, it turned out that neither had Mrs. Mortimer sent to Foyles in connection with her library. I began to feel suspicious of the affair, so the following morning I telephoned the Foyle office and learned that no representative had been sent to this part of the country for the past six months."

Belcher laughed. "That is an old trick with a new twist, Alicia, as Terhune here, being an amateur detective, will probably confirm. The man was probably a burglar spying out the land beforehand."

"For once you are wrong, Gregory," she snapped. "I discovered his reason for all those dreadful lies some weeks later."

"What was the reason?"

"To steal my dear father's genealogical history of this neighbourhood."

"But you showed the volume to me months later."

Mrs. MacMunn looked disconcerted. "He didn't exactly steal the volume, Gregory—I think my unexpected return home saved that tragedy from taking place. But he did steal part of it—he ripped out the first fifty pages——"

"Is that why A to D are missing? I concluded that your father must have unearthed some scandal connected with yourself, and that you had destroyed the evidence!"

"Nonsense!" She turned again to Terhune. "Now, Mr. Terhune, what do you think of *my* Mystery?"

"I think it is very extraordinary. But—but..." He paused.

"Well?" she prompted enthusiastically.

"Forgive my asking a personal question, Mrs. MacMunn, but had your father discovered—er—items of scandal which he had incorporated in his history?"

Her eyes twinkled. "You would be surprised to know how many families around here have skeletons in their cupboards."

"Then may not Mr. Belcher be justified in believing that the pages were torn out of the book in order to guard against some secret scandal being published—I mean published in its legal sense?"

Mrs. MacMunn was indignant. "I should not dream of mutilating my father's book, Mr. Terhune. Besides, I can assure you that there has been no scandal in my family for hundreds of years."

"I was not suggesting that you mutilated the volume, Mrs. MacMunn, but supposing that Major Blye—for the sake of example—learned that your father had mentioned, in his annotations of the Blye family, that Major Blye's mother was a mulatto from Jamaica——"

She leaned forward excitedly. "Surely not! So that explains why he is so dark——"

Julia sighed. "Mother dear! Do try to be more sensible and less catty. Mr. Terhune particularly pointed out that he mentioned

Major Blye as an example. He might just as easily have used George Brereton's name—or Gregory's——"

"Oh yes, of course!" Mrs. MacMunn acknowledged flatly.

Terhune continued hastily. "It might have happened that Major—that this person, whoever he was, learned of the existence in the history of the item referring to his mother's Negro blood—or some other secret—and, not wishing others to read of the scandal, employed a man to come here, on the pretence of valuing the library, for the specific purpose of tearing out the revealing pages."

Presently Mrs. MacMunn nodded her head. "Perhaps you are right," she agreed unenthusiastically.

Julia laughed. "Mr. Terhune, you have completely ruined Mother's evening for her."

"I—I do not understand——"

"For the past year Mother has revelled in what she calls her Mystery, and now you have stripped from it every possible romantic possibility. As a consequence of that man's visit, from the moment of discovering that he was an impostor in her secret thoughts, Mother has been fully expecting to wake up one morning to be told of a nice gory murder in the house. Me, for instance, or Phillips——"

"Don't be absurd, Julia." Alicia's lips became obstinate—Terhune realized for the first time why Julia had come to have an obstinate, sullen mouth. "You can joke about the mystery as much as you please, all of you, but I shall remain convinced that there was more to that man's visit than meets the eye."

"There is no reason why you should not, Mother dear. Meanwhile, having whetted Mr. Terhune's appetite by telling him so much about Grandfather's history, don't you think it would be nice to let him see the book? Do not forget that his only ambition in life is connected with books."

"Yes," her mother agreed eagerly, "I do." She jumped quickly to her feet and hurried from the room.

Julia turned to Terhune. "I am sorry your visit here tonight has proved such a damp squib," she said coolly. "But what could you expect from this neighbourhood? Serious crime, of the type which would interest anyone having real aptitude at detection, is only to be found in towns and cities, where the inhabitants are still emotionally alive."

Belcher chuckled. "My dear Julie, are you forgetting the case of Thomas Scott?"

She wrinkled her forehead. "What case was that?"

"Thomas Scott was charged three months ago with assaulting his mother-in-law. He was given six months, the chairman of the Bench remarking that, if the woman assaulted had been anyone else but Scott's mother-in-law, the accused would have been given a year."

Julia ignored her companion. "What made you interested in amateur detection, Mr. Terhune? It is the last hobby in the world I should have expected you to take up."

He was not tempted to ask her why; he could see the reply to that question in her contemptuous expression. Instead, he answered heatedly: "I am not an amateur detective, Miss MacMunn, and I have no wish to be one. The reputation for dabbling in the hobby, as you call it, has been wished upon me in the last few days simply because, quite by accident, I became involved in one or two minor affairs of which gossipers have made the most."

"Was it by accident that you shadowed that man in London?" Belcher asked drily.

Terhune reddened, but before he could answer, Julia continued: "If you are not dabbling in detection, Mr. Terhune, why are you here tonight?"

"I protested, but your mother insisted——"

"Enough said!" Belcher interrupted.

"Oh!" Julia exclaimed.

At that moment Mrs. MacMunn entered, carrying a large volume in her hands. This she handed to Terhune with: "You see now why the thief tore out the pages instead of taking away the volume?"

He did; it was far too bulky an object to be easily concealed. He examined the volume, but for several seconds did not open it, so that he could admire its binding; a beautiful and expensive piece of handcraft. At last he opened the book, to find that the interior consisted of thin, handwoven parchment, foolscap length, covered in small handwriting and illustrations in water-colours.

As Terhune turned over the pages of the book he thought of the work and care which Mrs. MacMunn's father must have put into the compilation of the history. Many of the pages contained hundreds of words in neat, scholarly handwriting; each little illustration was a gem in itself. To have mutilated such a work was a desecration which angered him; it was a pity, he reflected, that the author's daughter had not presented the book to the British Museum before it had suffered damage.

As he glanced quickly through the pages he recognized name after name: Hamblin, Kylstone, MacMunn, MacDonald (of Wickford Farm), Pemberton, Pearson (of Turnpike House, Bray), Pryce (Terhune had not realized that Edward Pryce, the artist, came of a local family, but there was his name at the end of the pages devoted to the Pryces, together with a list of his exhibited pictures), Reynolds (Wickford), and Robertson (Willingham)...

As he turned over the pages devoted to the Robertson family a piece of paper fluttered to the floor. He stooped to pick it up, glancing instinctively as he did so at the few words he saw written upon it.

Blondie,

26, Rylands Street, N.Y.C.

The Fourth Clue

Friday morning was always a slack morning in Bray; as though exhausted by the hustle and bustle of market-day the small town relapsed into an even more comatose state than usual. Terhune, particularly, suffered from this inactivity, which, in his case, sometimes lasted until the next day, when he became busier because many of his customers liked to take out fresh books for the week-end. Sometimes, on a Friday morning, not a soul entered the shop; for this reason he had long since made a habit of regarding Friday mornings as a weekly spring-cleaning day. On those mornings he inspected his lending library, withdrawing from it all books no longer in a fit condition to circulate, unpacking and adding to it any new publications which had arrived during the preceding seven days. On those mornings, too, he catalogued and priced any second-hand books purchased during the week, and, if there were time, balanced his accounts for the week.

On the morning following his visit to Willingham Manor he turned his attention to a large bale of books which had been delivered two days previously—the contents of a library which he had purchased from the executors of a resident of Tunbridge Wells. Whoever had baled the books had done so with scrupulous care; as he struggled to untie the tightly knotted rope he thought to himself that the books could not have been packed more securely had their destination been Bermuda instead of Bray. Having broken a finger-nail, and rubbed the tips of his fingers sore, he presently felt tempted to cut the rope—a temptation to which he would have given way only with extreme annoyance, for he was one of those precise, patient men who have a mania for never cutting a piece of string or rope which can be untied and used again. In his case this mania was pronounced, though not without good reason, for he did a considerable postal business, and often sent away parcels of second-hand books, not only to all parts of the British Isles, but also to distant corners of the Empire and America.

He stretched out his arm for the knife; as he did so he heard the door open. He was surprised; he could not think it possible that somebody wanted to change a book so early on a Friday morning. But there was no doubting the evidence of his ears, if not of his eyes (he had his back to the door), for the sound of the door's being opened was followed by the sound of its being closed, and then of feet on the floorboards.

He straightened up and turned. Then he exclaimed his astonishment, for he recognized the scarred, saturnine face of the man who had arrested him three days previously.

"Good morning, Mr. Terhune. You are busy, I see." The detective chuckled. "Surprised to see me?"

"I suppose I am," Terhune acknowledged.

"As I was passing through here on my way to transact some business in Ashford I thought I would take the opportunity of finding out whether you arrived home safely after your little adventure the other afternoon."

Terhune grinned. "Is that a diplomatic half-truth for concealing the fact that you came here specially to check up on me, Inspector? Bray is not on the way from anywhere to anywhere."

Sampson smiled grimly. "Humph! I can see that one mustn't take too many liberties with you, Mr. Terhune. Evidently you are not so sleepy as—well, this town, for instance. Still, I can assure you quite frankly that I did tell a half-truth—I really have some business in Ashford." He looked around at the hundreds of books which lined the shelves, and sighed. "A nice little place you have here. I almost envy you."

"Almost! But not quite, Inspector?"

The inspector laughed again. "Right again, Mr. Terhune. I may have the inclination to settle down, but not the nature. I have only to be off duty for a week or so to be roaring to get back into harness again. It's in my blood, I am afraid, and only old age will get rid of it. I am a natural-born man-hunter; I revel in the chase." He glanced through the glass panel of the door at Market Square beyond: a boy and a dog were ambling across the empty cobbled square where, yesterday, two dozen stalls or so had stood: on the far side a huge farm-horse was slowly clopping along the road to Wickford, drawing along a load of straw. Ten yards away two women gossiped.

"I can understand now what a sensation that affair at the church-yard must have caused to the local inhabitants. I suppose you have learned nothing new since Tuesday?"

"On the contrary! I have—last night," Terhune replied with elation.

The inspector's expression changed with astonishing rapidity. His body seemed to stiffen; his eyes to burn with eagerness; Terhune compared him with a terrier who scents a rabbit- or rat-hole.

"You work swiftly, Mr. Terhune."

Terhune shook his head. "No. I no more pursued the latest development than I did the former—it pursued me."

"You pursued Tony Malatesta," Sampson reminded him cheer-fully. "What happened last night?"

"You might not believe it, Inspector, but Bray and the surround-ing district is a hot-bed of gossip———"

"I should not believe anything to the contrary," Sampson inter-rupted quickly. "I know what these small country towns are—in spreading news the African bush telegraph is slow in comparison."

"You are right," Terhune agreed feelingly. "You will appreciate what happened when the news spread of what happened on Tuesday."

"Who put the story into circulation?"

"Not I. I suspect Lady Kylstone's butler."

"I know the type. Go on."

"Before long everybody living within miles was convinced that I was one of the Big Five in disguise. In consequence, more people visited this shop yesterday—yesterday was market-day—than ever before."

Sampson glanced at Terhune's inconspicuous figure, his round, serious face, and smiled grimly. Anyone less like the popular conception of one of the Big Five could hardly be imagined.

"Then business was good yesterday?"

"Very."

"It's an ill wind, et cetera."

"Yes, but the rush of customers had its disadvantage—two out of every three tried to question me about my exploits as a detective." Terhune saw the expression which crossed the inspector's face. "That is their description of the affair, not mine," he hastened to add. "Among the people who visited me yesterday was a Mrs. MacMunn—she informed me in a thrilling whisper that she had been haunted by a Mystery for the past twelve months, and asked me to dine with her last night for the purpose of investigating the circumstances."

"And you went?" Sampson gasped.

Terhune grimaced. "If you knew Mrs. MacMunn you would realize that the invitation was a sentence without the option of a fine. Well, I went to her house, and after the meal she imparted the details of her Mystery—she always speaks of it as though it were spelled with a capital M. Briefly, Inspector, her father was a keen student of genealogy and heraldry. During the last ten years of his life he amused himself by compiling what he called a genealogical history of the principal families of this particular neighbourhood. This history he wrote in longhand in a volume which he had had made for the purpose. He was just upon the point of completing the last entry under T when he died. Thereafter the volume occupied a place of honour in Mrs. MacMunn's library.

"About a year ago a man gained admission to the library when the family were supposedly absent for the afternoon. By sheer chance Mrs. MacMunn returned home some ten minutes later. She went into the library just in time to see the man thrusting some papers into his pocket. When she demanded to know the reason for the man's presence he fobbed her off with an excuse which thoroughly satisfied her—she is quite a simple soul."

Sampson nodded understandingly.

"Some weeks later she discovered the truth. Upon investigation she learned that the man had torn out and stolen all the pages containing the history of families with the initials A to D inclusive. Such was the sum total of her story."

"Did those histories contain any scandal?"

"That is a question I put to her. The answer is very definitely, yes." Terhune saw Sampson preparing to interrupt. "Wait a moment, Inspector. I haven't come to the point of *my* story yet. Mrs. MacMunn handed the volume for me to examine. I was glancing through its pages when a torn scrap of paper fell out and fluttered on to the floor. As I picked it up I saw a name and address written upon it; the address was Twenty-six, Rylands Street, New York City, and the name—Blondie!"

"What!" The Inspector's voice became harsh in his excitement. "Are you quite sure of that?"

"Positively."

The detective pressed his thin lips together before speaking. "What did you do with the paper?" he snapped.

"I was replacing it in the book when Mrs. MacMunn asked for it. I passed it over to her."

"What did she do with it?"

"Read it out aloud, and then said: 'Who in Heaven's name is Blondie? Is she a friend of yours, Julia?' Julia said. 'No——'"

"Who in hell is Julia?" Sampson interrupted roughly.

"Her daughter."

"Was she present when all this happened?"

"Yes. And a man named Belcher."

"Why didn't you say so at first, Mr. Terhune?" Sampson asked irritably. "The first attribute of a detective, amateur or otherwise, is to be clear and concise in repeating evidence."

"How many more times must I disclaim all responsibility for calling myself an amateur detective?" Terhune demanded warmly. "Besides, does it make any difference who was present at the time this happened?"

"It might make an important difference." The Inspector paused, to control himself. "I am sorry, Mr. Terhune," he apologized presently. "I am apt to lose my temper when I become interested. From which you can guess that I am interested in what you are telling me. Very! What happened when Mrs. MacMunn asked that question of her daughter?"

"Julia denied knowing anything of Blondie, of the address, or of the piece of paper, so Mrs. MacMunn threw it on the fire."

"Did you say anything about recognizing the name?"

"I said nothing, Inspector. I tried to act innocently, as though the scrap of paper bore no significance for me."

"Good! Good!" Sampson congratulated. He began to pace quickly up and down the small space which existed between the crowded book-shelves and the parcels of books which Terhune had brought into the shop to deal with. "You can accept it from one who has been in the police force ever since he was old enough to join it that something remarkably queer is happening in this sleepy neighbourhood of yours, Mr. Terhune. The fact that Tony Malatesta is mixed up in it is sufficient evidence to convince me that whatever that something is, it is big. I have already informed you that Malatesta doesn't have anything to do with petty crime.

"What is the situation as far as we know it? Malatesta has been brought over from New York for the purpose of committing a crime, and the person who sent for him was, presumably, a woman whose identity is hidden from us at the moment under the pseudonym of Blondie. Unfortunately, in criminal circles this particular pseudonym is not uncommon; any woman with outstandingly fair hair becomes Blondie almost as automatically as a red-haired man becomes Ginger.

"Right! Now the probability is that Blondie and Malatesta first met in New York, for we now have reason to believe that at one time Blondie was occupying an apartment on Rylands Street, while Malatesta, previous to his journey to England, was living in Worthington Street, which, if I can remember my New York, is not very far from the lower end of Fifth Avenue.

"Right! Now, having come to England, Blondie finds that she needs the services of Malatesta, so she sends for him, and he, tempted by the promise of a good reward, promptly leaves for this country, and within a few days is on the job. What is that job? As far as we can ascertain at this stage, to break into the Kylstone family vault, by fair means or foul. Due to some nice deduction on your part, Mr. Terhune, he fails.

"What was his purpose in breaking into the vault? According to you, the recovery of a gold fountain pen. You may be right, but I think it as well to keep an open mind on that point. To send to New York for a man like Malatesta to come over to England just to rob a vault of a fountain pen—even if it was gold—seems to me a ridiculous solution. For two reasons. The first; because there are hundreds of criminals in London who would have been willing to do what Tony did—or tried to do—for far less money. The second; because by waiting a matter of a few days, or a few hours, the pen could have been obtained merely by walking into the vault, on the morning of the twenty-fifth of October. Or, an application for the key could have been made at any time, to Lady Kylstone. But if we assume that the pen was not the object of the attempt to force the vault, then what was? There, for the moment, we come up against a blank wall.

"Right! But now your discovery of last night, and Mrs. MacMunn's story must be considered. Are we to assume that the man who tore out the pages from that genealogical history volume accidentally left behind the slip of paper containing Blondie's address? I think we may do so for the moment, and so arrive at this point: there is some connection between the theft of the missing pages, and the attempt to break into the Kylstone vault. But what is that connection? Eh, Mr. Terhune, what is that connection?" Sampson's eyes stared fiercely into Terhune's.

"By—by the way," Terhune stammered uneasily. "Have I mentioned to you that Lady Kylstone is American by birth?"

"What!" the Inspector exclaimed violently. His expression became grimmer than ever. "If that fact is a coincidence I will eat my hat! How long has she been married to Kylstone?"

"More than thirty years, I believe. She is a widow."

"Thirty years! Then Mrs. MacMunn's father would have mentioned her name in his history."

"In all probability. In fact, I know he did, now I come to consider the question."

"How do you know?"

"While I was looking through the volume last night I took a quick glance at the entry under Kylstone."

"Well, what did it say of Lady Kylstone?"

"Merely that, on such and such a date, Sir Piers Kylstone married Kathleen Cruikshank at St. Saviour's Church, Willingham."

"Is that all? Did it not give her genealogy, or biographical details?"

"Only *q.v.*, which I had no opportunity of doing."

"*Quod vide!* See under that name! Then Kathleen Cruikshank had an entry to herself?"

"Apparently."

Sampson laughed mirthlessly. "Apparently you do not yet appreciate the significance of the *quod vide*, Mr. Terhune?"

"Significance! No—I———" But just then he did so—Lady Kylstone's biography, under the letter C, had been entered on a page or pages included among those stolen a year ago.

II

The Inspector saw by Terhune's expression that no elaboration of his remark was needed.

"You see, your Lady Kylstone forms a possible link between the theft of those pages a year ago and the recent attempt to break into the Kylstone burial vault." He paused to offer a cigarette to Terhune, and to take one himself. His dark, snapping eyes stared at Terhune's glasses with embarrassing concentration as though he were trying to probe the mild blue eyes behind. "I should not be surprised to learn that Lady Kylstone is aware of that fact: hence her reason for not seeking the aid of the local police last Thursday."

The inference was obvious. "Piffle!" Terhune exclaimed indignantly. "You might as well accuse Helena Armstrong of being an accomplice. Besides, according to Mrs. MacMunn, I was the first person outside her family to be told of the theft of the pages from her father's local history."

If it were possible for Sampson's beady eyes to twinkle, they did so then, at Terhune's instant reaction to the apparent accusation against Lady Kylstone.

"Do not be so hasty, my young fire-eater. I was not accusing Lady Kylstone of complicity with either crime. All I was suggesting is that Lady Kylstone, besides having a skeleton in the vault, has one in the cupboard as well. Directly she heard of the attempt to break into the vault she realized that somebody was on the trail of her metaphorical skeleton, and as she did not want the skeleton exposed to public as well as private view, she did what she could to keep the police out of the affair. All of which is a complicated explanation, but I think you will understand my meaning."

"Yes," Terhune admitted slowly, "I think I do. But anyone knowing Lady Kylstone would hesitate to believe in the existence of that skeleton."

"Perhaps," the Inspector agreed promptly. "But you must acknowledge the significance of these facts: that Lady Kylstone, Blondie, and Tony Malatesta have all come from America, though at different times, that all have come together in this district, that Lady Kylstone's maiden name began with a C, so was among the pages stolen from the volume of local history, and that Blondie was probably involved with the theft of those pages."

Terhune nodded. He could find no flaw in Sampson's logical reasoning.

"Mind you," the Inspector continued briskly, "I do not suggest that one should give too much importance to this theory. Theories without evidence to substantiate them are dangerous, and we have very little evidence on which to work. But as a basis for investigation it is good enough to go on with." He paused. "I envy you, Mr. Terhune," he continued presently, with a casual air.

"Why?"

"This mystery has the beginnings of being an absorbing one. I admit frankly that I would give quite a lot to be able to work upon it."

"Which, of course, you cannot, unless the Chief Constable of this district asks for the co-operation of the C.I.D.?"

"Exactly. I suppose your information comes from those?" With a nod of his head Sampson indicated the book-shelves.

"Yes."

The Inspector chuckled. "One isn't able to keep much secret in these days of books, cinemas, and radio. Meanwhile, so long as the Chief Constable remains unofficially aware of what is happening round about here there is no chance of the C.I.D.'s being called in. A pity!" he murmured, shaking his head. "A great pity! But if I were you…"

There was something about the Inspector's manner which warned Terhune that the other man was leading up to something.

"If you were me, Inspector?"

"Listen, Mr. Terhune. I meant what I said when I told you how much I wish I had the opportunity of investigating this affair of the gold fountain pen and the missing pages of that history. It fascinates me. I believe there is very much more in it than meets the eye. The people at the Yard tell me I have a nose for smelling out a mystery. They taunt me about it, but they haven't proved my nose wrong yet. I have already told you that I suspect something pretty serious behind this affair, so I need not repeat myself."

"Well?"

"If you don't mind my saying so, I like you, Mr. Terhune. Unless I am very much mistaken there is plenty of grey matter behind those suspiciously mild eyes of yours. You are no fool. Right! Now Fate threw you headlong into this business, willy-nilly, didn't she, so why shouldn't you remain in it? You maintain that you are no amateur detective, but why shouldn't you be? You are here on the spot; you

know some of the people concerned; you have time to spare…"
His lips twitched as he glanced quickly at Market Square. "You
have discerning eyes, and you have, as you have already proved, a
brain capable of putting two and two together. Why shouldn't you
investigate this mystery?"

"I don't know the first thing about detection beyond what I have
read," Terhune explained helplessly, confused by the Inspector's
astounding suggestion.

"But you have read a great deal, I imagine. You may not know
much about detection, but I do, and if you are willing to co-operate
we will investigate this mystery together."

"Together!"

"Unofficially, of course, as far as I am concerned. In other words,
would you care to act as my eyes and ears while I am in London?
Act as my assistant, in fact? Well, do you think the scheme a possible
one?" Sampson saw the bewilderment on Terhune's face. "No," he
continued brusquely, "never mind about giving me an answer now.
Think the matter over, and give me a ring on the telephone. Here
is my private number." He passed over a card, and glanced at his
watch. "I mustn't stop much longer. Before I go—you didn't say
anything to Lady Kylstone of Blondie?"

"No."

"Nor of the piece of paper from the volume of local history?"

"I haven't seen her since my visit to Mrs. MacMunn."

"Well, if you decide later to investigate, tell her everything, but
while you do so, watch her face carefully; note every passing reflection, and link it up with what you are saying; you might possibly
learn a lot. Also, make discreet inquiries concerning all fair-haired
women living round about here; by doing that you might get on the
track of Blondie. Further, if you can do so without causing suspicion,
get Mrs. MacMunn to give you a description of the man who stole
the pages from her father's history. Lastly, see if you can unearth

any scandal involving local families with names beginning with A, B, C, or D." He glanced at Terhune with grim inquiry.

"There is a question I have been wanting to ask you, Inspector."

"What is it?"

"Why did you not trace the identity and address of Blondie from the cable which she sent to Malatesta? Surely all telegrams and cables are usually filled in with the name and address of the sender?"

"Good man! Naturally my first act upon receiving that cable was to check up on sender's name and address. Unfortunately, both were false. Now I must go. If I am not on duty I can visit you on any Sunday morning. I shall enjoy the run into the country." He held out his hand. "Telephone your decision as soon as you can."

"I do not need to—I have already made it," Terhune said as he took the Inspector's hand.

"Well?" Sampson snapped eagerly.

"What else could it possibly be but yes?" Terhune asked enthusiastically.

III

That evening Terhune cycled to Timberlands. Briggs answered the door to him.

"Good evening, Briggs. Has Lady Kylstone finished dinner?"

"Yes, Mr. Terhune, about five minutes ago. She and Miss Helena are in the sitting-room." As he held the door open for Terhune to enter the old man gazed at the visitor with admiring eyes. "If I am not being too bold, sir, may I ask whether anything more has happened?"

"That reminds me, Briggs; have you been gossiping?"

"Gossiping, Mr. Terhune?" The butler tried to appear horrified.

"Yes, about me. Have you told anyone about that little adventure of mine in London last Tuesday?"

The old man was too honest to deny the charge. "I did mention to a friend or two that I thought there was—er—that you were deeper than most people suspect..." His lined face crinkled into a disarming smile. "I am sorry, Mr. Terhune, if I have said something about you I shouldn't have done, but things have been happening that are more exciting than some of Edgar Wallace's books. The business at the vault was just like a story I read some time back by Leonard Gribble—or was it Sydney Horler?" he mumbled.

"All I know is that it wasn't Ursula Bloom." Terhune glanced significantly at the door of the sitting-room. "Did you say Lady Kylstone was in the sitting-room?"

Briggs took the hint. "I will tell her ladyship that you are here."

Some moments later Terhune entered the sitting-room. Lady Kylstone greeted him with a friendly nod, and as soon as he had shaken hands with her and Helena continued briskly: "Good evening, young man. Your fame is spreading rapidly, from what I have been hearing today. Now give Helena and me a cigarette, and then light one for yourself; sit down—not there, but there, in the chair you occupied the other night. I have told you once that I like a man to be comfortable, and to look contented. That is why I like a cat around me, because cats have a habit of making themselves comfortable." She pointed to a ginger cat that was curled up on the rug, close to the blazing fire. "So Alicia MacMunn has a mystery to be solved, has she?" Her eyes twinkled, as Terhune held a lighted match to her cigarette. "Trust Alicia not to let anyone else score over her. Before long I think you will find that Isabel Shelley will be asking you to solve a mystery for her. So will Diana Pearson, and Beatrice Robertson." Again her glance strayed toward the cat, and again her eyes twinkled.

"Mrs. MacMunn's mystery is a very strange one, Lady Kylstone."

Lady Kylstone's trim eyebrows were raised in surprise. "Do you mean to say that Alicia has become involved in circumstances which can truthfully be described as mysterious?"

"The circumstances were very peculiar—as peculiar as the affair at the vault last week."

Her lips twitched. "Are you reproving me, young man, for my remarks about Alicia MacMunn?"

He reddened. "Certainly not," he denied hastily. "I did not mean to infer anything of that nature——"

The twitch became an open laugh. "Of course you did not. I could not resist the temptation of teasing you, Mr. Terhune. You are such a teasable young man; your eyes become so shocked, and your cheeks so red! Well, well! You surprise me about Alicia's mystery. When Helena told me of it I was sure that Alicia had invented a mystery just to break even with me."

"On the contrary; it preceded yours by a year, Lady Kylstone."

"A year! More and more amazing! Are you seriously telling me that Alicia's mystery took place a year ago, and that she has kept the fact to herself?"

"Yes."

"Then that is yet another mystery!"

Terhune repressed a chuckle; he could not doubt the genuineness of her open astonishment. Then he sobered again. "Lady Kylstone, I have a confession to make."

"Really."

"I did not tell the entire truth of what happened to me in town last Tuesday. This was by no wish of mine, but upon the instructions of Detective-Inspector Sampson."

"Well?"

"The Inspector told me that the man I followed home, the one with whom I struggled in the vault, was a well-known American criminal by the name of Tony Malatesta. He then went on to say that Malatesta had been invited to come to England especially to carry out a criminal undertaking."

"Interesting, but why, are you telling me these facts, in the face of police instructions to do otherwise?"

"The Inspector said that I might do so."

"You have seen him again?"

"He called upon me this morning."

"Indeed! And why has the Inspector changed his mind about my being told of this man Tony Malatesta?"

"In view of what happened last night."

"You do not mean at Alicia MacMunn's?"

"Yes."

"What in Heaven's name has Alicia MacMunn to do with the affair at the vault?"

"It is a strange story, Lady Kylstone——"

"So I gather; I am becoming extremely curious to hear it," she interrupted impatiently.

"The person who sent for Tony Malatesta to come to England is known by the name of—Blondie!" As he pronounced the name, Terhune discreetly watched Lady Kylstone's face, but her only expression was one of perplexity.

"What a curious name—it sounds like a cartoon character!"

"I believe it is; it is also used as slang among certain circles for a woman with extremely blonde hair."

A strange expression flashed across Lady Kylstone's eyes, but all she said was, "Go on, young man; you are becoming very interesting."

"Knowing Malatesta to be a criminal, the police tried to trace the identity and address of Blondie, but she gave a false name and address on the cable form, so they are no wiser than before."

"A suspicious sign in itself," she commented shrewdly.

Terhune agreed, with a nod of his head. "Now for what happened last night." With that he gave his hostess an account of the theft at

Willingham Manor, ending with his reading the name and address written on the slip of paper which had fluttered to the floor.

By that time Lady Kylstone was sitting bolt upright, tense with interest.

"The story is the most amazing one I have ever heard," she snapped. "What possible connection can there be between the theft of those pages and the attempt to break into the Kylstone family vault?"

He became embarrassed. "There—there might—there is a faint possibility——"

"Humph! Now you are becoming embarrassed. I know what that means. You want to be personal. Well, speak up."

He nerved himself for the ordeal. "Lady Kylstone, have you a skeleton in your cupboard?" he asked tersely.

"A what!" For a moment she was profoundly puzzled by his question, then she understood. "Ah! Why do you ask?" she rapped out.

"You—you had an entry in the history—and some of the entries gave details of old scandals——"

She became excited. "I had an entry! How dare that old reprobate include me in his history! I was not born here. What did he say about me?"

"That is the point, Lady Kylstone. Your entry was one of those stolen."

"I thought she said that only the pages A to D had been stolen?"

"Yes, but your maiden name was Cruikshank."

Suddenly she realized the significance of his questions. "Ah!" she exclaimed grimly. "I am beginning to understand why your detective friend gave you permission to include me in your confidence. You are not very subtle, young man. But there. I like you the better for that. Unless I am making a mistake, what you want to know is this: could there have been any connection between my entry in the history and the Kylstone family vault? For instance, is there an illegitimate child of mine buried in the vault?"

"Lady Kylstone——"

She waved an impatient hand. "Don't start apologizing or remonstrating, young man. Perhaps you did not have that precise tit-bit of scandal in your mind, but if you had, you still have no need to apologize. I can assure you, Mr. Terhune, most solemnly, that at no time in my life have I committed any act of which I need be ashamed. I am sure it was not *my* entry which Alicia's thief was after."

"Or—or your family, Lady Kylstone? I mean, your blood relations?"

"What connection could they have with this matter, may I ask?"

"Only that you and your family are Americans, and that both Tony Malatesta and Blondie have come from New York."

Lady Kylstone was obviously startled by the suggestion. "Ah! The plot thickens, young man! The coincidence is strange! Very strange! But the fact is no more than a coincidence. The Cruikshank family is a particularly God-fearing one. To the point of smugness, some might say. Be it so, to the best of my knowledge there are no skeletons in the Cruikshank cupboards; all the Cruikshank skeletons have been buried in the proper place—in decent graves, I might add; not in damp, chilly vaults. No, Mr. Terhune; you must look elsewhere for the connecting link between Alicia's genealogical history and the Kylstone burial vault. Don't forget that many families must have been mentioned in those missing pages."

Her words suggested an idea to him. "You must know all the families included in the history——"

"Well?"

"Do you know anything about any of them which might have a bearing on the mystery?"

"Diana Pearson would prove a better source for information of that nature. She is a born osteologist where the metaphorical skeletons of the cupboard type are concerned. Still, I will do my best. The Abbots, of Windy Corner, I think, would come first in alphabetical order. Let me see, do we know anything about the Abbots which might prove of interest to our inquisitive young man, Helena?"

Helena spoke for the first time. "I have never heard anything against them," she replied in a low voice.

"I believe that Henry Abbot's aunt married beneath her, to the annoyance of the rest of the family, but I have heard of nothing worse against the Abbots. After the Abbots—let me see—oh yes, the Alcotts, of—of—what is the name of their house, Helena?"

Terhune supplied the answer. "Thrace House. Mr. Alcott buys books from me on Napoleon."

"That is it. Thrace House! I never can remember its name. Poor Mr. Alcott! Can anyone imagine that mild, gentle soul doing anything that was not strictly Christian? It is a pity that one cannot say the same of his wife, the termagant! I will say this for her, though; that if she had done something scandalous she would have enough courage to face the consequences." She shook her head, and smiled mischievously. "The Alcotts are newcomers—they have been here only twenty years or so; they came here from the north, where both have their family roots. I do not think there can have been anything in their entries to make the pages worth stealing.

"Who next? I wonder if George Barker, of Oak Forest Farm, was to be found among the élite? His family have farmed the same land for generations, but of course he farms his land for profit, which probably kept him out of the Earl of Fulchester's history." Both her voice and expression expressed her scorn, but not for long. She smiled apologetically. "I dislike snobbery, young man. That is the American in me. By the way, speaking of Fulchester, didn't his family name begin with B? Of course it did. I remember Alicia's lending me a book inscribed to Alicia Boileau. Ha! I wonder if Fulchester had a sense of humour, and included some scandalous episode connected with the family under the Boileau entry." She looked at Terhune with a significant expression. "Perhaps Alicia herself tore out those pages, and has invented a romantic story to conceal the fact?"

"You are forgetting the slip of paper, Lady Kylstone."

"Quite true! I am forgetting it. Still, I do not think you should lose sight of the fact that the Boileau history was among those stolen. Who comes after Barker? The Blye family———"

"The Belchers," Helena corrected.

"Ah, yes, the Belchers! It cannot have taken Fulchester long to discover the Belcher genealogy. With the exception of his cousin Gregory, old Jasper Belcher apparently hadn't a relation in the world when he died last year. When the solicitors traced him, two months later, he was in Cape Town. I wonder if Fulchester wrote about Jasper Belcher that he was fond of only two things in this world—his money and his house? And what a house! According to local tradition no woman has lived in that house for more than a hundred years."

"Why not?"

"Why not, Helena? Because Jasper lived in it as a bachelor owner for more than fifty years, and before that, while his father was still alive, for another twenty-five years."

"What about Jasper's mother?"

"She died, poor soul, in giving birth to Jasper. She had been married only a year, and at the time was living with Jasper's father somewhere in Devon, I believe, where they had lived for that year of marriage. Five days after her death, Jasper's grandfather, who had been living at Greenacres, a widower for Heaven knows how many years, died, so Jasper was taken there as a baby of two days old, and there he remained for seventy-five years, the old curmudgeon. As Jasper's uncle, John—Gregory's father—died, early in this century, a few months before Gregory was born, and as John's widow went to South Africa, Jasper has been the only member of the Belcher family living in England for more than forty years. I disliked Jasper intensely, but I cannot believe that he did anything which might have been considered scandalous—he was much too cautious. No, I do not think we need worry about the Belchers.

"I wonder if I can say the same about the Blye family?" Her eyes twinkled. "Have you ever seen the way in which the gallant Major eyes a woman? Bless the old reprobate! He even ogles me if Helena is not around. I am afraid that he has sown many wild oats in his day. I am sure Fulchester must have devoted several pages to the peccadilloes of the Blye family. For the Major has two younger brothers, and two sons, all of whom are quite as naughty as himself. Especially Reginald. Especially Reginald!" she repeated musingly. "I wonder! I recollect now a rumour I heard two or three years ago that Major Blye had to pay out a not inconsiderable sum of money on account of one of Reginald's scrapes. What the scrape was I know not, but, however bad it was, I cannot see what possible connection it could have with the Kylstone family vault."

"Was Reginald Blye's scrape connected with a woman?"

"I should not be surprised, but why do you ask, Helena?"

"I was wondering whether the woman was Blondie."

A significant silence followed Helena's question. Presently Lady Kylstone nodded her head approvingly. "My dear, that is the most sensible idea any one of us has put forward tonight. Do you not think so, young man?"

"Undoubtedly," Terhune readily agreed. "For the first time one can see a possible explanation for Blondie's share in the affair. Some years ago Blondie may have been involved in some sort of a scandal with Reginald Blye—or another man in this district. Lord Fulchester came to hear of this and incorporated the details in his biography of Blye—or the other man. Later, Blondie learned of the entry, and employed a man to steal the pertinent pages from Mrs. MacMunn's library." He paused, and pursed his lips in dissatisfaction.

"That explanation doesn't account for how Blondie came to hear that her name was mentioned in the history," he continued. "Nor does it help us to deduce why she should want to employ anyone to break into the Kylstone vault. Are there any other families worth keeping in mind, Lady Kylstone, who might be interested in the Fulchester volume?"

"Several. The Breretons, for instance. But probably you know as much about the Breretons as I do. George buys a lot of books from you, does he not? He is a dear old soul, but a frightful bore when he touches upon the subject of fishing—which he usually does, after half a dozen sentences."

"I—I suppose——"

"Well?"

"Olive Brereton's hair is extremely fair. And didn't she stay for two years, about four years ago, with an aunt in America?"

"She did," Lady Kylstone confirmed. "But I should hesitate to call her a true blonde."

"On the other hand, she is very friendly with Julia," Helena pointed out. "Julia might have passed on the information about her name's being mentioned in the history."

Terhune shook his head. "Don't you think, Helena, that if Julia had read anything in the history that was inimical to her friend she would herself have torn it out?"

Twin red patches glowed in Helena's cheeks. "You have more faith in Julia's friendship than I have."

Lady Kylstone glanced from one to the other, and smiled. "Young man, only a man accepts a woman as being above suspicion; never expect another woman to share such ideals. Meanwhile, I wonder if we are not wasting time, arguing about this possibility and that. If you were to go to the fountain head, Mr. Terhune, you might learn in five minutes all you want to know about the information in the missing pages."

Terhune looked puzzled.

"Alicia MacMunn," Lady Kylstone explained. "I cannot believe that she failed to read her father's work."

"Or, better still, ask Julie," Helena snapped.

"Julia was most objectionable to me last night," he explained hotly. "She insulted me with every alternate sentence."

Lady Kylstone appeared interested. "Is that really so, young man?"

"Definitely."

She nodded. "Then I think it extremely likely that you will see more of Julia very shortly," she said calmly. "It is a dangerous indication when Julia insults people instead of ignoring them."

IV

Lady Kylstone's prophecy was speedily fulfilled. About eleven o'clock the following morning Julia MacMunn entered Terhune's shop for the first time in her life. Three other people were already there; she looked at them with a smouldering expression in her eyes which Terhune translated as resentment.

"Good morning, Miss MacMunn. What can I do for you?" He addressed her shortly, and purposely in the typical style of the shop assistant, for he could not forget her attitude of Thursday night.

Apparently she appreciated the reason for his attitude. Her lips twitched. "Have you any books relating to—to—to Cuba? Travel books, I mean."

"I think I have two or three, Miss MacMunn," he replied briskly. "Would you care to look through them? You will find them on the shelf with books about the West Indies." He indicated the section of book-shelves concerned.

Julia approached the shelves and presently took down a book

which she opened and read. She continued to read while the three people in the shop, and others who entered subsequently, transacted their business with Terhune. It soon became apparent that she was only examining the books as an excuse to wait for a convenient moment to speak to him. The knowledge caused him to feel strangely exhilarated, and later, amused, for surreptitious glances in her direction warned him that she was becoming increasingly irritated by the constant stream of people who entered. She was still engaged in turning over the pages of the first book she had pulled down from the shelf when Arnold Blye entered—Arnold Blye was the younger son of Major Blye.

Upon recognizing Julia he whistled loudly as he advanced towards her. "Well, I'll be damned! If it isn't our Julia! What are you doing here, old girl? This is the last place in Bray I should have expected to find you in. I thought you hated books. What are you looking for? A book on cocktails?"

"Don't be so coarse, Arnold," she snapped. "Do not judge everybody by yourself."

He chuckled. "The symptoms are familiar. Don't tell me. Let me guess. The morning after the night before? Am I right?" Before she could reply he snatched the book from her and glanced at it. His chuckle became a full-blooded laugh. Chokingly he read out: "'Picture of a Cuban caballero on his way to serenade Señorita de Quevedo Segovia.' For the love of Mike! Don't tell me our Julia is going all romantic? What has the Cuban caballero got that the lads of Bray haven't got, Julia?"

Her cheeks burned as she snatched the book back again. "Manners!" she replied with a snap.

He grimaced. "Sorry, old girl! But seriously, what is the idea? You are not thinking of leaving us, are you, to go to Cuba?"

"I am not, though the idea is a good one. It just happens, Arnold, that I want to read about Cuba."

"But you have always said you hated reading."

"Will you be quiet?" she ordered angrily.

He grimaced again. "All right, Julia, all right! If you are in one of your moods I'll leave you. But if you feel like a quick one you will find me in the 'Almond Tree'."

"It is about the only place I know where I could be sure of finding you," she retorted sharply.

Arnold Blye looked discomfited as he sheered away from her and approached Terhune. "Is that latest book of Howard Spring's free yet?"

"Yes, Mr. Blye."

"Then give it to me quick. I want to clear off while my skin is still safe."

Blye took his book and departed, but other people continued to enter; another fifteen minutes passed before Julia and Terhune were left alone in the shop.

"I will take this book," she said, laying it down upon the desk which he used. "How much is it, please?"

He shook his head. "You do not really want it, Miss MacMunn."

"Don't be ridiculous. If I did not want it, why should I want to buy it?"

"As an excuse to speak to me."

"Really, you are insufferable," she began angrily. Then she checked her annoyance. "Very well, Mr. Detective. I plead guilty to the charge." She glanced at the crowded book-shelves. "You must do better business than I had imagined to be possible in Bray."

"Not everybody dislikes books as much as you do, Miss MacMunn."

"That was rude. Why are you being rude to me?"

"You were rude to me on Thursday night."

"Oh!" Her mouth twitched. "Well, I asked for that, so I must not grumble. I was rude, but I now humbly and sincerely apologize. Does that satisfy your *amour propre?*"

"Of course."

"Would you think me a very bold female if I were to ask you whether you would care to come driving with me?" She saw by the expression of his face that he was astonished. "Apparently you would, but I must take that risk," she continued. "Will you come?"

"Why?"

Her cheeks flushed resentfully. "There is no reason why you should have welcomed the invitation, Mr. Terhune, but I fail to see why you should be quite so suspicious of my motives. I am not planning to abduct you. I merely want to talk to you, and prefer the privacy of my car for that purpose to—to———"

Subconsciously she glanced around her.

"To these musty surroundings," he finished for her.

"You are a dangerous person to bandy words with. But I will be honest. That was the thought in my mind."

"I would love to come."

She looked surprised. "That was rather sweet of you. This afternoon?" she added eagerly.

"I am sorry. Saturday is one of my busiest days, Miss MacMunn."

"Of course. I was forgetting. Tomorrow morning, then?"

He nodded. "At what time?"

"Early? About nine-fifteen? Or is that too early?"

"For me the earlier the better, especially if there is a frost."

She glanced at him strangely. "That is when I also enjoy the day best. I am beginning to regret———"

"What?" he questioned curiously, as somebody entered the shop.

"That I did not begin reading books a year ago," she murmured, as she moved towards the door.

V

The morning was ideal for a winter's day. There had been a frost during the night, which still persisted, although an unclouded sun shone from a steel-blue sky, for a keen wind was blowing from the north-east; everywhere not yet warmed by the sun sparkled and glittered with silver-dust.

With half a minute still to tick away before nine-fifteen, a long-nosed, grey and chromium-plated roadster drew up before Terhune's door. Julia sat behind the wheel, her black hair free to the wind; her cheeks whipped a vivid pink; her eyes exhilarated. As he stepped out of the shelter of the door, where he had been awaiting her for the past five minutes, she waved her hand and called out gaily:

"The Clerk of the Weather has granted us our wish, Mr. Terhune. Isn't the morning perfect?" She opened the nearside door. "Hurry. I am impatient to be moving. The air is positively intoxicating."

She scarcely gave him time to arrange himself beneath the rugs before putting the car into gear and pressing her foot down upon the accelerator. The engine hummed musically as the car glided forward out of Market Square and on to the Ashford Road. In a surprisingly short time they were beyond the outskirts of the town; the wind against his face felt like something solid, something with the chill of an iceberg. He glanced at the speedometer, and was surprised to see it registering fifty; had he tried to guess their speed he would have judged it to be twenty-five miles per hour.

Julia did not talk; she stared ahead, with concentrated attention, at a road that was beginning to leave most of its curves behind. The whine of the engine rose to a higher pitch; he noticed that the telegraph posts were appearing and disappearing with incredible swiftness. He looked at the speedometer again; this time the needle was hovering at the seventy mark. He was sure that he ought to feel nervous, for he had often asserted that there were few roads in England which were safe for any speed higher than fifty, but he did not; Julia's deft handling of the car, and the note of power in the engine's throb, inspired him with confidence. He knew nothing would happen to them: he felt that he wanted to shout, to laugh, to sing; undoubtedly the air was intoxicating.

For fifteen miles or so Julia drove forward at consistent speed. Then the car breasted a hill; in front and below them they saw the sea, turquoise blue and scintillating, and nearer, the red and grey roofs of Dover.

The car slowed down to thirty as they began to descend. "There!" she exclaimed, speaking for the first time since they had left Bray. "That is that. Now I am satisfied. Thank you for not speaking. I should have hated you if you had spoiled the journey by insisting upon conversation."

"I was enjoying myself too much to wish to talk."

"You and I seem to have many tastes in common."

"Except about books," he said drily.

She laughed, but she did not continue the conversation. They drove through the rebuilt town, presently to emerge by the harbour, once more busy with continental traffic. After choosing a convenient spot she brought the car to a stop, and stared hungrily, first at the swelling glinting surface of the water, which was dotted inshore with small craft, and then at the Southern Railway ships tied alongside the quay.

"We are not really alike, you and I," she said unexpectedly. "You are content to vegetate at Bray; I am not. My one ambition in life is to travel."

"Why don't you gratify your ambition?"

"Because of Mother; I cannot get her to leave Willingham, even to visit Paris now and again. Of course, there is nothing to stop my going on my own, but that would hurt Mother; she cannot bear to feel deserted, which she would if I dared to go off without her. Perhaps you think I am a fool to allow so trifling a matter to baulk me——"

"I think you are extraordinarily unselfish," he interrupted warmly.

"Do you?" Her lips twitched. "You are the first person in years to say such a nice thing about me." She breathed deeply, and continued to watch the shipping. "Sometimes I think I must be a masochist; every time I visit Dover I become intensely unhappy at the thought of not travelling to all the many foreign countries I ache to visit, and yet I cannot keep away from here. I often come to this spot, at least once a week." She paused, then added: "Have you ever travelled?"

"I have never left England."

She turned and faced him. "Then how did you come to recognize the name of Blondie on that piece of paper which fell out of Grandfather's history on Thursday night?"

The direct question caught him off his guard. "I——I——what name—which piece——"

"It is no use trying to prevaricate," she told him coldly. "Just by chance I was looking at you at the moment of your reading what was written on the paper; by the expression which flashed into your eyes I knew that the name was familiar to you. Do you deny it?"

He had far too truthful a nature to lie. "No."

"Who is this woman Blondie? Why was her name and address in my grandfather's book?"

He countered her questions with another. "Did you ask me to join you this morning so that you might question me?"

"Yes," she admitted candidly.

He remained silent.

"Is your masculine vanity hurt?" she asked presently.

"A little, yes."

"Very well, then I shall ask you another question. Didn't you accept my invitation so that you might question me?"

"Yes." He laughed suddenly. Soon they were both laughing.

"So we are quits?" she asked at last.

"Quits, it is."

"Good! And here is a sop for that same masculine vanity. I like you better than I thought I should."

"Quits again," he stated sincerely.

"You can be very sweet when you wish. Before we start interrogating each other, what is your Christian name?"

He hesitated to tell her, for he was nervous of her caustic tongue. "Tommy," he said presently.

"I prefer Tom. Now, Tom, what about Blondie? Who is she?"

"That is one of the questions I was going to ask you, Miss MacMunn."

"Julia," she corrected sharply.

He grinned. "Julia."

She gazed searchingly at him. "You are not trying to prevaricate?"

"No."

"Then why did you recognize the name?"

The question placed him in an awkward predicament. He had no desire to take her fully into his confidence, but, on the other hand, he realized that secrecy would antagonize her and so make it impossible for him to obtain information from her.

"You remember that affair at the churchyard when some men tried to break into the Kylstone vault?"

"Yes." There was a note of surprise in her voice.

"I have reason for believing that the attempt was instigated by this Blondie person."

"Good Heavens!" For a moment Julia's astonishment kept her silent, but afterwards she continued eagerly: "What was her reason for wanting to break into the vault?"

"I don't know."

"You do not know!" There was a sharp note in her voice which suggested that she did not believe him. "People do not break into burial vaults without having a very good reason for doing so."

"I know," he agreed readily. "That is what made me so curious about the affair."

"Is it only curiosity which has made you turn amateur detective?"

He winced at the slight note of contempt in her voice as she pronounced the last two words. "The strangeness of wanting to open a burial vault was enough to turn anyone into an amateur detective," he told her sulkily.

She relented. "I suppose so," she admitted, touching his hand with hers as though to apologize for her attitude. "Is this Blondie woman an American?"

"I know nothing about her except that she was the prime mover behind the Kylstone vault affair, and that she had an address in New York according to that slip of paper which fluttered out of your grandfather's book on Thursday night."

"How do you think that piece of paper came to be in Grandfather's book?"

"You might be able to supply the answer to that question, Miss—Julia——"

"I?"

"Yes. That piece of paper suggests the possibility of there being a connection between the theft of the pages from the history and the attempt to break into the Kylstone vault——"

"Why?" she interrupted.

"Julia, that history of Lord Fulchester's contains very complete biographical details of the principal families living within several miles of Willingham, doesn't it?"

"Yes."

"Is it possible that some of those details might be of such a nature that the present members of the family will not welcome its publication?"

"Possibly. For instance, there was some scandal in it about Edward Pryce's grandfather, but I don't think Edward would mind anyone's hearing about it; on the contrary, he has often told his friends what a gay old spark his grandfather was, and of the affair he had with a London milliner's assistant."

"Have you read through your grandfather's history?"

"I have not; local affairs bore me sufficiently as it is. I am not in the least interested in anyone's family history." She could see by his face that her answer disappointed him. "Why do you ask?"

"I have a theory that the pages which were torn out might have contained some item of scandal which was of interest to the thief."

She nodded her head understandingly. "Perhaps. But still I do not see the connection between the book and the vault."

He decided not to mention that Lady Kylstone's maiden name began with a C in case Julia's sharp wits began to add up two and two. "Nor do I, except that the person who tore them out might accidentally have left behind the piece of paper with Blondie's address on it. That is why I was hoping that you would be able to throw some light upon the mystery. Has your mother read the history?"

Julia laughed. "Mother enjoys scandal, but not enough to have waded through all those pages of Grandfather's writing to find any; my dislike of reading books was inherited from Mother."

"Has nobody read through the history?"

"Nobody that I know of—which is a sad commentary on love's labour lost."

"But surely you have shown it to friends of yours from time to time?"

"Yes, but probably fewer than you imagine. There was no general interest in Grandfather's work, no more than in, say, an unproduced play written by Isabel Shelley. I am afraid both Mother and I were very heartless about it; we looked upon the history as a blessing because it occupied Grandfather's time and attention, but beyond that——" She shrugged her shoulders. "Why are you so anxious to learn the names of those who may have read the history? Do you think that one of them was responsible for the theft of the pages?"

"Possibly, but the person I really want to meet is he, or she, who can tell me the contents of the missing pages, or perhaps indicate to me which families, if any, might have had reason for wanting to secure the pages."

She gazed thoughtfully out to sea. "You are asking for the impossible. In the first case I cannot remember the book having been taken off its shelf for at least two years—except by the man who stole the missing pages. Of course, I speak now from personal knowledge only, but as I told you earlier on, I am so rarely away from home that I do not think much happens there with which I am not familiar."

"Have you any friends with blonde hair?"

"Several. Felice Quin. She has that lovely shade of hair which immediately attracts every pair of male eyes within sight. And female eyes, too, but they stare with envy rather than admiration. Then there is Vera Ritchie, and Evelyn Despard." She paused, then added: "They are the only true blondes I know."

"Have any of them looked through your grandfather's history?"

"Evelyn Despard glanced through it one day, but why——" She laughed suddenly. "Surely you are not trying to associate Evelyn or Felice or Vera with this mysterious Blondie? If so, you are on the wrong track."

"What about Olivia Brereton? Has she ever looked through the history?"

"Why do you ask specially about Olivia?"

"Hasn't she blonde hair? And didn't she stay with an aunt of hers in America some years ago?"

"Her hair was blonde when she went to America; it was auburn when she came back again." She started suddenly.

"What is the matter?" he asked sharply.

"Your mention of America has just reminded me of a strange fact."

"Well?"

"Do not hurry me, Tom," she urged, speaking slowly. "I want to be quite sure that my memory is not confused."

For what seemed to him to be an irritatingly long interval she remained perfectly still and silent. Soon he became fidgety with impatience, but, unheeding, she stared seawards, her dark eyes slumberous. At last she moved; he found himself gazing into eyes that were sparkling with excitement.

"I was wrong in stating just now that Grandfather's history had not left its shelf for at least two years; about fourteen months ago a man called at the house asking whether he might look through it. The man was an American," she added significantly.

"What!"

She nodded her head quickly. "Yes, Tom. I think I can remember his name. It was Jackson van Woude, Junior. Or van something or other, Junior."

"Go on; go on."

"It was round about the end of September. He called and asked to speak to Mother. Mother was out, so he asked Phillips whether there was anyone else in the house to whom he might speak. Phillips showed him in to me. Having described himself as a partner in a firm of New York attorneys, he apologized for disturbing me, but said that one of their clients, an Englishman by the name of Davis, had died recently, intestate, leaving a fortune of more than a million dollars.

"Then he went on to say that this Davis, besides being something of a recluse, had been very secretive about his past life in England before emigrating to America. All that was known of him was that he had come from somewhere near Ashford in Kent, England. In order to trace his family Jackson van Woude had come over to England to make the necessary inquiries."

"A tall story!"

"Perhaps. I did not think so at that time. At any rate, according to his story, he had first of all visited Howard, Son and Howard, the solicitors, because they handle the affairs of most of the families in the Ashford district. Mr. Howard, apparently, was unable to identify the Davis in question, but having told the American of Grandfather's history, suggested that he should call on Mother in the hope of finding a clue to the Davis family in Grandfather's book."

"So you let him look through the history?"

"Of course. There was no reason why I should have objected. He consulted several of the entries, but quickly expressed disappointment that neither of the Davis families in Grandfather's book appeared to be the family he was searching for. With that he thanked me and departed. From that moment until now I have not given his visit another thought."

"Do you remember van Woude's address?"

"He gave me a business card. I have it at home. Would you like it?"

"If I may. Tell me, Julia, did you have any doubts about the man's nationality?"

"Not at that time."

There was a significant note in her voice which made him ask: "Have you now?"

"I—I am not sure," she admitted with more uncertainty in her voice than he had yet noticed. "Perhaps my imagination is playing tricks, but in recollecting the interview it seems to me that there could be no doubting that he was American. I mean, he was obviously so; almost too obviously so."

"He might have been an Englishman trying to appear an American."

"Yes. His drawl was exaggerated, and he used all the American phrases which are put into the lips of an American by an English writer."

"'Sez you!' and 'Okay' and so on?"

She laughed. "He was not quite as bad as that; after all, he was supposed to be an attorney, not a film gangster. But there was no mistaking him for anything other than American, whereas I have met several Americans who only reveal their nationality by a word here and there."

"How was he dressed?"

"Just as the British imagine the average American business man to be dressed," she said, her voice testy with self-annoyance. "Of course, he wore horn-rimmed spectacles. His hair was very black, but speckled with grey round the ears. His shoulders were square. He wore pointed shoes."

"There cannot have been much about him which you missed. By the way, you didn't see the man who stole the missing pages from your grandfather's book?"

"No. I was at the Breretons' place, trying to comfort Mark's widow."

"Did your mother ever describe him to you?"

"She did," Julia admitted grimly. "According to her, the man must have looked like Charles Peace, Jack-the-Ripper, and Raffles all merged into one terrifying person. I am afraid it is no use your relying upon Mother for any help. Her vivid imagination would more than compensate for any deficiency in her memory. Do you think the two men were possibly one and the same?"

"Possibly. He might have discovered some item of information while he was looking through the book on the first occasion, but owing to your presence—you remained in the room all the time he was in your house, didn't you?"

"Yes."

"Then obviously he could not have torn out the pages while you were in the room, so he made plans for doing so at a later date. He used Mark Brereton's funeral as a convenient opportunity. Only your mother's illness spoiled—or half spoiled—his plan. Had it not been for your mother's early return you might not, even now, have become aware of the theft of the pages."

"That is quite true. But if we are right in assuming that, during the first visit to our house, this man Jackson discovered some item of interest from my grandfather's history, why did he take the trouble to return for the purpose of tearing out the pages in question?"

To this query he was unable to supply a possible answer.

VI

During their return to Bray Julia drove at a pace far more leisurely than that of the outward journey. Despite this they indulged in little conversation, probably because their thoughts were occupied with the extraordinary affair of the missing leaves from Lord Fulchester's book. It was perhaps fortunate that their pace was a normal one, for, without any warning whatever, Julia suddenly applied the brakes. To the accompaniment of a loud protesting shriek of the brake-bands, and a shiver from the rear end of the long, streamlined body, the car came to a sudden stop.

"What on earth——" he began, startled.

"Tom Terhune, I am a ninny. I have a memory which would disgrace a child of seven."

He imagined the occasion to be a special one, and himself a privileged spectator; it could be seldom, he believed, that Julia criticized herself. He chuckled.

She ignored his amusement. "You have been hoping to meet somebody who could tell you something of the contents of those missing pages—Tom, there is somebody. A woman—a woman with blonde hair."

"What!"

She continued breathlessly: "You remember Margaret Ramsay—she lives in the cottage next to Joe Richards, that surly gardener who used to work for Mother——"

"You mean the man who left the neighbourhood without a word about a year ago?"

"Yes, yes. He used to live on the road from Wickford to Bracken Hill, on the other side of the river. Well, Margaret lives with her father and uncle in the cottage this side of Richards'—a pretty little place on the bank of the river——"

"I remember her vaguely. Doesn't she work for Howard?"

"Yes, but she used to be Grandfather's secretary before she went to Howard. She helped Grandfather gather the material for his book right up to the day of his death."

"Good Lord!"

"I don't blame you for glaring at me, Tom. I ought to have remembered about her before. If anyone can tell you anything about what might have been in those missing pages, she is the person to approach. Would you like to call upon her?"

"Do you mean now?"

"Why not? Sunday morning is probably the only morning you would find her at home. We can take the road to the left we have just passed; it was seeing the road which reminded me of her."

"If you would care to take me——"

"Of course I should; that is why I stopped the car."

Without further waste of time Julia backed the car as far as the cross roads, then turned to their left.

"Margaret's hair is naturally blonde," Julia commented, as they drove along a narrow, hedge-bordered side-road. "Which is true praise, from one woman about another."

"But she is not Blondie?"

"Why not?" Julia challenged.

"Because Blondie had a New York address; Margaret, I take it, has lived all her life at Wickford."

"Oh!" For a short time silence succeeded this disappointed exclamation, but presently she added: "At any rate, I am sure she will be able to give you information about Grandfather's book."

They soon reached the riverside cottage. "Let me fetch her," Julia pleaded. "She has a very reserved nature, but I think I know her well enough to persuade her to be frank with you."

He was in no position to deny her request, so he remained seated in the car and watched her descend the few steps leading down to the cottage, which was built beside the river in a natural hollow below the level of the road. It was a charming situation, and helped to make the cottage one of the most picturesque in the district—in strange contrast to the deserted ramshackle affair some hundred yards farther along the road, which no longer bore any traces of having once belonged to a gardener.

Julia was not long absent. As she mounted the steps up to the road he noticed her peculiar expression.

"Well?" he questioned eagerly, as she approached the car. "She is not there," Julia said slowly.

"She has not lived there for more than two years."

He felt disappointed. "Where is she?"

"In America," Julia replied.

The Fifth Clue

Terhune felt that the news about Margaret Ramsay was far too exciting to be kept to himself. Directly he had finished his midday meal he telephoned Timberlands. Having spoken first to Briggs, he presently heard Lady Kylstone's pleasant voice.

"Well, young man?"

"Lady Kylstone, would you think me rude if I ask if it is convenient for me to call upon you tonight?"

"So dear Julia *was* able to give you some information?"

"How did you know I had seen her?"

She laughed. "A little bird informed me, young man."

"That little bird will soon be telling you tonight what I shall be doing tomorrow," he grumbled. Then he continued eagerly: "But she was able to tell me some interesting facts; I thought you might like to hear what they are."

"Of course I should. Already I am impatient for your coming. Is eight o'clock a convenient time?"

"Quite."

"At eight o'clock then—and young man——"

"Yes, Lady Kylstone?"

"Be sure you are warmly clothed. I am afraid you may find it chilly here tonight."

"Has the heating system failed?"

"No, I am glad to say. Nor have we run short of coal."

"Why is it so cold?"

She chuckled. "You will find out soon enough, young man."

Lady Kylstone's remarks mystified him during the hours which intervened before it was time to leave for Timberlands, but despite her injunction, he did not dress in warmer clothes than usual, for he was not a chilly mortal. Precisely at eight o'clock Briggs showed him in to the sitting-room with which he was rapidly becoming familiar.

His hostess greeted him with genuine warmth. Afterwards, he turned to Helena.

"Hullo, Helena. Have you finished the jumper?" This had reference to her knitting.

"I am not a magician," she replied shortly.

"But you are a fast knitter, aren't you? Or aren't you?"

"Haven't you seen for yourself?"

"I—I am not sure."

"That is because you are a man."

It seemed to him that she laid emphasis on the last word, and he could not think why.

"Isn't a man supposed to know anything about knitting? I have heard of men—sailors, cripples, and so on—who are pretty good at it."

"I was not referring to the knitting, but to your not noticing whether or not I am a fast knitter. Men never notice anything."

Her attitude was so obviously antagonistic that he was worried.

"That is the first time I have heard that accusation levelled against men. It isn't true, anyway."

"It is as far as you are concerned."

"Me! I don't understand, Helena. What makes you think that I don't notice things?"

"Your behaviour this morning when I waved to you."

"You—you waved to me——" he stammered. "When? I—I did not see you, Helena."

"Of course you did not. You were too busy looking at Julia to notice anything or anyone."

He realized suddenly the identity of the little bird who had informed Lady Kylstone of his journey with Julia. He grimaced.

"I am terribly sorry———" he began.

"There is no need to apologize," she snapped. "Julia made up for you. She noticed me. I know, by that nasty smirk of hers."

Lady Kylstone laughed. "I hope you carried out my suggestion, young man. Now you understand my meaning."

"Only too well," he admitted heavily.

"So Julia was not long in charming you."

"She had seen by my eyes that I had recognized the name on the piece of paper which fell from her grandfather's book, and wanted to question me."

"Naturally," Lady Kylstone agreed drily.

"Did she have to take you driving in order to ask you a few questions?" Helena interrupted in a sharp voice.

"My dear, Julia's technique is very subtle. So, young man, she questioned you about Blondie, and you told her, no doubt?"

"Only as little as I had to, not to make her antagonistic."

"Of course!" Lady Kylstone's lips twitched. "But from the excitement in your voice when you telephoned me this afternoon I should imagine that you consider the sacrifice of driving with a woman you dislike so much well worth the while."

"She is not so dislikeable as I had believed," he contradicted honestly. "But what I learned from her again connects up the affair of the vault with America."

"It does?" Lady Kylstone's eyes became keen.

"More than that," he continued triumphantly. "I believe we have solved the identity of Blondie."

Helena suddenly forgot her resentment. She dropped her knitting. "Who is she, Tommy?" she questioned eagerly.

"Margaret Ramsay."

"Peggy Ramsay! The name is familiar. Why, of course! I remember. Didn't she act as secretary to Fulchester just before his death?'"

"Yes, Lady Kylstone. She helped him to gather the material for his history."

"I see!" Lady Kylstone murmured softly. "Now I am beginning to understand. Now, suppose you stop teasing, and inform us of all you learned this morning."

This he did; by the time he had finished both his audience were frankly expressing excitement.

"Then what is your belief, Mr. Terhune? That while Margaret Ramsay was working with Lord Fulchester on that ridiculous history of his, she discovered certain information which Fulchester related fully in his book?"

He nodded. "Yes, Lady Kylstone. Heaven alone knows what that information was, but evidence suggests that while Margaret Ramsay was in America she must have passed it on to somebody who realized the possibility of gain. The man in question sailed for England to check up on the information he had gained from her. He did this by posing as a New York attorney and trumping up that story of the intestate Davis. Upon looking through Lord Fulchester's history he probably satisfied himself that Miss Ramsay's story was true, so he then made plans for stealing the pages which contained the pertinent information."

"I am sure your deductions are correct," Helena praised enthusiastically.

He shook his head. "There are weaknesses, Helena, which have still to be accounted for."

"You have blackmail in mind, young man?"

"Yes."

"Then one of those weaknesses must be, what possible connection can there be between the information in Fulchester's book and the Kylstone family vault?"

"Exactly, Lady Kylstone. If we can discount any suggestion of there being any buried treasure in the vault——"

"Which you most certainly can. If there had been anything in the vault worth finding be sure my husband's father would have discovered it. He was that sort of a man, according to what my husband told me."

"Then blackmail seems to be the only explanation to account for the several strange happenings which are coming to light. But I am not satisfied that this is so. Why was it necessary to break into the vault in order to levy blackmail? How did the gold fountain pen get there? What accounts for the long period—more than a year—which has passed between the theft of the pages from Lord Fulchester's book and the affair of the vault? If it were only a question of blackmail, why was Malatesta sent for? Why has Margaret Ramsay not informed her father of her return to England——"

"You told us she was at Hunzinger Building, East Fifty-fifth Street, Tommy."

"I know, Helena. That is the last address from which she wrote to her father some months ago. But the telegram from Blondie to Malatesta was sent from London."

"Dear me! You seem even better at presenting new questions than answering the old ones."

Terhune smiled ruefully. "I am afraid that is so, Lady Kylstone."

There was a long silence, broken at last by Lady Kylstone. "How many years have you lived in this neighbourhood, young man?"

"Twelve years except for an inglorious period in the Army."

"Twelve years! Then you know it well enough to answer this question: If two weeks ago someone had said that it was possible for the parish of Willingham to be the scene of a most incomprehensible mystery, would you have agreed with that person?"

"I should not."

"Nor I, and I have lived here for—well, apparently you will be able to see the date for yourself if you should ever find the missing pages. The nerve of that old fossil! But when I think of these strange happenings taking place round about sleepy Willingham I begin to wonder whether we are making a mountain out of a molehill."

"Is Willingham the principal scene of the mystery?" Helena asked. "Do you think that the solution of the affair lies here?"

"Where else, dear child?"

"In New York, at East Fifty-fifth Street."

"You think that Margaret Ramsay could supply the key to this mystery?"

"I am sure she could, Lady Kylstone. Five minutes' conversation with her might result in the entire affair being cleared up."

"But if Margaret is in England——" Terhune began.

"I do not believe she is," Helena stated emphatically. "I knew Margaret at school; we both went to the Ashford School for Girls. Of course, she was several years older than I, and in the Senior School. All the girls loved her, even the younger ones across the road in the Junior School. Margaret was the soul of honesty and truthfulness; I am quite certain that if she had returned to England she would have visited her father, or at least have communicated with him."

"If she has been mixing with criminals——"

"I am perfectly sure that Margaret would never mix with criminals. Never!" she flashed back.

"I agree with Helena," Lady Kylstone said. "Even allowing for a young schoolgirl's worshipping adoration for an older girl, I remember Margaret as having a sweet, simple nature."

"Lady Kylstone——" Helena began hesitatingly.

"Well, my dear?"

"Your brother is still at Albany, isn't he?"

"He was a month ago when last he wrote to me."

"Is the journey from Albany to New York a long one?"

"Not for Americans, Helena. Why do you ask?"

"If you were to send a cable to Mr. Wesley asking him to call at the Hunzinger Building he would be able to ascertain whether Margaret was still living at that address, and if not, her new address. He might—he might——" Helena paused, embarrassed.

"He might what, my child? Interview Margaret Ramsay and interrogate her as to what there was in Fulchester's history to set into motion the series of strange affairs which are so puzzling to us?"

Helena nodded.

Lady Kylstone's eyes twinkled. "So now you want to infect Wesley with the amateur detective germ?"

"An hour or so in New York might result in many questions being answered," Helena murmured, her cheeks reddening.

"Your suggestion is a good one, my child." Lady Kylstone gazed reflectively into the glowing heart of the fire. For more than a minute there was silence in the room, for neither Helena nor Terhune was anxious to disturb her, but at last she looked up. "But I think I can put forward a better. Dear Wesley would make a poor job of investigating; he is much too forthright and undiplomatic. I think the affair could be handled more skilfully by another person."

"A firm of inquiry agents?"

"Yes, but I have somebody else in mind, somebody who is already acquainted with all the circumstances of this affair."

"Not—not Detective-Inspector Sampson?"

Lady Kylstone smiled. "No, Helena, not the Inspector. No doubt he would prove an excellent man for the purpose, but I do not think the Commissioner of Police would see his way to releasing Mr. Sampson."

Helena looked puzzled. "Who have you in mind, Lady Kylstone?"

"You are fond of books, aren't you, child?"

"Yes, but——"

Lady Kylstone raised her hand. "Do you think yourself capable of looking after Mr. Terhune's business for two or three weeks?"

There was a startled gasp from both Terhune and Helena, but she was the first to speak.

"You mean Tommy?" she asked excitedly.

"If that young man considers himself capable. Well, Mr. Terhune?"

He was far too confused to answer coherently. "I—but you— New York—I——"

She shook her head. "I am sorry, young man, but I cannot comprehend a word of what you are saying."

"I should willingly go, Lady Kylstone, but——" He paused.

"Speak up. I like frankness."

"I have a small income inherited from my father, but it is not enough to keep me; I rely upon my business for the balance; I cannot afford to neglect it for several weeks. Besides, Lady Kylstone, I could not possibly afford the cost of the passage, and the expenses on the other side."

"I thought those were your reasons. I am going to dispose of them in their order. Firstly, Helena, if she will, can share with me the privilege of caring for your business while you are away——"

"*You*, Lady Kylstone!"

"Don't be so old-fashioned, young man. Do you think that I am not capable of being business-like just because I have a Lady instead of a Mrs. before my name?"

"I could not dream of allowing you to look after a shop," he protested. "What would your friends say?"

She brushed aside the objection with an impatient wave of the hand. "I am not in the least interested in what they might say. I study my convenience, not theirs. They know that, and have long ago given me up as hopeless. Besides, I should welcome the opportunity of having something to do; sometimes I am very bored doing nothing.

Of course, I should need help, and should prefer Helena's, but that is entirely a matter for her to decide."

"I should adore helping," she stated simply.

The embarrassed Terhune ruffled his hair; the effect was to emphasize his bewilderment. "I shall wake up in a minute," he gasped.

Lady Kylstone continued: "As for your second objection, I want you to understand that I am as keenly interested as you, young man, in clearing up the mystery of why your nasty Mr. Malatesta wanted to break into the Kylstone family vault. Indeed, if you were not already investigating the affair, I should feel tempted to employ the services of professional inquiry agents. So you see, you have probably saved me money. That money I am going to ask you to accept towards your expenses."

"No, Lady Kylstone; I could not do that——"

"If you speak out of your turn I shall become very cross," she interrupted. "I am a rich woman; I have an income that is bigger than my need—however rare a phenomenon that may be in these days. Why should I not devote a small part of that surplus income towards the investigation of a mystery which I am determined to have solved at all costs?"

"I do not know what to say."

"Have you any objection, other than the two already mentioned, to undertaking a voyage to New York?" she demanded briskly.

"No," he confessed weakly. "On the contrary, I—I should give a good deal to——"

"Then that is arranged." She picked up the *Sunday Times*. "How soon can you be ready to go? A week? Two weeks?"

"A week at the most."

"A week." She glanced at the advertisements of the shipping and travel companies. "The *Queen Elizabeth* leaves next Saturday. Would you like to travel in that floating palace, or would you prefer the intimacy of a smaller, slower ship?"

"I think it would be nice——"

"Well? Speak up."

"To go out on the *Queen Elizabeth*, and return on a slower ship."

Lady Kylstone nodded. "Sometimes you are not so slow on the uptake as your innocent appearance suggests," she commented drily.

I I

For Terhune the next few days passed with astonishing swiftness, for there was much to be arranged in a short time. At first the prospect of travelling to New York seemed little more than a dream; an incredible dream from which he was likely to awaken at any moment. For the past five years he had lived as sedate and as uneventful a life as it was possible for any man to live. Then in half that number of weeks a sequence of strange circumstances had overtaken him, beginning with cycling along a fog-bound road, and culminating with the preparations for a trip to the New World. Culminating? Perhaps not. There might be other equally strange circumstances to follow. The world—his world—had become suddenly topsy-turvy. Judging by the past week or so, anything might happen. Anything! Why not? Two weeks ago he had been a happy, contented nonentity. He was still happy and contented, but he was no longer a nonentity. Modesty tempted him to disregard the fact that he was now being accepted as 'somebody', but his innate honesty forced him to acknowledge that he was no longer just a bookseller, but a friend of Lady Kylstone and Julia MacMunn. Although shy and reserved, he appreciated friends.

Despite this sensation of living a dream existence, he wasted no time in making the necessary preparations for his journey. First of all there was the question of finding out from Miss Amelia how much time she could spare for the shop from her many regular engagements, and of arranging for Helena to attend the shop for the rest of the time. Then there was the question of booking the passage on the *Queen Elizabeth*, of buying clothes, being photographed and applying for a passport, and attending at the American Consulate for the necessary visa.

On Thursday night he had dinner with Lady Kylstone; on Friday he proceeded to town, and stayed the night at the Regent Palace; on Saturday he travelled to Southampton on the boat-train, and boarded the huge liner which lay alongside the new pier. The scene was colourful, cheerful, noisy, gay. Half the world seemed crowded aboard; despite its size, it was difficult to move along the passages, or through the many public rooms; sweating stewards had to plead almost tearfully for gangway. Only on one of the many spacious decks was there room to move.

Terhune proceeded immediately to his state-room, where he deposited the few things he had carried aboard. Then he proceeded to do precisely what seventy per cent of the other passengers were doing—explore the ship! This despite the knowledge that he—and they—had four days ahead in which to do that very thing, and in far more comfortable circumstances. He joined the pushing, thronging crowd, and slowly made his way to the shopping centre.

Although this was his first trip on an ocean-going liner the *Queen Elizabeth* awed him less than might have been the case had he not taken the opportunity offered by a visit to Southampton to explore the *Queen Mary* soon after her maiden voyage. Memories of the hour when he, and half a dozen sightseers, had toured the great deserted sister-ship crowded vividly upon him as he drifted from the *Queen Elizabeth's* shopping centre to the ballroom, from the ballroom to the dining-room, thence to the swimming-pool and the gymnasium, along to the tourist quarters, and up on to the sports deck. The two vast ships were not dissimilar in design, but the circumstances were, and it was this aspect which chiefly engaged him. He had seen the *Queen Mary* as a casual visitor, at the cost of a small subscription to a seamen's charity, in company with two men, four women, and a particularly annoying child, and had been conducted by a bored steward whose estimate of the total tip he might expect to receive had been far from flattering to the generosity of the small company—for his part Terhune had for ever ruined the steward's belief in his own judgment; he could still see the astonishment in the man's eyes, and hear the tone of the man's voice as he expressed surprised thanks. He had, indeed, toured the *Queen Mary* as an interested but impersonal sightseer who, in his wildest dreams, had never dreamed of sailing aboard her as a passenger for New York. To him, at that time, the beautiful sister ship, the *Queen Mary*, had been a museum piece.

Not so the *Queen Elizabeth*. He found himself comparing the two vessels with unjustifiable pride and prejudice biased in favour of the latter, not because she was bigger, or faster, or possibly more beautiful, but merely because he was to sail in her. For five days and nights, plus a few unspecified hours, he was to entrust his life and well-being to her; he was to become part of her, and she part of him. For that was the queer feeling which took possession of him; that a part, an infinitesimal part no doubt, but still, a part, of this huge floating palace belonged to him. No museum piece this, but a living entity which, within an hour or so, would pulsate with energy and power. As though this thought were a signal he heard, above the excited chatter of the crowd, a hoarse voice bellowing: "All visitors ashore, please. All visitors ashore, please."

All *visitors* ashore! That call did not apply to him. He was no visitor. He was a passenger. A *passenger*! He was on route for New York, for a New World which he had seen often enough at the cinema, but had never expected to see in real life—at least, not until he was a best-selling novelist. He was a passenger, entitled to live aboard her for the next five days!

His exuberance bubbled up beyond his control. He laughed loudly and excitedly. But fortunately nobody observed him, otherwise that person, or persons, might have gained a thoroughly wrong impression of Theodore Ichabod Terhune, Esq.

III

Had Terhune been on speaking terms with the Clerk of the Weather, he could not have ordered better conditions for the trip—at least, not for the time of year. It was cold, naturally, but the sun shone down from a steel-blue sky that was amazingly free from cloud; there was scarcely any wind, but what there was of it was so charged with oxygen as almost to intoxicate one; the sea did no more than heave in a most gentle manner—apologetically, it seemed to Terhune, for not living up to its reputation.

For him each second of the day was an exhilarating minute, each minute a happy hour. Awaking early, he was the first to invade the gymnasium, where he played medicine ball with the instructor, pedalled a stationary bicycle, rode an unknown number of miles on an electric horse, whirled Indian clubs, and generally enjoyed himself with all the other gadgets installed for the purpose of depriving middle-aged business men of a pound or so of comfortable fat. Afterwards he dived into the swimming-bath, where he swam to and fro, on the surface and under it, until he was almost too tired to climb out.

Then breakfast—and what a breakfast! He was almost ashamed to eat so much until the steward, a friendly fellow, assured him that he had no reason for going hungry; the sea was like that, it gave everyone an appetite except when it was in one of its bad moods, but that was a horse of another colour. After breakfast, the deck. Not the glass-enclosed promenade deck, but the sports deck above, where the salty head wind, slight though it was, pinked one's flesh, and raised one's spirits to soaring point. Later on, as other hardy passengers made an appearance, he played deck tennis and shuffleboard until cocktail time. Then, and not before, did he return to the heated part of the ship.

The mornings he enjoyed more than the afternoons, when there was less to do, except to jump into the pool for another swim, just before tea. But the evenings brought a different pleasure. Changing for dinner gave him an extraordinary satisfaction, which had its origin not in snobbishness, but in a boyish delight in something new. He enjoyed every moment of the meal, and later, dancing in the ballroom. He was not a good dancer; it was many years since he had last danced, but on the first night out a young American girl—she was just sixteen—had taken pity on him, and had boldly invited him to dance with her. Unable to refuse with politeness, he had ventured on to the floor with her. At the end of the dance Sally frankly informed him that he was a terrible dancer, but she was noble enough to persist with him, and before the evening ended he was dancing well enough to please his candid, critical partner.

So passed the first four and a half days of his trip across the Atlantic; four of the happiest days of his life. On the evening of the fifth he went into the ballroom as usual, but alas! Sally had found herself another partner, a handsome young fellow whom Terhune deduced (being now an amateur detective in real earnest!) to be a Yale man, returning home from a tour of battle-scarred Europe. He was wrong; the new partner was a Harvard man, but he did not know this as he sat in one corner of the ballroom and watched the two youngsters dancing together. After Sally and her partner had danced together for thirty minutes or so he was forced sorrowfully to recognize that Sally had forgotten him. Choosing a convenient moment, he slipped out of the ballroom, fetched his overcoat from the state-room, and went up on to the boat deck.

The sky was still as clear as it had been during the past five days. Riding the blue velvet arc was a glorious half moon which spread a scintillating white carpet from the ship's side to infinity. The scene was inspiring in its ethereal beauty; he was almost tempted to regret having wasted the previous nights in the stuffy ballroom. He advanced towards the rails; with elbows on the wooden top to support his arms, and chin thrust into his cupped hands, he stared at the moon, and for the hundredth time or so wondered whether or no he was dreaming a marvellous, happy dream.

He fell into a reverie which persisted for many minutes. Like a seabird skimming from one white horse to the next, his thoughts drifted aimlessly: trifling, unimportant thoughts, which, bearing little or no relationship to one another, made so slight an impression upon his mind that he would have found it impossible to remember them.

His reverie was rudely disturbed by a distant, warning shout. He stiffened with a start of surprise. At that same moment a pair of human hands clasped his ankles, and he felt himself being lifted into the air. His body described a semicircle as the top part of his body was thrust forward over the rails. Far below him he saw the hissing, bubbling wash. As he fell, head downwards, the instinct of self-preservation asserted itself. He clutched desperately at the rails, and miraculously his left hand caught hold of the bottom rail and held on. For the second time his body described a semicircle, but this time his legs fell downwards. The weight of his body very nearly jerked his bruised fingers from the rail, but he hung on desperately, and found himself swinging by one arm, like a crazy pendulum.

In a lucid moment he realized that he had merely delayed the drop into the icy water below: his nerveless fingers could not for long carry his suspended weight; in a precious moment or so they would have to relax their hold and release him. He struggled to stretch up with his free arm, to take a firmer hold of the blessed rail, but the sway of the boat defeated him. Then a voice shouted, "Hold on!" and a pair of arms came through the rails, and one strong hand grabbed the lapel of his overcoat and the other caught hold of his free wrist.

Even with help it was no easy matter to struggle into safety again, but somehow or other the two men managed it. As Terhune leaned weakly up against the rails he saw that his rescuer was one of the ship's officers.

"That was a narrow escape, sir. By God! I thought you were overboard. I should think it was only a miracle that enabled you to grab hold of that rail."

"Yes," Terhune gasped. "Yes. I thought I—I was———"

"In the ditch! I don't doubt it, sir, but don't think about it. Have a whisky or a brandy."

"I probably shall, but first I—I must thank you———"

"I don't want any thanks," the officer interrupted brusquely. "You saved yourself."

"No. I could not have held on any longer. By the way, did you shout just before I went overboard?"

"I certainly did," the other man admitted in a strange voice.

"Then you saved me twice. Your shout put me on my guard sufficiently to make me clutch at the rail. Otherwise———" Terhune paused—the prospect of what would otherwise have occurred was not pleasant. "Why did you shout? What happened?"

"What happened!" The officer laughed shortly. "Merely that somebody tried to murder you. That is all!"

"Good God!"

"I was just coming along the deck from the bridge when I saw a black shadow moving around in what struck me as a furtive manner. At that moment I saw the man creep up behind you and bend down. Something warned me what he meant to do, so I shouted. I was too late. I saw you both disappearing; you, overboard, and the other man behind that lifeboat there. I rushed here, and saw you hanging by one arm." He paused. "I shall have to report this business to the captain."

"Of course."

"He is on the bridge now, sir. I wonder if you would mind accompanying me, after you have had a drink."

"The drink can wait."

"Good." There was a note of admiration in the officer's voice. "This way, then, sir."

The story was soon told. The frowning captain stared at Terhune.

"In the face of what Mr. Carson saw there is little doubt but that you were the victim of a deliberate attempt at murder. It is the first time that anything of this nature has happened to one of my passengers during my thirty-odd years at sea. The attempt shall not go unpunished if I can help it, Mr.———"

"Terhune."

"There are not many hours left to us in which to work. We are due at quarantine by sunrise tomorrow. Now, Mr. Terhune, before I begin investigations, is there anything you can tell me which might be of assistance to me? To begin with, is there anyone aboard whom you suspect of having reason to desire your death?"

Terhune was unable to control his amusement at the thought of anyone's desiring *his* death. He laughed, but seeing Captain Moore's frown deepen, explained hastily: "I am really a most insignificant person, Captain. I live in a small town near the Romney Marshes, in Kent———"

"I know that part of Kent well. Which town, Mr. Terhune?"

"Bray-in-the-Marsh."

Captain Moore's frown vanished suddenly; he laughed in his turn. "I know Bray."

"Then, can you imagine a resident of Bray having an enemy desirous of killing him?"

"I can *not!*" the captain admitted, his words all the more emphatic because of his inspection of the man who stood before him. Most certainly the placid countenance, and the serious eyes, were not those of a man likely to make enemies of his own accord. "I suppose there is no doubt but that the attack on Mr. Terhune was deliberate, Mr. Carson?"

"None whatever, sir."

"It could not have been an accident, due to an unexpected roll of the ship?"

"No, sir, it could not. The ship was steady at the time. Besides, it was the furtive approach of the other man which made me shout. As I did so the attacker bent down, seized Mr. Terhune by the ankles, applied his shoulder to Mr. Terhune's—er—posterior, and heaved upwards."

"Humph! As you say, the attack was no accident."

"I wonder if I was mistaken for someone else," Terhune suggested.

"That, of course, is a very likely possibility, and one that would not help us to find your assailant. But first I should like to be quite sure that a mistake was made. Will you forgive my asking a personal question, Mr. Terhune? Are you a rich man? By rich, I mean would someone benefit by your death?"

"Rich!" Terhune chuckled. "'Whoever steals my purse steals trash'," he quoted. "I am worth three pounds a week live weight, less income tax, or roughly four thousand pounds in two-and-a-half per cent Consols, at present quotation, deadweight."

"I would commit murder for four thousand pounds," Carson rumbled.

"Are you in business?" Moore asked.

"I have a bookshop and lending library in Bray which pays me another thirty shillings to two pounds a week. I have no business rivals anxious to rid themselves of competition." As he said this Terhune saw a suspicious expression spring into the captain's eyes. For a moment he was puzzled to know why. Then the answer occurred to him. Moore was wondering how a man with a few pounds a week could afford to travel first class on the *Queen Elizabeth*.

"I am not paying for the trip to New York," he explained. "Somebody is paying all expenses so that I can meet a girl, for the purpose of asking her a few questions——"

He came to an abrupt stop as there flashed through his mind a possible reason for the attack upon him; somebody had learned of the reason for his journey to New York, and feared the consequences of the interview with Margaret Ramsay, even to the extent of committing murder!

I V

It took Terhune many minutes to dispose of Captain Moore's probing questions, but when at last he escaped from the bridge he proceeded directly to his state-room, and there sat down, to ponder over the remarkable possibility which had occurred to him.

If it had been definitely his life which had been attempted—if!—and if it were to be assumed that the purpose was to prevent his interrogating Margaret Ramsay—if!—then a new and uglier construction would have to be given to the strange doings at Willingham.

Hitherto, the affair had been too theatrical to be accepted seriously (despite Detective-Inspector Sampson's reaction to it). The plot might well have been lifted from a Lyceum melodrama, or a Drury Lane musical comedy, for it had also been somewhat, amusing in its way. That the events of the past and present suggested a crime of sorts, either committed, or about to be committed, was evident, but he had looked upon that crime, whatever it might be, as not being of a serious nature. But murder, the most serious of all crimes, was not likely to be attempted except as a means of covering up the existence of a crime equally serious.

Murder! A queer feeling possessed him as he reflected upon this question: had he stumbled upon the trail of a murder? Had the theft of the pages from Lord Fulchester's manuscript history, and the subsequent attempt to break open the Kylstone vault, been part and parcel of a homicidal crime? If so, and if it were likely that a conversation with Margaret Ramsay might reveal the existence of such a crime, then the attempt upon his own life was understandable. For murder begets murder. He had come across that theory in more than one of the books in his private library. The man who has committed one murder hesitates less at committing a second, especially if the second crime be the only means of protecting himself against the consequences of the first. Murder may even become a habit; the names of people who had committed a series of murders occurred to him without further prompting—Landru, Smith, of the Brides in the Bath case, Palmer...

Murder! But who was the victim? He tried to think of anyone who had died in suspicious circumstances during the past twelve months, but the only name he could remember was that of Mrs. Meredith. Mrs. Meredith, poor old soul, was found dead on the railway line, some three miles to the east of Willingham. A post-mortem examination had revealed her injuries to be multiple, not all of them the result of being cut in halves by the wheels of the Folkestone express. There was a severe bruise on her left forehead, for instance, which was believed to have resulted from having fallen on to the lines from the bridge above. Although there was ample evidence of her being an epileptic, an open verdict was found, because there was no direct evidence that she was not pushed over the parapet—he started as he reflected, suddenly, that such a push had very nearly killed him, not one hour ago. But then, Mrs. Meredith had nearly died once before through falling out of a window during an epileptic fit. Besides, there had been no proof of motive or reason for her death, for her sole means of subsistence had been an old-age pension.

Other people had died during the past twelve months, of course. Other people, whose death was of financial benefit to others; but none of these, to his knowledge, had died in circumstances that were in any way suspicious. Mark Brereton, for instance; old Mrs. Pearson; George Moore's young son, Alfred; Jasper Belcher; Dai Lluellyn's sister, Agatha. But to believe that one of these people had been murdered was unthinkable.

Murder! His mind revolted against the possibility of Willingham, or Bray, or Wickford, or any of the surrounding villages being the scene of that foul crime. The countryside was far too clean, too beautiful, with its rolling pasture land, its maze of winding, hedge-bordered lanes, its orchards, its hop-fields, its quaint old cottages (many of them one-time smugglers' haunts), its sheltered farms, and its sleepy villages. No. One accepted London, or Manchester, or Hull, or Glasgow as an environment in which the seeds of murder might flourish. But not Kent. The sweet south-westerly winds were likely to blow away that kind of seed before it could take root.

If not murder, then what other crime had been committed? To what pointed the clues of the gold fountain-pen, the missing pages of Lord Fulchester's history, the cable from Blondie to Malatesta? Whatever it might be, two facts seemed certain; one, that Margaret Ramsay could supply the key to the problem, and two, that it was of a sufficiently serious nature to provoke an attempt at murder. It was increasingly evident that he was not journeying to New York in vain.

V

The following morning came as a fitting climax to a voyage that Terhune was never to forget. As though the Clerk of the Weather was persistently determined that nothing should mar his first trip to the New World, once again the sun rose to a clear sky, and bathed that part of the universe in a misted golden mantle, through which he espied vaguely a distant isle of spires and tall, narrow buildings, floating, it seemed, in mid-air. As he stood on the boat-deck and stared eagerly ahead he was put in mind of the fairy books of his babyhood, with their pictures of armoured knights with tilted lance galloping towards a cloud-girt castle perched precariously on the spur of a rock-bound mountain. Not that he felt himself to be a knight in armour, or the *Queen Elizabeth* to be a mettlesome steed, or the nebulous skyline to resemble the crenelated fairy castle, but an uncontrollable excitement can play tricks upon one's imagination.

As the sun rose higher, the mist gradually dispersed; the strident whistles which had previously bothered him belonged not, he found, to railway locomotives, but to ferry boats gliding swiftly from all to all points of the compass; the heavy thumping, an outgoing oil-tanker; the sharper chug-chug-chug, a powerful tug-boat pulling behind it a line of barges. The strange, towering figure in the sky off the port side became the famous Statue of Liberty, the low squat building off the starboard side became an island. And, at last, New York City was revealed in all its defiant, magnificent grandeur.

He had read and heard so much of the famous skyline; he had seen it a hundred times on the screen, but it did not disappoint him. As the last remnant of the mist disappeared the stark outlines of the tall buildings lost their mellowness, but what was lost in fantasy was gained in realism; he saw the city as the epitome of constructional triumph, a monumental achievement to civilization. In consequence, his eagerness to step ashore increased; it was with a sense of impatience that he waited for the powerful engines to start up, preparatory to propelling the ship on its last, short stage to the disembarkation pier.

VI

From the pier Terhune later proceeded to the New Weston Hotel on Madison Avenue, which Lady Kylstone had recommended. There he booked a room, and as soon as he was installed, unpacked and took a shower. Then he had a quick, light meal, and afterwards went out for his first tour of exploration. Automatically he turned in the direction of Fifth Avenue, and within a few minutes was slowly strolling along the cheerful, noisy broadwalk.

The hours passed flashingly. He walked until his feet were tired; he visited a drug store and ordered an ice cream soda; he took a trolley-car and found himself at the extreme end of Manhattan, which he discovered was called Battery Park. He walked round the Aquarium; when he came out again night had fallen, and the city was blazing with light. He descended to the subway, and entered the first uptown train to appear. After a time he noticed that the train was passing through certain stations at a seemingly incredible speed, and rightly judged that he was on an express train. At 96th Street he left the subway, walked west to Riverside Drive, and took a bus back to Fifth Avenue at 49th Street. Then he returned to the hotel, and after a meal went to bed, tired out and as happy as a sandboy.

The next morning his inclination was to spend the day indulging in the fascinating pastime of further exploring the city, but he strongly resisted the impulse. True, one day more or less was not likely to affect his mission, but as Lady Kylstone was paying the expenses of his trip he felt that he owed a duty to her to settle first of all the business which had brought him to New York; there would be time enough afterwards, he hoped, to visit some of the many places on the list which Lady Kylstone had made out.

From the hotel to Margaret Ramsay's address in East 55th Street was no more than five blocks north, and some blocks east from the hotel's 50th Street entrance, so he decided to walk to his destination. He turned along Madison Avenue and soon reached the block of apartments which Ramsay had given as Margaret's address.

Upon entering the building he saw three elevators in front of him. Two of them had their gates closed; their indicators showed them to be soaring skywards, one at the twelfth floor, the other at the top. The third was on the ground floor, its gate open, its attendant waiting.

"Can you tell me the number of Miss Margaret Ramsay's apartment?" he asked the man.

"Ramsay." The elevator attendant shook his head. "Never heard the name."

"This is Hunzinger Building?"

"Sure thing."

"This is the address she has put on all her letters to her father."

"Sorry, buddy, but the name is a new one on me."

"Could she have moved?"

"Sure she could. Everybody moves around in New York. You a stranger here?"

"Arrived yesterday."

The elevator man looked interested. "From England?"

"Yes."

"My dad was born in London, England. Name of Sloane. I have a dozen relations over there still. Uncle Fred keeps a draper's shop somewhere in the west. Ever come across any of them? Sloane is the name. S-L-O-A-N-E."

"I am afraid not."

"Pity. You would have liked them if they were anything like my dad. How long ago was this Ramsay person supposed to be here?"

"Some months ago."

"Then you had better speak to George; he's on number three; he's been in this building nearly fifteen years; I've only been here three months." The man glanced sideways at the indicators. "George will be down in a moment."

"Thanks."

"You're welcome." The man closed the gate, and the elevator shot upwards.

George's elevator grounded a moment later. The gate opened, three people came out. Terhune approached George.

"Could you please tell me Miss Margaret Ramsay's apartment number?"

"Sorry, buddy, no can do. She moved from here two months ago." George saw by Terhune's expression that his words had caused dismay. "Do you want her bad?"

"I have come from England to see her."

"That's no mean journey to take to see even a good-looking dame like Miss Ramsay. Are you her boy friend?"

Terhune did not resent the question; Lady Kylstone had warned him of the friendly familiarity of Americans. "No. I—I just wanted to ask her a few questions."

George chuckled. "If I wanted to ask anyone some questions I should use the mails, or the Western Union, and spend the balance on the ring. But you don't need look like you've been sentenced to the long drop. Take the Seventh Avenue to Ninety-sixth Street, and try two-three-two Riverside Drive. That is the address she left with the renting office."

"Thanks very much."

"You're welcome."

Terhune was nearly at the door when George called out: "Hey, buddy."

Terhune turned. "Yes?"

"I hope she says yes." George's broad grin disappeared behind the iron gate, and the elevator shot upwards.

The journey to 232, Riverside Drive did not take long. Presently Terhune was once more inquiring of an elevator man—this time a negro—the number and floor of Miss Margaret Ramsay.

At the mention of her name the negro's white-rimmed eyes filled with apprehension. "Ah kain' tell you, boss."

"She is a newcomer to this building; she came here in September. She has blonde hair."

"Ah knows all dem things, boss, but Ah jes' kain' tell what you-all wants ter know."

"Why not?"

"'Cause it ain' none of mah bizness, boss. Ah 'spec' you-all should speak to the janitor." The negro left his elevator to approach a flight of stairs leading down into the basement.

"Hey, Tim."

From cavernous depths below a muffled voice bellowed, "Yeah?"

"Dere's a gennelman here asking fer Miss Ramsay."

"There is, is there? Okay, Sam, tell him I'll be right up."

Tim followed quickly on his words. As he approached he stared inquiringly at Terhune. "Well, mister, what can I do for you?"

"I want to know Miss Ramsay's apartment number. The elevator man at the Hunzinger Building on East Fifty-fifth told me that she moved to this address two months ago."

"Sure; she moved here right enough."

Terhune became impatient with the janitor's attitude. "Then perhaps you would be good enough to tell me the number of her apartment?" he said shortly.

"That is just what I can't do, mister. You see, this is her address right enough, for all her belongings are right where they should be, but she kinda ain't living here right now."

"I don't understand."

"It happened this way, mister. Miss Ramsay moved here from the Hunzinger Building last September, and everything was hunky-dory for a coupla weeks. Come the third week and she told Sam she was going away with some friends for the week-end. Well, I guess it was a swell party, for she ain't yet come back from it."

"You mean, she has disappeared?"

"That is what I'm telling you, mister."

"But—but—people can't just disappear like that."

"This dame did."

"Did you inform the police?"

"Yeah. A coupla dicks came along, and they gave her rooms the once-over, but all they found was clothes. I guess she destroyed all her letters before she left the Hunzinger. One of the dicks told me they couldn't find an address of anyone to tell of her vanishing trick."

"So that is why her father has heard nothing from her for several months," Terhune reflected aloud. "What on earth could have happened to her?"

Tim became more alert "Say, mister, do you know her pop?"

"Yes. He lives in England."

"Then I guess Lieutenant Kraszewski would like a word with you, mister, at the local precinct—two two nine West one hundred and twenty-third in case you don't know. He's after finding somebody who can tell him the address of her folk."

"I will go and see him."

"Thanks, mister. That will ease my mind. I didn't see much of Miss Ramsay, but I liked her well enough, so I guess her pop did, too. By the way, mister, how many of you has her pop asked to look her up?"

"What do you mean?"

"You ain't the first to come here asking for her in the past twenty-four hours. Yesterday afternoon, about three o'clock, another man was wanting to know where she was. That's what made me look queer at you just now."

At first Terhune was interested in the workings of the long arm of coincidence, thinking that the other man was probably one of Margaret Ramsay's New York friends. Then a horrible suspicion occurred to him.

"Was he from England?"

"That was his story."

"Was he an Englishman?"

The janitor rubbed his black fingers through his shock of hair. "Now you puts it into me mind, mister, I ain't so sure that he wus. He tried to talk like a Limey, but he looked more like one of them Bowery Eyetalians."

Tim's answer helped to confirm Terhune's fears that the man who had yesterday inquired for Margaret Ramsay (perhaps Malatesta himself) was probably he who had tried to commit murder aboard the *Queen Elizabeth*. Having failed in one attempt to prevent the girl's being interrogated, he had tried to tackle the problem from the other end, by hurrying directly from the ship to her address (probably via the Hunzinger Building) in the hope of persuading her to maintain silence, if not by fair means, then by foul. If this were a true explanation to account for the previous caller, then it was increasingly obvious that somebody was very desperate in his anxiety to block all trails which might lead back to the crime at Willingham (whatever it might have been).

He questioned the janitor for a while longer, but Tim had no further information to divulge, so Terhune left, and proceeded to the Twenty-eighth Precinct of the city police, which he found to be also the local headquarters of the detective district. Fortunately Lieutenant Kraszewski was in, and gave Terhune an immediate interview. Having announced his name, Terhune said:

"The janitor at two three two Riverside Drive suggested that I should call upon you to give you the address of Miss Margaret Ramsay's father."

"Huh!" The lieutenant's hard eyes stared into Terhune's. "What do you know of that woman?" he rapped out.

"Only what the janitor told me."

"What did he tell you?"

"That she went away for a week-end trip a few weeks ago and hasn't been seen since."

"What made him tell you that?"

"I was asking him for her apartment number."

"Why?"

"Because I wanted to meet her, and give her a message from her father in England."

"Are you from England?"

"Yes. I arrived yesterday on the *Queen Elizabeth*."

"The *Queen Elizabeth*, eh! A fine ship that. What was the number of your state-room?"

"D.16."

"Any objection to my checking up with the shipping company?"

"None whatever."

"Where are you staying?"

"At the New Weston."

"Right." The detective looked up from the notes he had been jotting down. "You were snappy on looking up the Ramsay woman, weren't you?"

"Not considering that the purpose of my journey to New York was to see her."

"You came to New York just to see a woman?" There was sharp suspicion in the lieutenant's voice. "All right, carry on."

"I was wondering if you could be of assistance to me in tracing Miss Ramsay's whereabouts."

"Do you want her that bad?"

Terhune could see that Kraszewski was suspicious; he decided to try a long shot. "Do you know the name of Tony Malatesta?"

The lieutenant's eyes narrowed. "Do I know what a rattlesnake is? The point is, what do you know about that four-flusher?"

Terhune felt in a mischievous mood. He grinned. "I know that he was in England a week ago."

"In England! Say, young feller, you seem to know more than is good for you. I think you and me must get to know each other better. What are you? Why have you come to New York? What do you want with Tony Malatesta? How do you know he was in England?"

It was apparent to Terhune that it might repay him to be frank with Lieutenant Kraszewski; the detective looked a decent fellow behind his hard, disillusioned mask, and might prove a useful ally. So the Englishman related something of the events which led up to his arrival in New York, not forgetting the attempt to murder him aboard the liner. Although the lieutenant looked somewhat contemptuous when his visitor began by describing himself as an amateur detective, his expression became more and more interested as Terhune continued, and he listened to the end without once interrupting.

"Let me tell you this, young feller," he then said, "your Inspector Sampson knew what he was saying when he warned you that if Smart Tony—our name for Malatesta over here—was connected with a crime, there was big money in it. Tony lives up to his name. He's smart all right; too smart for us, I don't mind telling you. We could name a dozen crimes we suspect him of, but so far we haven't been able to pin anything on him. Take my word for it, if Smart Tony reappears in New York during the next few days you will know that it was he who tried to push you over into the ditch.

"Meanwhile, this is what we have found out about your Margaret Ramsay. For the past three years she has been employed as a stenographer by the China Import and Export Corporation. She has a good reputation both at business and privately. Her best friend was Netta Pouskin, but unfortunately, on the Tuesday before Margaret disappeared, the two girls had a quarrel and parted bad friends. On the Thursday Netta rang up to ask Margaret to stay with her at Port Jefferson, Long Island, for the week-end, so they could kiss and make up, but Margaret said that she was already dated. Netta was so surprised that she asked, 'Who with?' To which Margaret replied, 'Wouldn't you like to know?' and rang off.

"Now, it's darned funny, Mr. Terhune, but we haven't traced a soul who is able to tell us for certain who Margaret went away with. All we know is that she was seen in a Buick with another girl and two fellows. What we do know is that three other people disappeared that same week-end; one of them was a girl and two of them young fellows. There's not much doubt but that they all went away together on a secret jaunt, but why, where, and as to what happened to them we know no more than you do."

"They may have had an accident."

"That is what we reckon, but a check of all the mortuary and hospital cases has failed to bear any results. Those four week-enders made a neater job of disappearing than Aladdin's slave of the lamp."

"Were her companions of good reputation?"

"Yes, sir, they were. One of them was one of Netta's best boy friends, so you know why the girls quarrelled. Why did you ask?"

"I was wondering whether Margaret's disappearance had anything to do with the events in England."

Kraszewski shook his square, shaven head. "Not a chance! No, what probably happened was that they began celebrating the week-end too soon, and drove into the Hudson, or some other deep water. Maybe we shall not hear of them for months yet."

"Poor devils!" There was a slight pause, broken presently by Terhune. "My journey to New York seems to be wasted."

"It seems like that," the police detective agreed sympathetically. "But a visit to Netta Pouskin might be worth your while. The two girls were pretty close until the boy friend came between them." He grinned, then added: "Would you like her address?"

"Please."

"Here it is. One hundred and three, West Fifty-fourth." The lieutenant wrote something on a piece of paper which he presently passed over to Terhune. "Good luck to you, young feller. If anything turns up about Margaret Ramsay I'll let you know. Meanwhile, if there is any other help I can give you, ring me up. You will find the number there, and also my name, which nobody ever spells right." He held out a hard, knotty hand. "And say, young feller, if you are interested in crime and would like a tour around this burg one night, what about you and me dating up?"

Terhune accepted with alacrity.

VII

A telephone call to Netta Pouskin at her office quickly brought about an arrangement for dinner that night—after Terhune had disconnected, bemused by her endless flow of conversation, he tried to work out how he had come to extend such an invitation, for he had had no previous intention of doing so; he reached a conclusion that she must have dragged it from him by some subtle method of painless extraction. Not that he regretted the engagement; on the contrary, from her conversation Netta seemed to be an extremely vivacious, entertaining person.

So she proved to be. He was shy with her, as with most young women of that age, but it would have been all the same had he been inclined the other way. She soon talked him into a state of silent camaraderie. Nevertheless, he thoroughly enjoyed the meal, and by the time coffee was served she was, he believed, likely to be more pliable to his questions.

"How long have you known Margaret?"

"Ever since we were at school together."

He was astonished. "Were you at the Ashford School for Girls?"

"Yes. For two years. My father was sent to England in connection with some engineering business. He sent me to the Ashford school as long as we were in England. It was I who was responsible for Margaret's coming over to New York, and I who secured for her the post in the China Import and Export Corporation."

"Did you see much of her?"

"We roomed together until eighteen months ago. Then my sister came to town, so Margaret found an apartment for herself on East Fifty-fifth."

"I suppose you met each other's friends?"

Netta energetically nodded her pert little head. "Of course."

"Tell me, did you ever call Margaret by the nickname of Blondie?"

"No." Netta giggled. "The name would not have suited her."

"Why not? Wasn't her hair blonde?"

"Yes, but Margaret was not the kind of girl we would have called Blondie. She was much too quiet and strait-laced."

"Did other people ever call her Blondie?"

"Not as far as I know."

"Do you know anybody else who is known as Blondie?"

"Only the peach on the strip cartoon."

"You knew, of course, that she was working for Lord Fulchester before coming to America?"

"Yes. Wasn't he writing a scandalous history of the people living in his neighbourhood?"

Terhune started. "What made you call it a scandalous history?"

Netta looked vague. "I don't know. Wasn't it scandalous?"

"Did Margaret ever tell you that it was?"

She shook her head. "She never said much about the silly old book."

"Did she ever discuss it with you?"

"I wasn't interested enough."

"Did she never tell you anything of any scandal connected with one of the local families?"

"Not that I remember."

"Then what made you describe it as scandalous?"

"My! You are inquisitive."

"Please tell me; please try to remember; it is very important."

She patted his hand. "You look so sweet when you have that expression on your face. Now don't talk to me. Let me try to think." She placed one elbow on the table, rested her chin in one cupped hand, and stared at the surrounding people.

Time passed; but just as he began to think that her reverie was permanent she exclaimed loudly, "I know."

"Well?" he barked.

"Don't hurry me. I think it was one night when Margaret had had too much to drink—the only night I have ever known her drink too much, the poor darling. But then it was both a jolly and a sad occasion. It was her birthday and also the last night we were to room together. We gave a party, and Margaret brought along that Englishman of hers—what was his name?—oh! I remember— Jimmy Lewis, or some name like that.

"I remember she and Jimmy getting into a huddle in a corner of the room. I heard them talking about Kent and Willingham and Lord Fulchester's book. I knew by Jimmy's eager expression, and the way he whistled now and again, that she was telling him some choice low-down. I guess that is what you want to know, isn't it, my pet?"

Terhune nodded. He was too excited to make any attempt at masking his feelings. "Did you hear any name mentioned? Please try to remember. Please."

"There was one name," Netta admitted slowly. "It was Jack—no, Joe—Joe somebody or other."

"Joe who?" he pleaded.

"Joe—Joe—say, isn't there a gardener fellow living near her pop over in Kent?"

"Joe Richards?"

"That's the johnny!" she confirmed triumphantly.

The Sixth Clue

The discovery that Joe Richards was apparently connected with the affair at Willingham was one which kept Terhune awake that night for two hours or more while he lay flat on his back, staring upwards through the darkness, and listening to the noisy traffic which slackened off after midnight, but did not cease.

Many facts pointed to Margaret Ramsay's conversation with the Englishman, Jimmy Lewis, as being a clue of sorts in the inexplicable business which he was trying to solve, but if it were he failed utterly in interlocking it with the other clues which had come to light. In the first case, who was this Jimmy Lewis? Netta Pouskin, despite persistent questioning, had remained delightfully vague about him. What was he like? Oh, much like any other Englishman. Was he tall? Yes, about six feet or thereabouts. Was he young? No, he was not young; but neither was he old; about early middle-aged, with greying hair. Did he live in New York? Heaven alone knew! Maybe he did, maybe he didn't; she never remembered having heard his address; she wasn't interested, that was why. He was not her type. How had he come to be at the party? Margaret had brought him. Was he a friend of hers? They had met at a night-club some weeks before; subsequently he had taken Margaret out to dine once or twice. What was the name of the night-club? The "Green Parrot", in 43rd Street. Had the friendship continued? She couldn't say for certain, but it had seemed to her that it had cooled off after the night of Margaret's birthday. Although Margaret had not said much, she,

Netta, had gathered an impression that Jimmy Lewis had proved to be just another man—which cut no ice with Margaret, for she was not that kind of a girl.

Terhune asked a score or more questions, but none of Netta's subsequent answers proved to be of any help to him. Apparently Margaret and Lewis had met as ships in the night, and after spending a few evenings together during a period of a few weeks, as ships in the night they had parted, never, to Netta's knowledge, to see each other again.

Nevertheless, it was no difficult matter to make significant deductions from this short-lived friendship. It might be, Terhune reflected, that what had happened was this: Lewis had, at the first meeting, liked Margaret for her own sake; perhaps because she was of his own nationality. On the night of Margaret's birthday she had drunk more alcohol than was good for her; in consequence, she had relaxed the discreet guard which normally, it seemed, she maintained over her tongue. She had probably started by telling Lewis of her work in England, and had finished up by disclosing information which she had helped Lord Fulchester to collect and collate. It was this information which might have put into motion the sequence of events which had led, more than a year later, to the Kylstone vault's being opened by Malatesta and his accomplices.

So far so good. But what was the information which it was assumed Margaret Ramsay had revealed to the man Lewis? Had Netta overheard the name of Kylstone, or MacMunn, or Major Blye, or Pearson, or any of the people whose biographies were certainly included in Lord Fulchester's history, then one might go on to assume that Lewis had appreciated the possibilities of reaping gain from the information which Margaret had unwittingly betrayed. But the only name Netta had overheard was that of Joe Richards, jobbing gardener, almost the last person in the world from whom or through whom anyone might hope to benefit financially, and possibly one of the last people round Willingham likely to find any place in the Fulchester history.

True, there were three significant facts about Richards which Terhune did not overlook. The first was that Richards had once been Margaret's neighbour. This fact-bore two inferences. The first, that it was through being his neighbour that she had discovered that certain information about him which Terhune was using as the basis of deduction. The second factor was Richards's one-time employment by the MacMunns as their gardener. Terhune felt that that should be of importance, but he could not imagine why. Unless... Another possibility suddenly occurred to him. Richards had been employed by Mrs. MacMunn at the time her father was preparing the history. Perhaps Richards, during the course of employment with other people, had come into possession of some biographical details which he had passed on to Lord Fulchester for inclusion in the history: the story that Margaret had told of Richards might have been of how the gardener had learned of this item of information.

A third complicating circumstance was Richards's departure from the neighbourhood of Willingham. He had left for North Wales, Terhune seemed to remember, roughly about the same time that the pages had been stolen from the Fulchester history. Had he had an indirect hand in their theft? Or—yet another possibility—had Lewis, in consequence of Margaret's revelation, gone to England, and there, in collaboration with Richards, planned the theft of the pages, and the mysterious crime, whatever it might be, of which the sundry clues Terhune had unearthed were part and parcel?

The more time he devoted to the problem the more endless became the possibilities. He became bewildered by their variety, and despaired ever of solving the mystery. He asked himself, by what right had he accepted the money from Lady Kylstone to pay for the journey to America? How could he, an amateur, hope to chart a course through a fog of perplexing circumstances which might have baffled even an expert—Detective-Inspector Sampson, for instance? He bitterly regretted having accepted Lady Kylstone's generous offer—until commonsense reasserted itself. Only Fate had robbed his journey of success, he angrily reassured himself. Had he been able to meet Margaret Ramsay, the key to the riddle might, by now, have been his. But Fate had decreed otherwise—his one hope now of achieving any result from his stay in New York was to get on the track of the elusive Blondie.

II

The next morning Terhune went downtown to Rylands Street. Here he found a different New York, a New York for which his slight acquaintance with the skyscrapers of Fifth Avenue, Broadway, and 42nd Street had made him quite unprepared. Here, in Rylands and the surrounding streets, there were no skyscrapers—the tallest building was no more than four floors in height—no immense blocks of offices or apartments, no palatial shops, no bustling crowds; even the traffic seemed slight and slow-moving. As he stepped out of the subway stairs it seemed to him that he had not merely travelled a few blocks from one quarter of a city to another, but rather, from the middle of the twentieth century back into the dying years of the nineteenth.

In many ways Rylands Street reminded him of Soho crossed with Chelsea; there was the same atmosphere of unreality, of a stage *décor*, as it were; the same 'arty' buildings, with their gaudy curtaining, their green doors and their pillar-box-red window-boxes (or their pillar-box-red doors and their green window-boxes), the same little intimate restaurants, with names suggestive of Montmartre or Montparnasse, the same small shops, with names above to remind one of every quarter of Europe, the same dark-haired, dark-eyed children playing in the streets, the same clop-clopping horses and rumbling carts, the same studio windows, the same collection of strange people. Even the same smells.

Twenty-six, Rylands Street he found to be a three-storeyed building, of the type he would have described as double-fronted. Its front door was four steps high; it had shutters of the French variety (the paint had long since lost its colour), its walls were of brown stone.

He mounted the few stone steps and pressed upon the electric bell. Presently the door was opened by a yellow-skinned, slant-eyed, slippered Japanese, who stared at him with a dazzling, white-toothed smile.

"Can one rent rooms at this address?"

" 'Scuse, pleese, me fetch missee."

As the little man began to hurry away Terhune called out: "Just a minute."

The Japanese turned. " 'Scuse, pleese?"

"I don't want to rent a room; I just want to ask somebody a few questions."

The man nodded his head understandingly. " 'Scuse, pleese, me fetch missee." Again he hurried away along a dark-looking passage, creating in Terhune's mind the impression that the answer would have been the same whatever his question. Presently a very stout woman made a waddling appearance. She puffed and gasped as if from great exertion, but Terhune noted that she eyed him with a hawk-like, calculating scrutiny.

"Good marning to ye. I have only but one room lift, an' that is me best, so it is. What are ye prepared to pay, now?"

"I am sorry, but I do not want to rent a room."

"Thin what do ye want, worrying a poor woman at this time of the day? If you be one of thim insurance men, thin begod, it is a piece of me mind I'll be giving ye——"

"I am not selling anything," he hastily interrupted.

"Be you not selling anything? Thin it is a rare sort of a caller ye are, to be sure. What is it ye want?"

"I must apologize for taking up your time, Mrs.—Mrs.———"

"O'Connor."

"Mrs. O'Connor, but I am anxious to trace the present where-abouts of somebody who rented a room at this address, probably more than a year ago."

A gleam of interest revealed itself in the woman's eyes. "Are ye one of thim detectives?"

"Not exactly, Mrs. O'Connor—not officially, that is to say———"

"Thin ye are one of thim amatoor detectives me old man used to read about in books whin he wasn't at work, the lazy good-for-nothing."

"Well, sort of," he admitted cautiously.

"Hum! In that case I'm not saying that I'll tell ye anything of what ye want to know, me man, for I don't hold wid such underhand business as snoopin' around by some whipper-snapper. If anyone wants to ask me any questions let them come here and ask thim to me face." She paused. "What was the name of the man ye'll be after tracing?"

"It isn't a man, Mrs. O'Connor, but a woman."

"A woman!" She broke into a high-pitched cackle of laughter. "A woman or a girl, me man?"

"I—I am not sure."

"You're not sure?" She stared at him with amazement. "What was her name?"

"I don't know, but———"

"The Saints preserve us!" She stared at him. "Is it crazy ye are, coming here to ask me questions about a woman whose name you don't know, and whose probable age you don't know? Do ye know anything about her at all? How am I to know who ye mean?"

"I can describe her, Mrs. O'Connor. She has blonde hair."

"God save us! I very two out of three women have blonde hair," Mrs. O'Connor exaggerated. "Did ye say this blonde-haired woman had one of me rooms here?"

"So I understand."

"Thin it is Mary Watson ye be after, me man, for she is the only blonde lodger I mind at this moment."

"Was she very blonde?"

"As blonde as a bottle of that peroxide stuff could make her."

"Can you tell me her new address?"

"New address me foot! She's occupied that room above me head for the past four years, and it's me hope she'll stay there for another four years, for she pays her rent, bless her, as regularly as me old man gets boozed up."

He was disappointed. "Then Miss Watson is not the woman I want to find; the one I am looking for has sailed for England."

Mrs. O'Connor snorted her scorn. "What for?"

"I don't know. Are you quite sure you haven't had another blonde-haired woman staying with you during the past year or so?"

"Thir was Mrs. Kostromiten; thir might be found some to call her hair blonde, though to me own way of thinking it is light mousey. But thin she can't be in England, to be sure, for it was meself that set eyes upon her in Fourteenth Street not two weeks gone. Thin thir is Agnes O'Grady, but she married, like a sinsible girl, and went to live in Arkansas. 'Tis less than a month ago I had a letter from her telling me that thir's a baby on the way." She shrugged her fat shoulders. "But thir's the lot, me man, and if ye are not satisfied wid what I have told ye, thin it's elsewhere ye must find out what ye want to know."

"Are you quite sure, Mrs. O'Connor, that there is nobody else you can think of?"

"Quite sure, me man," she confirmed decisively. "Most of me roomers stay wid me a tidy time for they have the sinse to realize whin they are well off. And now, me man, if that is all ye want to know, I have me work to do, though ye being a man wouldn't know that a woman's work is niver done. Good day to ye." With that Mrs. O'Connor firmly closed the door in his face.

Terhune walked slowly back to the subway. His mood was disconsolate. Following upon the news of Margaret Ramsay's disappearance, the disappointment of being unable to trace Blondie's identity and present whereabouts made it seem all the more as if his journey to America was proving to be an utter waste of time and money. Of the three addresses at which he had hoped a personal call might yield useful information—the addresses of Margaret Ramsay, Blondie, and Malatesta—two had already failed to produce any worth-while result. Of the third he had no genuine hope; he did not think it likely, from the little he had seen of the New York underworld, that anyone associated with Malatesta was likely to betray the Italian. Nevertheless, it was his intention to pursue his inquiries at 145, Worthington Street, for inquiries there, and at the "Green Parrot" night-club, represented his last hope of achieving good results from his visit to New York.

While he was studying a map of city communications to ascertain the route to Worthington Street he remembered unexpectedly Lieutenant Kraszewski's willingness to help if there were any way in which that were possible. In dealing with inquiries about Malatesta, Kraszewski's assistance might be invaluable in unloosening lips which otherwise might remain sealed. Acting upon impulse, Terhune entered the nearest drug-store and telephoned the 28th Precinct. In less than a minute he heard the lieutenant's guttural voice at the other end of the connection.

"Hullo there! How goes it? Was that Pouskin girl helpful?"

"She was helpful, but not too useful. She told me of one occasion when Margaret Ramsay had too much to drink, and went into a huddle, as she called it, with an Englishman. From the little she heard and saw she is sure they were talking of Willingham, and believes that she told him some of the scandal from Lord Fulchester's book."

"You are getting warmer. Did Netta tell you this guy's name?"

"Yes. Jimmy Lewis."

"Never heard of it," Kraszewski volunteered promptly. "I'll have him looked up for you. Anything else on your mind?"

"Although I doubt its usefulness I am anxious to make inquiries about Malatesta in the hope of learning something more of the blonde woman I mentioned to you. I have the feeling, however, that I shouldn't get very far on my own."

"You are dead right, Mr. Terhune. You wouldn't. You can take it from me that anyone associated with Smart Tony is a bad egg; it's dollars to cents you wouldn't get no place on your own." He chuckled. "I guess you would like me to accompany you."

"That is what I had in mind if it would not be asking too much of you, Lieutenant."

"You bet it isn't. Glad to give you a helping hand any time, Mr. Terhune. I hope to be free tonight; would eight o'clock suit you?"

"Excellently."

"I'll call for you at the New Weston. And say, don't trouble to eat. If it appeals to you we will have a bite at Smart Tony's favourite hide-out—I am told that you Britishers know a thing or two about mixing business with pleasure." The lieutenant's genial laugh robbed his words of any sting.

So it was arranged. After ringing off, Terhune took the uptown subway and returned to his hotel. There he got into communication with Lady Kylstone's brother, Wesley Cruikshank, who was at Albany. In consequence, he received a hearty invitation to spend the week-end of the 22nd at the capital city, an invitation which he accepted eagerly, for he was anxious, not only to visit the capital city of New York State, but also to see something of the American countryside en route.

During luncheon he decided to devote the afternoon to business of his own, for he could think of nothing more he could do, meanwhile, in connection with the Willingham affair. Afterwards, therefore, he paid visits to the principal book dealers, where he not only made several purchases (including two volumes on American fly-fishing for Sir George, a book of theatrical memoirs which he felt convinced Isabel Shelley would buy, and a book on American art for Edward Pryce), but also sold more than a dozen titles (to be despatched as soon as he returned to England) and established a number of valuable connections likely to prove of great benefit to him. Indeed, before the afternoon ended he began to have rosy dreams of an extremely interesting future, as he foresaw the possibilities of greatly extending his sales by circulating to American buyers lists of certain books already in hand.

At five minutes to eight Lieutenant Kraszewski called for him at the New Weston and took him down town.

"I am going to take you to Willy's," the American explained. "Half a dozen crooks have an interest in Willy's; probably the only honest interest they possess. Six of these birds—Smart Tony was the guiding spirit, and chief investor—whipped up the capital between them to establish the place, and then ordered all the small-timers of the neighbourhood to eat there, or know the reason why. The owners keep the business on the level as an insurance against the failure of crime to pay dividends. I tell you, young feller, Tony is as smart a guy as you'd meet anywhere in this burg."

There was nothing startling about Willy's. The restaurant consisted of a moderately large room, in which were set out tables and chairs, and, at the far end, a raised platform reached by mounting a flower-bordered staircase of five stairs. The length of this platform was occupied by a bar, behind which served two white-coated bartenders. Room and bar alike were generously mirrored, and garish with hard-gloss paint. A number of amplifiers, spaced at regular intervals, diffused music from the radio.

As Kraszewski strode along the table-bordered gangway which led to the bar he was greeted from all sides, in some cases by insincere words of welcome, in others by sullen, hostile glances. The dumb hate the detective ignored; the other salutations he acknowledged with a curt nod or a brief word.

Followed by his guest, he mounted the stairs to the bar and sat down upon one of the high stools. The bartender gave a sickly smile.

"Hullo, Lootenant."

"Hullo, Al. So your sins haven't found you out?"

"Aw, you're always joshing me, Lootenant. Why don't you pick upon somebody else for a change? You know me; I ain't done nothing nor nobody wrong."

"Maybe you haven't since you've landed this job, Al."

"We ain't seen much of you lately, Lootenant, since you moved uptown. Only the other day the boys was saying that times aren't what they used to be when you was around. Name your poison, Lootenant."

Kraszewski glanced at his companion. "A highball, Mr. Terhune?"

"I should prefer a dry Martini."

"One Martini and one highball, Al."

While Al prepared the drinks the lieutenant jerked his head backwards at the crowded restaurant. "There are enough convicted criminals down there right now to fill a small penitentiary. Have you a money wallet in your pocket?"

"Yes."

"Well, if it weren't for me you wouldn't leave this place with the wallet still there. There are three of the slickest hands in New York not a dozen yards from you. There is a white slaver over there in the left-hand corner of the room by the door—you can see him in the mirror just to the left of Al's ears. At the table next to him is

Strangler Lloyd. He is not an all-in wrestler, as you might think, but a cold-blooded murderer. Two members of Ruffini's gang have been picked out of the East River, but it wasn't water which croaked them, it was a couple of thumbs. Dollars to cents, the thumbs were Lloyd's, but they might have belonged to one of seven odd million other citizens of New York City for all the evidence we could pin upon him. With him is Kansas Annie—the stoniest-hearted dame as ever spilled a sob-story to a hick pastor." Kraszewski shrugged his shoulders. "I could tell you something about almost every man or woman here, but what's the use? He is the man who should interest us right now." He nodded at Al, who was turning about at that moment.

"Here you are, Lootenant. The real McCoy."

"It had better be," Kraszewski muttered. "Don't go away, Al," he added quickly. "You and me are going to have a conversazioni."

Fear blazed from Al's eyes. "You've got nothing on me. I ain't done nothing since I've been here. You know that. You know what our orders is, while we are here——"

"Yeah, I know," the lieutenant agreed. "I also know something else, Al, and the name is Nazerbeck—Mrs. K. Nazerbeck."

Tiny beads of perspiration suddenly made their appearance on Al's forehead. "I don't know nothing about her, Lootenant. Honest to God, I don't!"

"That's as may be, but she isn't my pigeon, see! And I don't *have* to drop a hint to O'Farrell, if I don't feel that way inclined. Get me, Al?"

Al mopped his damp forehead with his handkerchief. "I get you, Lootenant."

"Right! When did you last see Smart Tony, Al?"

"Tony!" Al started. "Yesterday," he muttered in a low but relieved voice.

"Yesterday!" Kraszewski leaned forward. "You are quite sure you aren't trying to cross me, Al?"

"Honest to God, he was, Lootenant. Ask any of the boys if you don't believe me."

"Perhaps I do, after all," The lieutenant turned sideways. "Does that solve one of your problems?" he asked Terhune.

Terhune nodded. Kraszewski faced the bartender again.

"When did you last see him before yesterday?"

Al moistened his lips. "About five or six weeks ago."

"Haven't you seen him between whiles?"

"I can't say I have."

"He's been away, hasn't he?"

"How should I know?" Al asked sullenly.

"He's been away, hasn't he?" the detective repeated.

"Yes," Al admitted at last.

"Where did he go to?"

"How should I know? I didn't buy his ticket."

"He's been to England, and you know it, Al."

"Well, what if he has? I ain't his nurse. I couldn't stop him going, could I? Besides, it wasn't his first visit there. He was there last year, but you didn't ask no questions, did you?"

"I suppose you didn't know what he was going there for, either?"

Al laughed hoarsely. "Have you ever met anyone to know what Tony was doing? He ain't Smart Tony for nothing."

"All right, skip it. What about that blonde woman of his—where is she now?"

Al stared at the lieutenant with an unmistakably genuine look of surprise on his face. "What dame?" he demanded.

"The one with the blonde hair he was trailing around with."

The bartender laughed—somewhat maliciously, Terhune thought. "You've got Tony wrong, haven't you, Lootenant? Tony's never teamed up with a blonde; he don't like 'em. He likes them ginger or black. Besides, you don't think Zola would stand by and see her boy friend tag around with another dame, do you? She's poison to other dames where Tony is concerned."

"Listen to me, Al. I want this straight, see? Never mind what you haven't seen. Have you heard any talk of Tony having a blonde as his girl-friend?"

Al shook his head with a decisive manner that was unfortunately convincing. "No, I ain't, Lootenant, and I'll bet you a five spot that you don't find anyone that has."

Nothing the lieutenant said shook Al's testimony, so, having finished their drinks, Kraszewski took Terhune to a vacant table and ordered a meal of Blue Point oysters, blue-fish, and ice cream. During the course of the meal he kept his visitor entertained by innumerable anecdotes of the people who surrounded them. Despite his book knowledge of crime, the Englishman was astonished to learn how much positive knowledge the police could have concerning a man's connection with a specific crime, and yet not be legally entitled to make an arrest. Kraszewski told him, also, of the extensive use made in America of the writ of *habeas corpus*, and of its hampering effects upon police efforts to check crime.

From Willy's the detective took Terhune to other haunts where information concerning Malatesta and his associates was to be obtained. During the course of the next few hours Kraszewski questioned more than a dozen people concerning the blonde woman, but from none of them did he obtain any useful hint or lead. Although many were aware that Malatesta had visited England twice in eighteen months, and knew other things about him, too, about which they let drop certain hints, nobody had ever seen him with a fair-haired woman; as for other blonde women with a criminal or near-criminal reputation, all of these could be accounted for in or near New York City.

Towards midnight the lieutenant abandoned his efforts for the time being. His manner was quite abrupt as he parted company from Terhune; it was obvious that he was nettled by his failure to get on the trail of Blondie. Terhune was sympathetic to the police lieutenant's feelings; his own mood was equally dispirited, for it seemed to him that his last chance of making a success of his trip to America had failed. All that he could now do was to visit the "Green Parrot" nightclub in the hope of finding out more of Jimmy Lewis—and that hope was a slender one. Assuming that he was lucky enough to discover Lewis's New York address, it was unlikely that he would be any nearer to solving the Willingham affair, he thought, for the probability was that Lewis was in England.

The next day, being Sunday, he spent amusing himself. In the morning he visited the Zoological Gardens; in the afternoon he went to a movie at Radio City. In the evening he went to the "Green Parrot". Many years had passed since his last visit to a night-club— his last visit had been as a guest of an Australian who wanted companionship in painting London red—but the "Green Parrot" appealed to him no more than the three or four he had visited in London. The "Green Parrot" differed very little from the others—the same habitués, with their tired, blasé expressions, the same thick fug of smoke, the same crowded tables, the same microscopic floor space for dancing, the same noisy dance band—no, even noisier he soon decided—the same false and forced gaiety, the same cabaret turns, the same undressed chorus.

Having, as an unaccompanied man, and a stranger, been given a small table in the most inconspicuous and uninteresting corner, he ordered supper and half a bottle of Spanish wine. When the first course was brought to him—he experimented with cherry clams— he asked the waiter if he knew anything of Jimmy Lewis.

For once luck was with him, the inquiry proved fruitful.

"Sure I know Jimmy Lewis," the waiter replied. "Was he a pal of yours?"

"No, but I am a friend of one of his friends. He used to come here regularly, didn't he?"

"Sure, three or four nights a week mostly."

"Is he here tonight? I have a message for him."

The waiter laughed. "You are more than a year too late. I was talking about the past, not the present."

"Doesn't he come here any more?"

"Not since way back last year—I guess it's more than twelve months since he showed up here."

Terhune tried to look dismayed. "The message was very important," he explained. "Is there anybody here who knows his telephone number, or address?"

"Not a chance. Jimmy Lewis doesn't live here any more. I guess you come from England, don't you?"

"Yes."

"Then you'll have to go back there if you want to deliver a message to him, for that is where he went to."

Beyond confirming the fact that Lewis had, as Terhune suspected, gone to England, the waiter was unable to disclose any further information of value, so, disappointed, the Englishman devoted the remainder of his time at the nightclub to the dubious pleasures of the cabaret, and the contortions of the chorus girls who had been chosen, he judged, less for their merit than for their willingness to expose, discreetly but tantalizingly, their intimate but overplump charms.

III

As the days went by it seemed to Terhune that his initial failure to achieve any success in his inquiries had set the tenor for the rest of his stay in the New World. He left for Albany on the Friday afternoon with the sad reflection that he would have almost no fresh news to follow up the letter which Lady Kylstone had sent to her brother in order to make him fully acquainted with the sequence of strange events which had terminated in her paying the expenses of Terhune's journey to New York.

Yet the week had not passed entirely without slight progress having been made—thanks to Kraszewski. Perhaps because of a feeling that the police department had been put to shame because of his failure to trace Blondie, the lieutenant had busied himself in investigating some minor developments. For instance, he had ascertained from the Cunard-White Star people that Malatesta had arrived on the *Queen Elizabeth*, and that he had only booked his passage, tourist class, two days before she sailed. This, as Kraszewski pointed out, was a significant point.

"Somebody tipped him off that you proposed coming here in the *Queen Elizabeth* in order to question Margaret Ramsay. Did anyone in London know of your journey?"

"Only the shipping company, the passport officials, and the man at the American Consulate who vised my passport."

"You can cut all that crowd out, and listen here! It was for the purpose of learning your identity and address that Malatesta tried to rob you of your wallet. Well, he didn't get it, so unless one of his accomplices followed you from the police station back home again, we are safe in assuming that he didn't learn what he wanted to know. Yet he knew you were to be on the *Queen Elizabeth*. In short, young feller, it was somebody from Willingham or Bray who gave him the low-down, and if you want my guess that somebody was Blondie. What is more, it's dollars to cents that Blondie suggested that an accident of some sort might overtake you."

"Having failed once, why didn't Malatesta have another shot at silencing me?"

"Because one man's meat is another man's poison. Margaret's fate was your gain. No doubt Malatesta reckoned that so long as you couldn't untie Margaret's tongue you couldn't do much harm running round the town."

Kraszewski also supplied some meagre information concerning Jimmy Lewis. Lewis, it seemed, had been known in New York for about three years previous to his departure for England (the lieutenant easily traced Lewis's address). He had arrived there, according to his own story, from Scranton, Pa., but the Scranton police being unable to confirm this, the lieutenant doubted the truth of this story. At any rate, during his three years in New York Lewis had spent money freely, and had mixed with all types of society, from the ranks of the extremely exclusive on the one hand, to the extremely dubious on the other.

"He was a crook, right enough, and a pretty smart one, too, to have kept out of our clutches. If you want my guess he was a blackmailer. That is what you suspect, isn't it? Though what blackmail has to do with that old burial vault, and why Lewis sent for Malatesta, is something that don't make sense to me if blackmail is the only crime that bird Lewis is mixed up in. It's dollars to cents that Lewis is one of those smart guys who move on from city to city, stopping at each place long enough to skim the cream from the crime jug but not long enough for the police to become properly acquainted with him. A slick feller can get away with a hell of a lot if he takes care to keep clear of federal crimes, and confine himself to non-extraditable offences. If he does that, all he has to do is to slip across the state line every time he knows the red is showing."

If Terhune arrived at Albany feeling moody and disconsolate, he left there, on the following Monday morning, still warm (despite the bitter wind) from the effects of an exceedingly happy week-end. Everything that could be done to please a guest Cruikshank did; Terhune was never to doubt America's claim to be one of the most hospitable countries in the world. This glowing happiness lasted until he reached the New Weston and was told that Lieutenant Kraszewski wanted him to telephone the 28th Precinct.

"I have news for you, Tom," the lieutenant announced over the 'phone. "Margaret and her pals have turned up."

"Are they all right?" Terhune asked eagerly.

"No," Kraszewski replied shortly. "They were found just where I was afraid they might be—at the bottom of the Hudson. The poor devils were trapped and drowned before they could open the doors and escape."

Within an hour of hearing the lieutenant's sad news Terhune was on his way to the steamship office to book his return passage to England. There seemed nothing more for him to do in New York, so conscience dictated that he should leave by the first available ship. At the shipping office he was told that two ships were due to leave for England the following Saturday; the *Queen Elizabeth* and the *Samaria*. Anxious to discover for himself the difference between the palatial luxury and speed of the faster vessels, and the more friendly intimacy of the slower, he selected the *Samaria*, and was allocated a starboard state-room on C deck.

It was a miserable Terhune who left the heated building and faced the bitter wind that was blowing up Broadway from the direction of Battery Park. Although he suspected that too long a stay in New York might rob it of its novelty, that stage, as far as he was concerned, had not yet been reached. The city fascinated him; the people, also, with their incisiveness, their hospitality, their easy familiarity. He would not have cared to face the prospect of living there for years, for he loved the peace and serenity of the English countryside too much to desert it for so long. But meanwhile, he would gladly have welcomed the opportunity of staying in New York for at least another month. Preferably two, with perhaps a trip to Niagara Falls, another to Boston, and a Greyhound coach trip south into Colonial America.

Another reason for his reluctance to return to England so soon was his failure to achieve any useful result. The money which

Lady Kylstone had given him had been wasted. In all the eleven days of his stay in New York he had learned nothing new, with one exception—that he now knew that an Englishman by the name of Jimmy Lewis might be somewhere in the background, and that Joe Richards, also, had some possible, but inexplicable, connection with the events in Willingham. No audit, he felt, however optimistic, could manipulate a profit from that balance sheet.

As he passed by a subway entrance a gust of warm air tempted him to go below, for the ice-chill of the wind nipped his ears and nose (he noticed that a number of people were wearing ear-flaps). He hesitated, but not for long; less than two minutes' walk away was Battery Park, his favourite spot in New York; from it was to be seen Upper New York Bay, busy with shipping (even the largest ships afloat passed within a stone's-throw of Battery Park), the Narrows, with the ocean beyond, the shipping piers of New Jersey, Ellis Island, the Statue of Liberty, Governor's Island, Brooklyn. He braced himself against the wind, and moved on past the subway entrance.

As if annoyed by his defiance the gusty wind blew with added violence. Hats blew off half a dozen heads near by; his own started to lift, but a quick snatch saved it. He stopped to jamb it more firmly down upon his head; as he did so he saw, to his right, several feet above the entrance to a skyscraper, a bas-relief in stone which set his nerves jumping with excitement. The sculptured design was that of an automobile tyre outstretched in Mercury's hand, similar in every detail to the one ornamenting the gold fountain-pen found in the Kylstone burial vault. Beneath the bas-relief were carved the words: Tunkhannock Building.

He did not pause to reflect upon what he should do in the matter; prompted by impulse, he forced his way into the building through a crowd of men coming out. The design was a clue; it must be; it had to be! Somehow or other Tunkhannock Building was mysteriously linked up with the Kylstone burial vault; somebody must be found who could explain why and how.

His eager gaze raked the directory board; there were a hundred names upon it, but his eyes focused upon the outstanding one; the Tunkhannock Tire Corporation. Mercury and an automobile tyre! Of course! Ruefully, he chided himself upon not having realized the possibility of the design's being a commercial trade-mark. A hasty, second thought was in the nature of an excuse—why should one connect motor-car tyres with gold fountain pens? Perhaps that was a question which somebody in the Tire Corporation could answer.

The Corporation, according to the directory board, occupied the twentieth to the thirtieth floors inclusive. Inquiries, he noticed, were to be made at the twentieth. He hurried towards the line of nine elevators. Three of these were marked 'Tunkhannock Tire Corporation Only', so he entered one of these; a few seconds later the elevator was mounting rapidly, non-stop, to the twentieth floor.

He alighted at the twentieth, stepping immediately from the elevator into a huge, spacious office in which thirty or forty people of both sexes were at work, each at his or her own table. Close to the elevator doors he noticed a long table marked 'Inquiries'. Three women clerks sat behind the table—three chairs were placed in front, on the near side of the table. Before each young woman was a telephone, and papers of some kind upon which they were at work. One of the three chairs on the near side of the table was already occupied by a man; Terhune sat down in the next chair.

The girl opposite gave him a pleasant smile. "Yes, sir?"

"I—I want to make an inquiry."

"Home or export?" she asked briskly.

"Not—not that sort of inquiry."

She looked oddly at him. "Well, sir?"

"Do you make only automobile tyres?"

"Yes."

"You don't make fountain pens?"

"Fountain pens!" She laughed in perplexity. "Good heavens, no! I am afraid the Tunkhannock Tire Corporation can be of no assistance to you."

"Then I should like to ask you another question. Does any other company use the design of the winged automobile tyre?"

"Certainly not. It is our trade-mark."

"Then how came your design to be on a fountain pen?"

She pursed her lips with annoyance. "I really cannot say. You must have made a mistake."

"I assure you that I have not."

She made an impatient gesture. "I am sorry, sir, but I can see no way in which we can be of assistance to you. I should advise a visit to one of the better known fountain-pen manufacturers—Waterman's, or Conway Stewart, for instance. They might be able to supply the information you want."

Her officious manner annoyed him. "Nevertheless, I should be glad if you will put my request before somebody in authority," he requested sharply.

The glance she gave him was venomous. For a moment or two he anticipated a refusal, but with a slight shrug of her shoulders she picked up the telephone before her.

"Mr. Matthews, please—Mr. Matthews, I have a gentleman here who is making inquiries about fountain pens—yes, sir, I have informed him that we are only interested in automobile tyres—I will ask him..." She looked at Terhune.

"What is your name, please?"

"Terhune," he informed her. Then added, as an afterthought, "from England."

"Mr. Terhune, of England," the girl passed on to Mr. Matthews. "Yes, sir." Again she addressed Terhune. "Have you business relations with the Tunkhannock Tire Corporation?"

"I have not," he replied testily. "But please tell your Mr. Matthews about the pen bearing your trade-mark."

"Mr. Terhune has no relations with us, sir, but he asks me to tell you that the pen apparently bore the Tunkhannock trade-mark upon it—I have already told him that he must have made a mistake, but he insists upon speaking to somebody... Very well, sir." She replaced the receiver and said: "Mr. Matthews will be down within a few minutes if you will kindly take a chair over there." She pointed to four easy chairs which stood in a carpeted space railed off from the office by low, ornamental iron scrollwork, in which, Terhune was interested to notice as he sat down, was interweaved the design of Mercury and the tyre.

Ten minutes passed before Matthews made an appearance. "Mr. Terhune?" he asked crisply, in an impatient voice.

"Yes."

"Apparently Miss Kleinmann did not make it clear to you, Mr. Terhune, that this Corporation has no interest whatever in the manufacture of fountain pens——"

"Miss Kleinmann made that all too clear to me," Terhune interrupted. "But in view of the fact that I have crossed the Atlantic for the purpose of making these inquiries I was unwilling to accept her authority." He excused himself the white lie on the grounds that he did not like the staff of the Tunkhannock Tire Corporation.

"Then will you accept mine, Mr. Terhune?"

"When you have heard what I have to say," he agreed coolly. He was beginning to enjoy himself. "Some weeks ago a fountain pen was found in a burial vault. Circumstances point to the pen as being a clue to a crime. As the pen in question bore a design similar to the Tunkhannock trademark I had hopes that you might be able to give me some information concerning it."

"An interesting story, Mr. Terhune, but I cannot account for the design on the pen. I repeat; we make tires, not fountain pens."

"Then can you tell me why a fountain-pen manufacturer should have copied your design on a gold fountain pen?"

Matthews started. His expression became strained. "Did you say a *gold* fountain pen, Mr. Terhune?"

"I did."

"Then I—I—must apologize to you for my—my hastiness," Matthews stammered. "If you would kindly wait here for a few minutes I might be able to give you some information." He hurried away.

More minutes passed. Then the telephone before Miss Kleinmann jangled. She picked it up. From where he sat Terhune could see her flabbergasted expression. She replaced the instrument on its receiver, rose from her chair, and walked towards him.

"Mr. Wildenbruch, our President, would like to speak to you, Mr. Terhune. Would you please go up to the twenty-fifth floor?" she said, in a civil, awed voice. "Mr. Matthews will be there to take you to Mr. Wildenbruch."

Terhune winked, deliberately. He couldn't resist the impulse.

As promised, he was met on the twenty-fifth floor by Matthews, who took him along a short passage to a carved wooden door at the far end, which the American tapped discreetly, then opened, as he waved to the visitor to precede him. Terhune entered a large, luxuriously appointed room, in the middle of which was set a plain but expensive-looking table. Behind was a tall man with a keen alert face and snowy hair, who rose from his seat and advanced toward Terhune with outstretched hand.

"Good morning, Mr. Terhune. Will you sit down?" He waved his hand towards a deep, easy chair near, and facing, the table. As Terhune sat down, Wildenbruch did the same.

"Mr. Matthews informs me that you are making inquiries regarding a gold fountain pen bearing upon it the device of Mercury holding in his hand an automobile tire."

"That is so."

"Did it resemble this, Mr. Terhune?" Wildenbruch picked up a pen from his desk and passed it to his visitor.

One glance assured Terhune that the pen was a facsimile of the one he had picked up in the Kylstone vault.

"In every detail," he confirmed.

Wildenbruch pursed his lips. "Do you know that there are only seven such pens in the world, Mr. Terhune? All seven of them were made specially for me fifteen years ago. One of them I retained— the one you hold in your hand. Of the remainder, five were presented by me to certain associates of mine in the Tunkhannock Tire Corporation in celebration of a record sales year."

"And the seventh?"

"I presented to an Englishman, at that time in our employ, as a memento of his gallantry in saving my daughter's life," the President replied gravely.

"What was his name?" Terhune asked eagerly.

"Jimmy Lewis," Wildenbruch told him. "Known more familiarly to the staff, on account of his extremely fair hair, as Blondie."

The Seventh Clue

The clerk of the weather, hitherto Terhune's friend and ally throughout his journey to America, and his stay there, deserted him on the day before he was due to return to England. Early Friday morning a storm began to rage along the streets of New York; by dawn it had developed into a blizzard which made progress by any means a hazardous adventure.

Terhune had to venture out into the streets to obtain the necessary exit permit from the Excise authorities. Soon after breakfast he left the hotel and emerged into the teeth of the blizzard. The effect was staggering; literally so, for as the blast of the wind struck against his unbalanced body he reeled against the wall, and only prevented himself from sliding to the ground by a desperate clutch at the handle of a shop door. No gale he had experienced in England had ever been possessed of such savage intensity, such bitterness; or such solidity; it seemed to him as if a sheet of ice was pressing against him in an effort to propel him forward. Even as he paused to recover his balance snow filled his ears, his eyes, and his mouth. When he ventured from the shelter of the shop porch he saw that visibility had been reduced to a few yards by a moaning, tearing white cloud. With some difficulty he battled his way to the subway.

The blizzard ceased an hour after noon, but the gale continued blowing at full strength. It persisted all night and the following morning. Even the surface of the Hudson, normally so sedate, was whipped up into a flurry of small but vicious looking white horses.

The ship left on time; cautiously she crossed the Bay and passed through the Narrows. There she began to meet the full force of the turbulent seas. Within an hour Terhune, in company with fully eighty per cent of the passengers, was lying on his bed, sad and sorrowful, and harbouring a personal grudge against those early pioneers who had discovered the New World.

Eventually, after two days of intensive effort, the gale blew itself out, but not before stirring the Atlantic into a sullen, resentful swell, which the stewards cheerfully predicted would last for the remainder of the journey. Events justified this forecast, but most of the passengers soon gained their sea-legs, and began actually to appreciate and enjoy the pitch and toss. Terhune, for one, enjoyed the latter stage of the voyage.

For all that, the first sight of land thrilled him as he could never have anticipated. He had enjoyed every minute of the four weeks he had been away, yet his heart beat quicker with excitement at the thought of returning to Bray-in-the-Marsh; and Wickford, and Willingham, with their simple, kindly inhabitants; and at the prospect of handling his beloved books again; hearing all the latest gossip from Miss Amelia; listening to the story of Sir George's latest piscatorial triumphs, smelling the earthy scent of the countryside, appreciating the brooding, undisturbed silence of the nights, the dawn crowing of distant cockerels, the unsophisticated bustle of market-days...

He received his first surprise within two minutes of his stepping ashore. From among a thin line of people at the far end of the customs shed he heard a voice call: "Tommy! Tommy!" When he looked in that direction he saw Helena and Lady Kylstone.

Leaving his luggage to look after itself, he hurried towards the barrier. Excited greetings were exchanged, but very soon Helena asked eagerly: "Was your journey successful, Tommy?"

"There will be plenty of time for questions later on, my child," Lady Kylstone said firmly. She looked at Terhune. "When your luggage has been cleared Gibbons will collect it."

"My—my luggage!" he stammered. "The stewards can take it to the train."

"Nonsense! You are not going by train—unless you have a special reason for wanting to go to London." He shook his head. "You are coming back with us in the car, young man. Surely you do not think my patience will last until tomorrow before hearing the result of your journey?"

"It is very kind of you, Lady Kylstone, but I am afraid the journey has not been as successful as we had all hoped."

"Never mind. Run along, now, and clear your luggage. We have a long journey before us."

Within thirty minutes the car was threading its way through streets that only here and there revealed scars of the ordeal through which they had passed; most of the cleared sites were already occupied by fine new buildings.

"Now, young man, we are all attention," Lady Kylstone said presently. "First of all, did you meet Margaret Ramsay?"

"She is dead—she died in a car accident some time before I reached New York."

Lady Kylstone looked shocked, but presently her face tautened. "Her death was—an accident?" she queried sharply.

"Definitely," he reassured her, and followed this up by giving a full account of everything that had occurred from the day he had left England, including the attempt to murder him. At this point Helena gasped and her face paled, but Lady Kylstone prevented the flood of questions which threatened to escape her eager lips by an authoritative: "Wait, my child."

At last his tale was told. Then it was not Helena but Kathleen Kylstone who spoke first.

"It would be stupid not to assume that Malatesta tried to kill you in order to prevent further inquiries being made," she commented gravely. "Surely so desperate a step suggests that the crime which your death was to cover up must have been a serious one?"

He nodded. "The same thought occurred to me."

"In those circumstances, young man, it is time for us officially to advise the police of the events which you have been investigating. As you know, I had no wish to have the police meddling in the affair; I value my privacy highly, and thoroughly dislike publicity, particularly the type of publicity which usually results from sensational crimes."

"But Lady Kylstone——"

She raised her hand authoritatively. "I know what you wish to say, and I sympathize with you. Of course, you wish to finish what you have begun? But, after all, my dear boy, you are only an amateur detective; it is not right that you should risk your life doing work which it is the duty of the police to do."

"With Malatesta in New York there is no danger of another attack on my life," he protested.

"No? Is it not evident that the man Jimmy Lewis is in England—living, in all probability, somewhere in the neighbourhood of Willingham? For how, otherwise, would he have learned so much about your private affairs, and the reason for your journey to New York? If Lewis was so anxious for your death that he sent Malatesta back to New York on the same ship as the one you were travelling on, does that not indicate that he may try to succeed where Malatesta failed?"

"I am able to take care of myself."

She smiled. "I believe you are. From what I have heard of your fighting abilities on the night of the fog you are very capable of defending yourself. But I do not think you would have to fear only an honest, frontal assault. The attack would be mean, treacherous, in the back." She shook her head. "No, young man, what you must do is to give a full account of your investigations to that Inspector Sampson of yours, and let him take what action he thinks best in the matter."

Observing the obstinate expression on Terhune's face Helena added anxiously: "Lady Kylstone is perfectly right in asking you to do as she wishes. Mr. Sampson could do in safety what might be—be dangerous for you."

He did not speak, because he felt bitter and humiliated by the suggestion that he should retire from the strange affair he was investigating. It was not fair of the two women to make such a suggestion, he reflected rebelliously. Damn it! He had done the spade work, why shouldn't he reap the reward of his labour—the reward being the satisfaction of discovering a crime from the most meagre of clues? Besides, was he not finding the investigation far too fascinating a mental tonic thus tamely to relinquish it? His mood was firmly to refuse Lady Kylstone's request. Unfortunately, this he could not, in decency, do, because he was under an obligation to her on account of his expenses throughout the New York trip. So he sat dumb, and glowered at the passing scenery. Damn all women!

Lady Kylstone easily divined something of his thoughts. She placed her gloved fingers on his hand. "You don't want to stop now, do you?"

"No."

"And nothing I could say would persuade you to do otherwise, would it, if it were not for the fear of proving yourself ungrateful? Now, when answering, remember my pet aversion—prevarication!"

"No," he admitted frankly.

She sighed. "Then it is not fair of me to insist. I do not want to have you feel that you owe me an obligation. But nor do I want you to come to harm in consequence of your having done a kindly action to Helena one certain foggy night. You must carry on, dear boy, but please do nothing rash."

"I promise," he agreed readily, therefore breaking the promise even as he made it.

Lady Kylstone became briskly business-like. "What else did you learn of Jimmy Lewis beyond the fact that his friends called him Blondie?"

"Not very much. He seems to have been a bird of passage, and a very cautious one, too. From the little Lieutenant Kraszewski subsequently discovered, Blondie had first entered the United States between nineteen-twenty and nineteen-twenty-two. For some years he was employed by the Tunkhannock Fire Corporation, during which period he saved the life of Wildenbruch's daughter, and was rewarded by a rise in salary and the gold fountain pen. His future with the Corporation seemed assured and rosy. Then, one day, he gave notice and left the firm. Nobody knows why. Nor where he went to. In fact, from then until I walked into their offices nobody in the firm had heard of or from him—Wildenbruch kindly made inquiries on my behalf from some of the older members of the staff.

"It is almost certain that he left the Corporation to begin a life of crime. He became a sort of Lone Wolf, restraining himself to crime of the type which involved him in the minimum of physical activity—blackmail, confidence tricks, and so on. Apparently he is good-looking, dresses well, spends freely, and is possessed of a manner which inspires confidence in all who meet him.

"He has a reputation of sorts in the United States underworld, where he was known as Blondie. It seems that his surname Lewis was almost unknown in those circles, that is why Kraszewski was unable to tell me much about him until I told him of Lewis's nickname. Directly I spoke of Blondie—as a man and not a woman—then the lieutenant was able to give me the few facts I have just passed on."

"He was called Blondie, I take it, because of the colour of his hair."

"Yes. He has the genuine blonde hair which one associates with the Scandinavian—in fact Kraszewski had been told that he was a Swede."

Lady Kylstone nodded her head reflectively, then glanced at Helena. "You go about more than I do, child. Do you know of a blonde-haired man living or staying in the neighbourhood of Willingham?"

"No."

"Nor do I. Theodore Terhune, your visit to New York has not made matters any easier to understand. Suppose that Lewis gathered information from Fulchester's stupid history to enable him to levy blackmail on some unfortunate resident of our neighbourhood, what connection has that mean crime with our family vault? How came his fountain pen there? Why? And why did he send for Malatesta a year after he—if it were he—had stolen the missing pages from the manuscript history?"

"And what part does Joe Richards play?" Terhune added.

"Ah! I had forgotten Richards. Wasn't he that dirty-looking man with ginger hair, and a cast in his eye, who used to work for Alice Hamblin, Helena?"

"Yes; that was before he worked for Mrs. MacMunn."

"I thought him a most unpleasant-looking man."

"He had a reputation for unpleasantness, but perhaps his looks were to blame."

"And his dirty face," Lady Kylstone added drily. "Nature cannot be blamed for the dirt on his face—at least, not for the fact of its remaining there."

"He was a very good gardener, I believe."

"No doubt he was. Did you say that he no longer lives in this neighbourhood?" The question was directed to Terhune.

"So Julia told me. She said he had gone to live in Wales. At any rate, his cottage is empty."

Lady Kylstone laughed shortly, in irritation. "It is difficult to imagine what interest poor Margaret Ramsay had in Joe Richards."

"They were once neighbours," Terhune pointed out.

"Were they? I did not know that. Dear me! How puzzling everything is. As you insist upon remaining a detective your next move will be to go to Wales and talk with Richards."

"That was my intention," Terhune confessed.

I I

It was good to be home again, Terhune decided, as he let himself into Number 23, Market Square late that night after dining with Lady Kylstone. The musty smell of the books from the shop—the narrow staircase up to his small flat on the first floor—the four sketches on the wall of the staircase (originals, picked up from time to time at sales)—the spotless kitchen—his book-lined *sanctum sanctorum*—all these things were his; they were an integral part of him; as he stood still, surveying his possessions, an unexpected wave of emotion made his eyes prickle, and his heart warm with delight. For all the enjoyment he had had from his journey across the Atlantic and back, this moment was very, very sweet. He grinned confidingly to himself; Julia's scornful appraisement of his character was apparently well-founded; he was a home-bird at heart, content with the simple and domestic pleasures of life. New York was New York, America was America, exhilarating, dynamic, thrilling, but—home was home; the peace of his few rooms was sublime.

Gibbons helped him up with his luggage; they shared a drink. After Gibbons had gone, Terhune undressed for bed. He shivered while doing so, and reflected ruefully that, thanks to central heating, he had not felt cold indoors for the past four weeks. He wasted no time about slipping under the sheets. Then he switched off the light, and, for a short while, luxuriated in the glowing warmth of the bed. Then he began to feel that all was not as it should be; something, somewhere, was different. He chuckled when realization came to him. All that was wrong was the steadiness of the bed; although instinctively he expected to feel it sway beneath him, and subconsciously stiffened his limbs to counteract the expected motion, it remained still and unyielding. It took several minutes for the effect to vanish, of waiting for the ship's movement and feeling abnormal when it did not come.

No sooner had he adjusted himself to the steady bed when he was influenced by another peculiarity. This time, the stillness of the night. For four weeks he had slept to the accompaniment of sound; at sea the even thump-thump of the ship's heart-beat, on land the roar and rumble of New York's unceasing traffic. But tonight the stillness, solemn and undisturbed, impinged upon his senses, and kept sleep at bay. How quiet the world was. So quiet that the ear which pressed into the soft pillow picked up the faint beat of his heart. His own body was noisier than the world outside! A humorous reflection. The world was not dead; its heart, too, must be beating. Surely somewhere near something was making a sound which was to be heard if one listened carefully. A night bird? A car? The whistle of a distant train? The rustle of evergreens? The coughing of a sheep in the field behind the 'Almond Tree'? He strained his ears—but no! The night was utterly and completely silent. Strange, but after New York it seemed impossible that such silence could exist.

Presently he fell asleep. The day had been a long and tiring one.

III

But for Mrs. Mann he would have slept on the following morning long after his normal hour for rising; she, however, entered the kitchen earlier than ever before, and awakened him by her clatter as she prepared his breakfast for him. Hearing her, he grimaced ruefully; the reason for her early arrival was not far to seek; she was anxious to hear all his news. As there was no way of avoiding the ordeal, except at the risk of offending her, and losing the use of her services (like all country-bred people, she had a fierce, touchy pride), he dressed, and offered himself to the slaughter.

And what a slaughter! Mrs. Mann was normally garrulous, but this morning she surpassed herself. There were so many questions she was anxious to ask that she did not allow him to finish his answer to one question before asking another. What did he think of New York? Was it larger than London? What were the people like? Was it really true that even the charwomen went to work in their own cars? How much did it cost him to have a hair-cut? Had he come across Mr. Boles's brother George, who went out to find work in America fifteen years ago come next January the ninth? What were the shops like? And, above all, had he solved the mystery? (She was hazy as to the precise nature of the mystery, but that was an unimportant matter. Everybody in Bray knew that that there Mr. Terhune had gone to America to solve a mystery. Just like the films, it was.) Even the presentation of a small gift which he had bought for her did not still her tongue. It was a beautiful present; he shouldn't have worried about thinking of one; but did it come from one of them big stores you see at the pictures? Was it true that some of them employed thousands of people?

He escaped from her at length—only to fall a victim to Miss Amelia, likewise earlier than ever before, on the plea that she was anxious to give an account of her stewardship. This she did, most conscientiously, but directly he expressed himself as satisfied with her account (which he did automatically, knowing Miss Amelia to be incapable of chicanery) she eagerly plied him with questions.

So did one half of the inhabitants of Bray, of Wickford, and of Willingham—at least, it seemed to him that the number of people who entered the shop that morning totalled fully half the local population. They besieged him in a never-ceasing stream; many of the callers had never entered the shop before. Business might have reached a record high level had he not been compelled to talk so much; as it was, nearly every time one person started to question him, another six people or so gathered round to hear his news. To his dismay, he presently realized that he had become a person of notoriety.

Among his callers were Julia and Belcher. They, calculatingly, waited until it was time for him to close for the evening before entering.

"Hullo, Tommy. Have you had a successful trip?" she greeted.

"Not particularly. Good evening, Mr. Belcher."

"Good evening, Terhune." He glanced at the door. "Were you about to close the shop?"

"I was, but there is no hurry."

"On the contrary, Tommy, we want you to bolt the door," Julia said coolly. "We did not come before on purpose, for I hear you have had an extremely busy day."

Terhune wearily admitted the fact as he pulled down the blind covering the door. "I never realized before how many amateur detectives live in Bray or round about. I have not stopped answering questions all day long."

"If that is intended as a reproach, my pet, it is wasted upon us. After all, you owe a duty to me; if it had not been for my telling you of the work Margaret Ramsay did for my grandfather I doubt whether you would have left here to visit New York. As a matter of fact, I have regretted telling you as much as I did."

"Why?"

"Because it gave you the chance of going to a place I would have given my soul to visit," she admitted viciously.

"Bit of a dog in the manger, aren't you, Julie?" Belcher asked, chuckling.

"Yes," she agreed waspishly. "I have never taken enjoyment in other people's pleasure."

"There is nothing to prevent your mortgaging your soul for a trip there," Belcher continued suggestively.

"Shut up, Gregory, and don't be so crude," she snapped. She turned to Terhune again. "I had planned to meet you at Southampton yesterday, but fortunately I heard, just in time, that others had already formed a reception committee. I don't like joining queues." Her manner changed. "Did you meet Margaret?" she asked eagerly.

"No."

"No!" She appeared astonished. "But, Tommy, I thought that your principal reason for going to New York was to meet Margaret Ramsay."

"It was, but Fate was unkind to me. And to Margaret," he added guiltily. "She was drowned in a car accident some weeks before I arrived in America."

"Oh!" Julia's expression was more disappointed than sympathetic. "Then your journey was wasted?"

"Yes," he said, abruptly, and to his own surprise, for it had been his intention to give her as full an account of his investigations as he had given to Lady Kylstone and Helena; after all, as Julia had pointed out, his journey across the Atlantic was indirectly due to the information she had given him concerning Margaret. Yet even as he was on the point of relating the few discoveries he had made, caution prompted him to maintain silence: too much information concerning his activities had already spread through the town. If Lewis were hiding in the neighbourhood it was better for him to believe that his presence there was unsuspected, so that he should not flee or be on guard. It was evident that he had learned of Terhune's proposal to visit Margaret Ramsay, and had made plans to checkmate this move. If he were now to hear that Margaret had died without revealing her secret, and that Terhune's visit to New York had been a total failure, he might be lulled into a feeling of false security. Indeed, Terhune experienced a passing feeling of regret that he had been so frank with Lady Kylstone and Helena, in case information leaked out from Timberlands via one of the servants. But it was too late to cry over spilled milk, besides, surely Lady Kylstone, of all people, was entitled to his full confidence.

"Surely you must have discovered something," Julia persisted. "Did you visit the firm of attorneys—Jackson van Woude, and MacDonald?"

"I visited the address you gave me—the firm was a bogus one. I could find no trace of them."

"I am not surprised. But I was hoping you would find out something useful. What are you going to do now towards solving the mystery?"

He grinned.

"What is the matter?" she asked sharply.

"I never want to hear those three words again; I have heard them all day long."

"That is the penalty of fame, Terhune," Belcher said smoothly.

"Pig!" Julia ejaculated. "Do not take any notice of him, Tom; he is merely expressing his jealousy."

"Jealous of what, Julie? Notoriety? No, no; I have little wish to become famous or notorious. But if you mean that I am jealous of Terhune's journey to the New World, then I plead guilty. I have always wanted to see America."

"There is nothing to prevent your going," Terhune said pointedly.

"I do not agree with you. England has too many attractions for me to wish to leave them." He glanced at Julia, then, antagonistically, at Terhune.

Julia ignored the inference underlying Belcher's words. Looking at Terhune she asked: "Has Margaret's father heard of her death?"

"No. The police were going to cable, but I told them it would be kinder for me to give him the news personally. I have several messages for him from Margaret's friends and her employers. It might console him to know how much she was liked. I proposed cycling there tonight."

"That sounds very much like a hint," Belcher sneered.

"It was not meant to be," Terhune protested, not very sincerely. Nevertheless, his visitors left soon afterwards, Julia adding as they went out: "I have started to read books, Tom. Will you put some aside for me which you can recommend?" There was a flash in her eyes which warned him of events to come as she quickly disappeared without waiting for his reply.

After his evening meal Terhune cycled to Ramsay's home. From the road above, the cottage appeared to be in pitch darkness, but, having knocked, he heard sounds from within, and presently the door opened, to reveal a stooping, bespectacled man holding an oil-lamp aloft in his left hand. Terhune recognized the clerk—he worked for a firm of Ashford estate agents—whom he had visited before leaving for the States.

"Hullo, Mr. Ramsay."

The man held the lamp nearer to Terhune's face, at which he peered short-sightedly.

"Mr. Terhune, isn't it? So you're back." He spoke in a flat voice that was devoid of eagerness or feeling. "You didn't see my Margaret, did you?"

"I—I am afraid I—did not."

"She's dead, isn't she?" Ramsay asked brusquely.

"I—I am sorry——"

"I knew she was dead," the father interrupted tonelessly. "I knew my Margaret was dead. It wasn't because I hadn't received a letter from her for some time. It was because God told me. I knew she was dead before you went to America, but I didn't say anything. I hoped against hope. But come inside, Mr. Terhune; it is cold out there. I want to hear the—details."

Ramsay led the way through a narrow passage into the kitchen. The tiny, low-ceilinged room was small enough in itself, and made smaller by the quantity of furniture in it, but a glowing coal fire in the open kitchener made it warm and cheerful. A bowed, white-haired man sat crouched up in a high-backed kitchen chair beside it.

"Samuel Leach," Ramsay announced, "Margaret's uncle on her mother's side. He was out when you came here the last time. Samuel, this is Mr. Terhune."

Leach held his hand behind his ear. "What name?" he asked in a loud, rasping voice.

"Samuel is deaf," Margaret's father explained unnecessarily. Then, to Leach: "Mr. Terhune. The gentleman who went out to America to see Margaret."

Leach nodded his head at Terhune. "Did he meet her?"

"Margaret is dead," Ramsay replied loudly.

"So you were right, Fred." The old man turned his head and stared at the fire; tears rolled down his furrowed cheeks. "She was a good girl, Margaret," he mumbled. "The spit of her ma."

"Aye," the father confirmed heavily. "She was that. How did she meet her end, Mr. Terhune?"

Terhune related the story of Margaret's death, softening, as far as possible, the more tragic details. Then he went on to give all the verbal messages which he had been charged to deliver to the bereaved parent.

Ramsay listened to the end without interrupting. Then he nodded his head once or twice. "Aye! Everybody liked my Margaret," he muttered. "So you weren't able to see her, and learn what you wanted to know?"

"No, Mr. Ramsay," Terhune admitted awkwardly, for he was embarrassed by the thought of having his mission intrude upon the father's grief. He made a movement as if to rise, but Ramsay restrained him.

"Can you stay a little longer, Mr. Terhune?" he pleaded. "Perhaps I might be of help to you. I know Margaret would wish it."

"Hey?" said Leach loudly.

"I was asking Mr. Terhune to remain."

"What about Margaret's death? I didn't hear a word."

"I will tell you everything later, Samuel." Ramsay lowered his voice. "You must excuse Samuel's impatience, Mr. Terhune, but he became almost a second father to her when her mother died, eighteen years ago."

"Nineteen years ago," Samuel interrupted loudly.

"You see, he hears odd words here and there. He is right—it was nineteen years ago." Ramsay shook his head. "While you were away I spent some time in trying to remember if Margaret had ever told me anything of her work for Lord Fulchester which might be of interest to you, but I did not succeed. Margaret was very conscientious about her work. Once I asked her if her employer had found out anything about the Blye boy—there were strange rumours about Reginald Blye at one time," he explained apologetically. "Margaret said he had, but she never let me know what it was that Lord Fulchester had discovered; she told me I must wait for the book to be published."

"I did receive one hint," Terhune began hesitatingly. "Netta Pouskin told me that, one night, she overheard Margaret talking to an English friend of hers about Joe Richards——"

"Joe Richards!" Ramsay interrupted with astonishment. "Do you mean our next-door neighbour?"

"Yes."

"Why should Margaret discuss Joe Richards with anyone?"

"That is the question I was about to put to you, Mr. Ramsay. Is there any mystery about Richards?"

"Not that I know of. I didn't like the man, mind you. Nor did Margaret. Although she befriended the mother on one occasion, she refused to speak to the son, if she could help herself, beyond saying good morning and good evening."

"Is there anything about him you can tell me?"

"I can tell you what I know, which isn't much. He came to this neighbourhood, and the cottage next door, when he was a boy of five or six; that would have been about twenty-seven or twenty-eight years ago now, I suppose. Samuel and his wife were living here at that time—Margaret and I came here to live after his wife's death.

"The boy lived with his mother; they were supposed to have come here from North Wales. I don't wish to insult the poor woman, but the rumour spread around that she was not entitled to call herself Mrs. Probably this was due to the fact that as long as she lived, nobody ever saw her husband."

"She might have been a widow."

"That is the most charitable explanation, but she never referred to herself as a widow, and always acted in a most mysterious manner whenever she spoke of her husband or family."

"Who kept her?"

"Nobody. She worked for her living as a daily woman, to Jasper Belcher. As soon as the boy was old enough to leave school he was employed at Turnpike House, as an assistant to Harry Gibbs, who was Mr. Pearson's gardener at that time. I must say this for Richards: he was an excellent gardener. When Gibbs died Mr. Pearson kept Richards on as gardener in Gibbs's place. Afterwards he went to work for Colonel Hamblin, afterwards for Mrs. MacMunn, and later for the Abbots. Mrs. Richards died about seven years ago, but the son remained on at the cottage and looked after himself."

"He didn't marry?"

"No, and it is no wonder that he remained single. I don't think any girl could have faced the prospect of marrying him. And he was never one to run after the girls. I believe he had no liking for their company."

"Why did he leave this neighbourhood?"

"It is no use asking the reason for anything Richards did. Besides, I am not sure that he has left the neighbourhood for good."

"What do you mean?"

"He was always disappearing at odd intervals, without saying a word to anyone of where he was going, or afterwards, of where he had been. It is my opinion that he used to go off on a drinking bout, for he always returned with a bloated face, and bloodshot eyes. I believe Mr. Pearson's only reason for discharging him was on account of such absences."

"Had he ever been away before for as long as one year?"

"Well, no," Ramsay admitted. "But there, as I have told you, he has an unstable character."

"Do you know where he has gone to?"

"No, but some time after he had gone Mr. Kelly had a note from him enclosing stamps worth two shillings and ten-pence, in payment of a debt for groceries. Mr. Jones told me that there was no address on the note, but that the envelope was postmarked Betws-y-Coed, in North Wales. As Mrs. Richards came from a place near there, no doubt he is living with his mother's family for the time being."

"What happened to all his personal belongings and furniture? Do you know where they went?"

"They are still in the cottage next door, going to rack and ruin."

"How is that?" the surprised Terhune asked. "Hasn't the landlord moved them out?"

"It was his own cottage. Mrs. Richards bought it before moving in."

"How did a daily woman get enough money together to buy a cottage?"

"She said that her husband gave it to her."

Samuel interrupted the conversation. "Hey? What are you two talking about? I can't hear a word you say," he grumbled loudly. "Are you talking about Margaret?"

"No; Joe Richards."

"Hey?"

"Joe Richards."

"What about him, the good-for-nothing?"

"Nothing important, Samuel," Ramsay said patiently. Then, to Terhune: "That is all I can tell you about Joe Richards." And after a slight pause: "I wish I knew why Margaret discussed him with that friend of hers. It was not like my Margaret to talk scandal."

I V

The following night Terhune called at Timberlands to give Lady Kylstone the gist of his interview with Ramsay. As was rapidly becoming the habit, two bottles awaited his ministrations; his favourite Manzanilla for himself, and the sweeter Solero for Lady Kylstone and Helena. At a sign from Lady Kylstone he filled their glasses; afterwards he pulled a chair into the semicircle around the fire and gave an account of his talk with the bereaved father.

"Well, young man, what do you make of Joe Richards's disappearance?" Lady Kylstone asked presently.

"I don't know," Terhune confessed. "It seems a strange thing for a man to leave his home without a word to anyone, and go off to live in another part of the country. But then, by all accounts Richards was a strange character who was always liable to act strangely. I think that the most extraordinary aspect of his departure was his sending to Kelly the two-and-tenpence which was owing for groceries."

"Why?" Helena asked. "Wasn't his doing so proof of his intention to return here later?"

"It might bear that construction, Helena, but Richards was not noted for being conscientious about paying his debts. I was talking to Pearce, the coalman, this morning, and he told me that none of the local tradesmen willingly gave credit to Richards; apparently whenever they had done so they had had subsequent cause for regret."

"Then why did he trouble to send the money to Kelly?"

"To establish the fact that he was in North Wales, Helena."

"Why should he want to do that?" she asked, her expression puzzled.

"Exactly! Why?"

"To conceal the fact that he is elsewhere," Lady Kylstone answered quickly.

"Yes," Terhune agreed crisply. "Possibly I am allowing this amateur detective business to colour my perspective, but certainly that explanation might account for Richards's having taken the trouble to send a letter to pay a debt which, normally, Kelly might have had trouble in collecting."

"I agree with you. Tell me, Theodore, did Richards leave his home before or after the theft of the pages from Fulchester's manuscript?"

"Afterwards, but how long afterwards I have so far failed to establish. He was out of work at the time, and being a man of solitary character he had probably been gone from home for several days, perhaps longer, before it occurred to some people that nothing had been seen of Joe Richards for some time."

"Was his disappearance reported to the police?"

"No, because everybody believes, in consequence of the letter to Kelly, that he is in Wales."

"What an extraordinary situation!" Lady Kylstone exclaimed. "How can a man leave his home for more than a year without some authority or another making inquiries for him? The rating authorities, for instance? Haven't they been after him to pay his rates? I am sure they would never allow my rates to go unpaid for so long."

Terhune grinned. "There is a pile of unopened letters inside the door—they can be seen from the back through the kitchen window. Possibly some of them are Final Demands."

"If Richards is not in Wales, where do you think he is, Theodore?"

"Somewhere within a reasonable distance of here," he answered promptly. "It may have been he who informed Blondie that I was going to America in the hope of interviewing Margaret Ramsay."

There was a momentary lull in the conversation; Helena was the first to speak. "Didn't you propose to visit North Wales, Tommy, to question Richards?"

"Yes, why?"

"As you have been unable to discover his address it is no use your going."

"I don't agree with you, Helena. If Richards is in North Wales there are two clues to his possible whereabouts: the postmark, Betws-y-Coed, and the fact that his mother's family are supposed to live at Tyn-y-gwer. If I visit that neighbourhood to make inquiries I might come across him, if he is there. And if he is there I can question him. If, on the contrary, I fail to trace him, then we shall have all the more reason for believing that he had an ulterior motive in sending the money to Kelly."

"A sound plan," Lady Kylstone confirmed. "When do you propose we should go to Wales, Theodore?"

Her words startled him. "*We*, Lady Kylstone?"

"Yes, *we*, young man, unless you have any objection to our company! In the first place, it will be easier and quicker for you to get there and back by car, and in the second, I am becoming far too thrilled to remain at Timberlands doing nothing, while you keep all the fun of the chase to yourself. If you would like me to give you a third reason, it lies in a wish to visit Wales; a country to which I have never been. Well?" she challenged.

"I suggest Sunday morning," he suggested promptly. "Miss Amelia is usually free all day Monday."

V

During Friday morning Julia visited the shop again, this time unaccompanied.

"Have you chosen a book for me?" she demanded.

He had put several aside for her, which he showed her. For fifteen minutes or more she kept him busy describing the books to her; plot, type, and why it should appeal to her. At last she carelessly picked one from the pile and tucked it under her arm.

"Will you come driving with me again Sunday morning, Tom?" she asked.

"I am terribly sorry, Julia, I—I have already arranged to go out with Lady Kylstone."

Malice flared up in her eyes. "And Helena Armstrong too, I suppose?"

"I—I think so."

She pressed her lips into a thin line. "How much do I owe you for the book?"

"Please do not worry about—about that——"

"Most certainly I shall," she snapped. "I am not in the habit of putting myself under *obligations* to people."

It was impossible to mistake the inference behind her words. He felt his face beginning to burn. "You do not understand, Julia——" he began.

"Am I supposed to understand? Why should you believe that I have the slightest interest in your reasons?"

"Damn!" he exploded. "Threepence for seven days, and three-pence for each part of a week thereafter. Older books are twopence for the same period, if you would prefer to change——"

Inexplicably, and to his utter astonishment, all signs of ill-humour suddenly vanished from her face. She laughed and strolled towards the door. "I like you in a temper, Tom—it makes you become human," she said as she passed out of the shop.

VI

Long before they reached their destination Terhune had to admit that Lady Kylstone's idea of accompanying him to Wales was a good one. No journey could have been gayer. Lady Kylstone was in high spirits; she was more like a schoolgirl on her way home for the summer vacation than the even-tempered, sedate chatelaine of Timberlands. Helena was equally excited, but there was a strange, deep expression in her eyes which he could not analyse. He marvelled that the fascination of playing the role of amateur detective could be so general.

They reached Betws-y-Coed just before nightfall, and booked rooms at the Royal Oak Hotel. In the morning, after breakfast, the three people stepped out into the cold wind which blew from the west. As they walked slowly along the main street Lady Kylstone gazed up at the black-clouded sky, majestic in its ominous threat of snow, at the looming, white-capped mountains, at the picturesque slate-roofed, stone cottages, at the tumbling, noisy stream.

"It is beautiful, even at this time of the year," she exclaimed presently. "I am glad we came." She tightened her grip on the walking-stick which she had purchased just previously. "I shall not be content until I have climbed high enough to look down upon the village from above. Come, my child, we will go exploring, while Theodore makes his inquiries. Where do your propose to start, young man?"

"At the post-office."

"Then we will meet at the hotel in time for pre-luncheon sherry. Are you ready, Helena?"

The post-office was fortunately empty. "Good morning to you, sir," greeted a pleasant-looking woman.

"Good morning. I wonder if you can be of service to me? I am anxious to talk with a man named Richards."

"Richards! Would it be Dai Richards or Evan Richards you'd be wanting, sir? Dai Richards, now, he lives beyond the village at Machynlleth Farm, look-you———"

"Joe Richards is the man I want."

"Joe Richards!" The woman puzzled over the name, frowning. "You wouldn't be meaning Jack Richards of Trefriw?"

"Has he a cast in one eye?"

"Lord bless you, man, Jack Richards's eyes are as straight as mine, so they are."

"Joe Richards came to this neighbourhood a little more than a year ago."

"Then it isn't Jack, or Dai, or Evan, indeed, for they have lived here all their lives." She shook her head. "There is no Richards in Betws-y-Coed with a cast in his eye, nor any Richards who has come here a year ago."

"He posted a letter from here."

"Then he was no more than a visitor like yourself, man, for if there was a Richards living in this village I should know him."

The start was not a promising one, but Terhune resolved to try another tack. "Richards's mother came from Betws-y-Coed; she left here nearly thirty years ago, when her son, Joe, was about five or six years of age."

"Indeed, she did now." The woman appeared interested. "I have lived in this village all my life, so I should know her. What was her name?"

"Richards."

She looked at him with an expression which made him feel uncomfortably like a child being admonished. "It's her family name I am asking for," she explained patiently.

"I don't know it," he answered weakly.

"What was her husband's Christian name?"

"I am afraid that also is unknown to me."

"Don't you know anything, man? But look-you, I call to mind this minute the name of Gwyn Richards. He married Bessie Morgan of Llanfairfechan about the time you mention."

"Did his wife leave the district?"

"She did, and her child with her."

"That must have been the boy Joe," he told her excitedly.

"A boy! I thought it was a girl Bessie Morgan bore, indeed. But there, my memory isn't what it was."

"Tell me about Bessie Richards and the boy. Did Gwyn Richards go with him?"

"Indeed he did," the woman replied firmly. "Would any Christian wife go without her lawful wedded husband? And he is still with her now, for it was no more than a month gone——"

"Still with her?" he interrupted.

"That is what I said, man."

Her news was disheartening, it was all the more bitter coming as it did just at a moment when he was beginning to believe that he was on the right track.

"Joe Richards's mother is dead," he explained dully.

"Well; Bessie isn't. As I was saying, it was no more than a month gone that her old father came into this very place and said he had just heard from his daughter Bessie in America——"

"America?"

"Yes, America," she replied firmly, apparently determined to finish her story. "He said he had heard from Bessie that she and the family were moving from Baltimore to Philadelphia because he had been offered a better job."

"Quite!" He raised his hat. "Thank you for your help, but Mrs. Richards—Joe's mother—moved from here to Kent."

"Kent!" she repeated, interested once more. "I wonder if she met Megan Rees there. Megan went there soon after Gwyn Richards had taken his wife to America. Do you come from Kent, man?"

"Yes."

"Then perhaps you have news of her, man, for it is many long years now since her family have had news of her."

"Megan Rees!" he acknowledged politely. "I am afraid I have never met her."

The woman laughed. "Away with you, man! Rees was her father's name. She married an Englishman, look-you. What was his name now?" She turned to a woman who entered at that moment. "Good morning to you, Mrs. Jones. There's snow on the way here, by the looks of it. It will be a treat when this cold wind stops blowing. I shall be with you in a moment." Then to Terhune: "I have just remembered the name."

She looked at him skittishly, obviously waiting for him to request the name. He was impatient to be off, but she had tried to help him, so he asked:

"What was the name?"

"Belcher!" she told him. "Jasper Belcher."

The Crime

"Jasper Belcher!" exclaimed Lady Kylstone. "It isn't possible. That old curmudgeon was a misogynist, like his father before him."

"There is no doubt about Megan's marriage to Jasper Belcher," Terhune assured her. "I have examined the records and also spoken to one or two of the older inhabitants who remember him, and the details of the marriage."

"You work fast for an amateur, young man," she approved. "Tell me all you learned."

"Briefly, what happened was this: thirty-seven years ago Jasper Belcher visited Betws-y-Coed on holiday——"

"A surprising event!" Lady Kylstone interrupted drily.

Terhune chuckled. "There was an explanation. He had recovered from some illness or other, so Dr. Edwards had insisted upon a recuperative holiday in Wales."

She nodded her head. "Of course! Old Dr. Edwards' panacea was the Welsh mountains; his son, Dai, has more faith in the West Indies. So Jasper actually spent money on a holiday! Dear me!"

"He took care to spend as little as possible. He wouldn't even go to one of the smaller hotels. He made a round of the cottages in order to find one where he could lodge as cheaply as possible. He found one at last——"

"Don't tell me, Theodore. With the Rees?"

"Yes. That is how he met Megan. She was employed as a daily

servant to the local doctor. Misogynist or no, Jasper must have fallen in love with her, for he returned to Betws-y-Coed the following year, and again stayed with the Rees. He proposed to her after he had been there a week, and was married as soon as all arrangements could be made. He remained with his bride for another three weeks and then returned to Kent—alone."

"Whatever for?"

"One can only guess his reasons, but I believe they were two; the first, because he didn't want a woman permanently in his home, and secondly, to save the expense of keeping a wife. It was cheaper for him to let her remain in Wales, working for her living, than to take her with him to Kent."

"How mean!" Helena exclaimed indignantly.

"He was that sort of a man," Lady Kylstone told her.

"In due course their son was born, but Megan still remained in her native village, and Jasper visited her each August. However, when Joe was about six years of age Megan left Betws-y-Coed to go and live in Kent. For reasons which we may never know, however, Jasper must have insisted that she was never to let it be known that she was his wife.

"What happened in Kent we know: Jasper gave his wife the money to buy a cottage, and then arranged for her to visit his house daily as a servant. Megan consented to this arrangement——"

"Heaven knows why!" Helena interrupted hotly. "He was a beast to be ashamed of his wife."

Lady Kylstone smiled wistfully. "Women are funny creatures where their men are concerned. Sometimes they will submit to all kinds of indignities to retain their mate's love."

"I would not describe that man's feelings as love."

"No! You are young, my child. When you grow older you will understand, even if you refuse to condone. But continue your story, Theodore."

"There is not much more. Jasper's wife remained his servant until the day she died."

"Do you think that the son was aware of the identity of his father? But there, that was a stupid question to ask. Of course he was not."

"Why not?" Helena asked.

"Surely it is safe to assume, my child, that if Joe had known he was Jasper Belcher's son he would have claimed his father's inheritance?"

"Of course. How silly I am." She paused. "But, Tommy, didn't Joe leave home before Jasper Belcher died?"

He nodded.

"Then Joe may be unaware of Jasper's death?"

"Helena is right, Theodore."

"But if Joe had known that Jasper was his father, wouldn't Mr. Howard, the solicitor, also have been aware of the fact, either from Jasper direct, or most certainly from Joe? In view of the fact that Jasper was on his deathbed for two or three months before he died, it seems most likely that Joe would have taken care to give warning of his identity and claim to the estate."

Lady Kylstone nodded her head. "Of course he would," she agreed incisively. "I think it is time for someone to interview Howard, don't you, young man? He might be able to impart some very useful information."

"I am afraid it would be useless my calling upon him."

"Why?"

"Professional etiquette would not allow him to betray any of his clients' secrets."

Lady Kylstone's face assumed an expression of obstinate determination. "Leave Howard to me," she said confidently. "I consider myself capable of dealing with him. And what is more," she added eagerly, "I shall not waste any time about doing so. We will call upon him at his office on our way back to Willingham." She paused upon observing Helena's face. "What is the matter, my child? Why are you suddenly so pensive?"

"I was thinking of poor Mr. Gregory Belcher."

"What of him?"

"I have just realized that, when Joe Richards reappears, he will have to relinquish both the lovely property and the fortune which he inherited from his cousin. I should hate to do that."

Terhune scowled. "I am sure Gregory will be able to take care of himself even if he does have to part with the Belcher estate... Good Lord!" he exclaimed, unexpectedly.

"What is it, Tom?"

His eyes bright behind his tortoiseshell glasses, he gazed with excitement at each woman in turn. "Lady Kylstone—Helena—I believe I can supply an explanation to almost all the problems we have been puzzling over. Listen!

"Begin by assuming that Margaret Ramsay had known for some years that Mrs. Richards was really Mrs. Belcher—remember she was kind to Mrs. Richards on one occasion, and might have learned the secret at that time. Margaret kept the knowledge to herself until after Mrs. Richards's—or, if you like, Mrs. Belcher's—death. One day, however, she divulged it to Lord Fulchester so that the fact might be incorporated in his genealogical history.

"Now bridge the years until the night she took Jimmy Lewis to her apartment in New York. In consequence of celebrating too well and not wisely she gave him the whole set-up, as they say on the films—including the facts that Jasper had, presumably, made no will, and that the estate would descend, through intestacy, to Gregory Belcher, which facts she may have learned through working at Howard's, the solicitor's. Lewis, being a confidence trickster and blackmailer, realized the possibilities of taking advantage of the situation. He sailed for England, and began operations by robbing

Mrs. MacMunn of the pages in Lord Fulchester's manuscript relating to the Belcher family."

"Why?" Helena interrupted. "If he already knew those facts why should he have taken the risk of being caught stealing them? Alternatively, he need only have read the pages in question, he could have left the volume intact."

"There was no great risk; had he been caught he could easily have made up a story which would have saved him from anything worse than a fine. The reason of his stealing the pages was, I think, to prevent their being read by anyone else. Also he had a use for them."

"What was that?"

"I will tell you in a moment. Lewis had now to wait for certain events to happen. These, as he had probably anticipated from what Margaret may have told him of Jasper's state of health, were not long in materializing. Jasper died—intestate. His money descended to Gregory. Gregory entered into his inheritance. And then——"

"Lewis began to blackmail him," Lady Kylstone interpolated.

"Yes. Doubtless he showed Lord Fulchester's pages to Gregory Belcher. Gregory must have realized immediately that the moment it was known to the authorities that Jasper had a legitimate son, every penny of the inheritance would go to that son. As half a loaf is better than none, he must have paid Lewis to keep his mouth shut."

"In doing that Gregory must have known he was deliberately robbing Joe Richards," Helena protested.

"I believe him capable of that," Terhune said drily.

"Why don't you like Gregory Belcher?" she asked suspiciously.

"That is Theodore's business," Lady Kylstone said hastily. She faced Terhune. "Do you think Lewis engineered Joe Richards's disappearance?"

"Yes."

"Why?" she asked shrewdly. "If Richards was unaware of his true identity there was no danger of his spoiling Lewis's chances of blackmailing Gregory?"

This question stumped Terhune.

I I

"Ah! Good morning, Lady Kylstone, good morning," Mr. Howard welcomed effusively, warmly holding her gloved hand in his two. Then his sparse grey eyebrows lifted high in his domed forehead as he saw Helena and Terhune entering his office.

"I have taken the liberty of bringing two companions with me," Lady Kylstone explained rapidly. "Miss Armstrong, my secretary and companion, you have met before."

"Of course we have, dear lady," Howard murmured as he took Helena's hand. "Twice, if my memory serves me well. Once in this office, and once at your home, Lady Kylstone, when I had the duty of handing the key of your family vault into this young lady's charge."

"Yes, yes, I had forgotten that fact, although that key has bearing on the business which brings me here today."

"Indeed."

"But first, Mr. Howard, I should like to introduce Mr. Terhune to you. Mr. Terhune is responsible for the cultivation of literary taste in our neighbourhood; he owns a lending library and book-shop in Bray."

"Indeed!" The solicitor looked bewildered. "I am pleased to welcome you to my office, Mr. Terhune," he said as he offered his hand. "Would you be seated, please, ladies? I will have another chair brought in for Mr. Terhune." He stretched out his hand towards the button of an electric buzzer.

"Don't worry about another chair, Mr. Howard," Lady Kylstone interrupted impatiently. "He is quite capable of sitting on the arm of Helena's chair."

"Well, of course..." Howard glanced helplessly at each of his visitors in turn as he sat down, following their example. "But it will be no trouble, I assure you———"

"It will be a waste of time, I have a long story to tell you."

"A story, dear lady!"

"Oh, don't look so surprised, my dear man; at least, not until you have heard what I want to tell you." Her lips twitched.

"Well?" Howard murmured in a resigned voice.

"First of all, I want some information from you about Jasper and Gregory Belcher."

The spectacles very nearly dropped off the solicitor's nose. "Information?"

"About the extent of Jasper's fortune, and who Gregory is, and how you traced him."

An expression of horror crossed Howard's face. "My dear Lady Kylstone, you cannot mean what you say! Are you asking me to betray professional confidence?"

"Fiddlesticks! I am asking you to give me some information which I could surely find out from other people with some difficulty, but which you have at your fingertips."

He shook his head. "With my humblest apologies, I must ask you to forgive me———"

"How long has your firm represented the Kylstone family?" she snapped.

He tittered. "For more years than I care to estimate."

"I suppose you wish to continue to act for the family?"

"I should be more sorry than I can possibly express to know that such a long, such an esteemed, such a loyal———"

"Yes, yes. So should I. But please understand this, my dear man.

If you do not tell me what I want to know this will be my last visit to your office."

"Lady Kylstone!"

"I mean what I say."

"But professional etiquette——" he began protestingly.

"I know, I know! Believe me, I respect you for your firm stand, which is what it should be in all cases—except this! Let me add that, even if you refuse to give the information to me, you will have to give it to the police."

"The police!"

Lady Kylstone smiled: his unhappy, woebegone expression was too marked not to appeal to her sense of humour. "You poor man! Perhaps I am not being fair to you. But I am surprised that you permitted Gregory Belcher to inherit an estate that should have descended to Jasper's—son!"

Howard nearly leaped out of his chair. "His *what*?"

"His son," she repeated coolly.

"My dear Lady Kylstone!" His voice quavered. "Surely you must know as well as I that Jasper Belcher has no son." He coughed. "At least, not a legitimate one, for he was never married."

"That is where you are mistaken. Jasper was married, and he has a son. I am afraid you may have to answer several awkward questions about your carelessness in not making inquiries," she taunted.

Howard looked miserable. "You are joking, Lady Kylstone. You are teasing an old man."

"Then ask Mr. Terhune," she retorted. "He will tell you the locality of the church in which Jasper was married, the date, and the names of people still living who witnessed the marriage ceremony. To say nothing of the midwife who helped to bring the son into the world."

"But—but... Oh dear! Oh dear! I do not know whether I am awake or dreaming." In his distress Howard rubbed his bony hands together. "If this story be true—and I am compelled to emphasize the word 'if' lest some mistake has been made—if it be true, I say, why did Jasper Belcher never inform me of his marriage, why did he not make a will in favour of his son, why has not the alleged son claimed the inheritance?" He came to a breathless pause.

"No mistake has been made," Lady Kylstone informed the solicitor. "So set your mind to rest upon that point. With regard to your questions—Jasper, for reasons best known to himself, apparently informed nobody of his marriage. As for his son's not claiming the inheritance, perhaps this was due to his not being aware that Jasper was his father. Did you ever visit Belcher at his home?"

"Several times."

"Do you remember a daily woman by the name of Mrs. Richards, who used to work for him?"

"Vaguely! Vaguely! Wasn't she short and plump?"

"Heaven knows! At any rate, Mrs. Richards was Jasper's lawfully wedded wife, and Joe Richards his legitimate son."

Howard gasped. "Richards the gardener?"

"Yes."

"Oh dear! All this is much too fantastic not to upset me. Will you ladies permit me to take a glass of water?" At, a nod from Lady Kylstone he swung his chair round so that he could reach a carafe of water.

Lady Kylstone relentlessly pursued the matter. "What you have heard so far does not compare with what you are about to hear. For instance, the attempt to break into the Kylstone family vault."

Howard wilted completely; he slumped back in his chair and stared bewilderedly at Lady Kylstone while she gave him the gist of all that had so far happened.

"Now that you have heard the complete story, Mr. Howard, you will realize how you can assist Mr. Terhune by giving information concerning Jasper's affairs."

"I do not know what to say, dear lady. Professional, etiquette——"

"Supposing Detective-Inspector Sampson were to request you to do so! Would you refuse?"

"The police have powers, dear lady."

"Then remember that Mr. Terhune has been asked by the inspector to investigate this strange affair—in giving information to Mr. Terhune you are really giving it to Inspector Sampson."

Howard sighed. "You make it hard for a professional man to follow the dictates of his conscience." He took off his pince-nez and began to polish the lenses. "What do you want to know?" he asked finally.

"Could Margaret Ramsay have known that Jasper had made no will—that is, up to the time of her leaving for America?"

"I believe so. I seem to remember dictating a letter to Mr. Jasper suggesting that he should make a will—she might have been the young lady who typed the letter. The initials on the copy could be looked up."

"Later will do, thank you, Mr. Howard. Even if she did not type the letter herself she might have seen the copy. What was the value of Jasper Belcher's estate?"

"In the neighbourhood of one hundred and fifty thousand pounds."

"Phew! The stakes were high enough to be worth a gamble."

"No stakes are high enough to make a criminal offence worth committing," Howard rebuked severely.

"What relation was Jasper to Gregory?"

"Let me see... One moment..." The solicitor rang the buzzer. When a clerk appeared he asked for the Belcher Estate deed-box. While the clerk was carrying out this errand Howard explained that he had prepared a genealogy at the time of Jasper's death.

As soon as the deed-box was in front of him he opened it, and having rustled among the documents inside, presently produced a paper.

"Here it is. It goes back to George Belcher who was born in the year eighteen-eighteen. George married in the year eighteen forty-one. Henry was born two years later, and John, in forty-eight. Two other children were born in between, but both died as infants, and need not concern us now. Henry married at the age of twenty, in sixty-three. The following year three events happened, within a few weeks of each other. George Belcher died, Jasper was born, and Henry's wife, Jane, died. Henry inherited the Belcher estate and lived there, wifeless, until eighteen eighty-nine, when he died, leaving the property to Jasper. Jasper, as you know, occupied the house thereafter for the next fifty-six years, dying last year at the ripe old age of eighty-one.

"At that time his only living relation was Gregory Belcher, the only son of John, who, you will remember, was Henry's younger brother. John married comparatively late in life, at the age of forty, his bride being South African by birth. John died in South Africa. Early in this present century his son, Gregory, was born posthumously. According to the laws of intestacy, Gregory, his first-cousin, became, in the apparent absence of nearer blood relatives, the heir to Jasper's estate." Howard paused; his expression was most miserable. "Gregory Belcher has always impressed me as being of the type of healthy upright British gentleman whom it is a pleasure to meet and do business with. During the first six months of his residence in England he paid many visits to this office, but the last one was several months ago. Let me see, when was it?" He ignored the obvious signs of impatience betrayed by his audience, Terhune in particular. "Ah! I can tell you the precise date. Friday, the eleventh of October: I was telling Mr. Belcher of the picturesque ceremony of the yearly opening of the Kylstone family vault, and suggested that he might be interested in visiting the vault. I remember adding that the vault would be opened to the public precisely two weeks later."

Terhune took advantage of the pause to continue his interrogation. "Did you advise Gregory Belcher that he had become heir to the estate?"

"I did, Mr. Terhune. By cable. As a matter of fact, but for a strange coincidence, I might have had considerable trouble in doing this, but fortunately, two weeks before Jasper died, I received a letter from Gregory saying that he had written to his cousin several times in the past twelve months but had received no reply; would I be so obliging as to assure him that Jasper was still well?"

"Did that letter come from South Africa?"

"It did. From Aberdeen, in Cape Province."

"How long had Gregory been in South Africa before returning to England?"

"How long? All his life, Mr. Terhune. His mother returned to her parents within a month of her husband's death."

"What!" In his excitement Terhune jumped to his feet. "Gregory has lived in South Africa all his life?"

"That is what I said," Howard replied testily.

"Then, in God's name, Mr. Howard, what proof have you that Gregory Belcher is Gregory Belcher?"

The solicitor stared at his visitor. "What do you mean?" he asked irritably.

"What proof have you, for instance, that Gregory Belcher is not Jimmy Lewis?"

A long silence followed Terhune's words. Howard stared at the deed-box.

"None," he replied at last, in a strained voice. "None that could not have been forged by a clever criminal."

III

It was obvious, even to Terhune, that the case had reached a point beyond which an unofficial investigator could not, and should not, proceed. Upon arriving home, therefore, he telephoned Sampson to suggest a meeting. This was arranged for ten-thirty the next day at New Scotland Yard.

Early the following morning he cycled into Ashford and caught the early train to Cannon Street. It was more than usually crowded; in addition to the normal complement of business men, many women were travelling to London to complete their shopping for Christmas, now exactly a week distant. Indeed, it seemed to Terhune that the train was already infected with the Christmas atmosphere; the chatter of conversation was louder than usual; there was much laughter, and nearly everyone looked happy—even the business men, which was extraordinary, for they usually resented chance travellers.

It was the same in town. From the top of the bus which took him to Charing Cross Terhune saw the efforts which were being made to make this Christmas the brightest for a decade; to celebrate, not only a Christmas festivity, but also what everybody felt instinctively to be a turning point in world history, a milestone marking the end of the immediate postwar period of reconstruction and the beginning of a happier era of creative endeavour. Shop windows, filled to bursting-point with seasonable goods, were profusely decorated; the shops themselves were thronged with buyers. The pavements were equally crowded; street hawkers did a flourishing trade. Traffic was at its worst; every private motor-car, every taxicab, every bus and every transport lorry in London and the Home Counties appeared to have converged upon the Strand; every Vehicle crawled at walking pace. But, for the most part, tempers were good—after all, Christmas was Christmas!

Terhune arrived at New Scotland Yard well before time, so he strolled along the Embankment for the next twenty minutes, admiring the improvements on the opposite bank. Precisely at ten-thirty he entered the rather forbidding entrance, and sent his name up to Detective-Inspector Sampson. A few minutes later he was giving the saturnine inspector a full account of his investigations in New York, and subsequently in Betws-y-Coed and Ashford. As usual, Sampson listened without once interrupting, but the play of expression in his penetrating eyes revealed his acute attention to every detail.

"So your reasoning is this," he commented after Terhune had finished speaking. "Jimmy Lewis meets Margaret Ramsay in New York. They become friendly, and meet frequently, probably because he is attracted to her. One night she drinks too freely; her tongue is loosened; she begins to tell him about Lord Fulchester's history, and about Joe Richards, who is heir apparent to Jasper Belcher, and is not aware of the fact. Perhaps she tells him that the man who will inherit the property is Gregory Belcher, last heard of in South Africa, where he has been all his life.

"Right! You next deduce, do you not, that Lewis, being an Englishman by birth, and a criminal by profession, foresees the possibilities of turning the extraordinary circumstances to his own advantage. Gambling on this chance, he sails for England, steals certain pages from Lord Fulchester's manuscript, studies them, and is thereby satisfied that he can pass himself off as Gregory Belcher. His next move is to travel to South Africa by air, where he despatches a letter to the solicitor Howard inquiring about Jasper Belcher's health, at the same time making arrangements for someone to act as post box for him." The Inspector looked at Terhune inquiringly.

Terhune nodded.

"Right! Having made all necessary arrangements in South Africa, Lewis, you think, returns to England. Here he intrigues to dispose of Joe Richards, by bribing the gardener, or perhaps using other means, to leave the neighbourhood of Willingham to go and live in Scotland, or Ireland, or perhaps Australia—anywhere, in fact, other than Wales. To allay suspicion, and draw a fresh herring across the trail, Lewis then goes to that part of Wales which is known to be the birthplace of Joe's mother, and from there sends the letter, presumably from Joe, containing money to pay a small bill owing to the village grocer.

"Then he awaits the death of Jasper, which is obviously only a matter of time." The detective paused to consult some notes he had jotted down while Terhune had been talking. "As a matter of fact, Jasper's death followed very quickly. Howard, believing that Gregory is the only surviving relative of the deceased man, cables Gregory to come to England at once to enter into Jasper's estate. Warned by his friend in South Africa of this cable, Lewis later presents himself at Howard's office, pretending to have just arrived from the Dominion, and presenting forged credentials. Having no reason to be suspicious of Lewis, Howard accepts Gregory in good faith, and Gregory, after legal formalities have been complied with, enters into possession of the intestate estate. Right?"

Terhune nodded again, adding: "Probably I have been drawing upon my imagination——"

"There is no need to apologize," Sampson interrupted sharply. "I congratulate you on some fine work. Now what do you want me to do? Trace, firstly, Joe Richards, and secondly, through the police in South Africa, the real Gregory Belcher?"

"If you could, Inspector."

"I do not say I *can*, or rather, that the police *can*, but I think I can arrange for the police to try and trace the two men. It may not be easy. But meanwhile there is something you can do for me."

"What is that?"

"Find out from Lady Kylstone in what circumstances her sister-in-law lost the second key to the Kylstone vault."

IV

There was no difficulty about finding out how Mrs. Kylstone had lost the vault key—her maid had been "careless" and had accidentally thrown it away with some rubbish. Afterwards, when a search was made for the key, no trace of it could be found. Terhune telephoned this information to the Inspector. Sampson grunted, but said nothing beyond expressing his thanks. Terhune was disappointed; he had hoped the Inspector might have had news for him with regard to the missing gardener. However, early Sunday morning, Sampson appeared in Bray.

"I have news for you concerning Gregory Belcher," he announced as he sat down before the blazing fire and began to toast his toes. "Disappointing news!"

"The South African police cannot trace him?"

"On the contrary. They were able to send me all the information we wanted within twenty-four hours." He paused, mischievously.

"Well?" Terhune was at last compelled to ask.

"Your Gregory Belcher is the real Gregory Belcher."

Terhune wilted. He glanced ruefully at his visitor. In a flat voice he said: "So all my deductions were pure nonsense."

Sampson chuckled. "Not altogether. Gregory Belcher left South Africa seventeen years ago—for his own good! He emigrated to— the U.S.A.!" He saw the light of comprehension flare up in Terhune's eyes. "You have guessed right. He landed as Jimmy Lewis. But even in South Africa he was known as Blondie.

"I think we can assume this," the Inspector continued before Terhune could comment on the new discovery. "Until he met Margaret Ramsay, Gregory Belcher may have known very little of his relative in England. He may have known only that he had several relations living in this neighbourhood—I know what it is to have relations living abroad; I have three cousins somewhere in Canada, but where they are now, whether they are still alive or not, and whether they are rich or poor I haven't the slightest idea. When Margaret mentioned that she came from this part of Kent I can well imagine his asking curiously but casually: 'Do you know anything of the Belcher family? Are they still living round about there?' Whereupon, her tongue loosened by drink, Margaret related all she knew of Jasper and his son. To his great surprise Gregory Belcher learned that he was second in succession to a very sizeable fortune. Indeed, as long as Joe Richards remained in ignorance of his real identity, Gregory was first in succession. With the one difference that Jimmy Lewis did not impersonate somebody else, but merely reassumed his real identity, I think your deductions are substantially correct."

For nearly a minute the two men stared into the fire. Then Terhune asked slowly: "Have you any news of Richards yet, Inspector?"

"No," Sampson replied shortly.

"Why did Belcher send for Malatesta?"

"To recover the gold fountain pen from the Kylstone family vault?"

"That does not make sense," Terhune protested.

"Doesn't it! Why not?"

"Malatesta wouldn't have crossed the Atlantic without expecting a handsome reward."

"Belcher was willing to pay for it."

"If he wanted to recover the fountain pen so desperately why didn't he himself break into the vault?"

"Kraszewski told you why—a fact which the South African police have confirmed. Belcher was a mental crook, not a physical crook. That sounds stupid, but what I mean is this: if he had to use only his brains he would undertake most crimes, but he fought shy of any which necessitated using any physical means, such as breaking open a safe, entering a house, or anything of that nature."

"I see!" Terhune agreed slowly. "I think I can understand the psychology of his limitation. Probably he is afraid of the dark, to begin with."

"Quite likely."

"But why send to New York for Malatesta? Surely it would have been cheaper and simpler for him to have paid a London crook to break into the vault."

Sampson shook his head. "Cheaper, perhaps, but not simpler. Your question of psychology comes into the picture again. In America Blondie was known as a crook; in England Gregory Belcher was a wealthy landowner, without a criminal record. Belcher had been a blackmailer for too many years not to fear becoming a victim in his turn. Perhaps he knew he could trust Malatesta; he certainly would have had good reason to be afraid of trusting his reputation to London criminal circles."

"Then we are back at the old question again: how did the pen get into the vault in the first case, and why wasn't Belcher content to wait until the public opening of the vault on the twenty-fifth of October in the hope of recovering the pen before it was found by anyone else? For that matter, why didn't he go frankly to Lady Kylstone, and ask to borrow the key of the vault so that he might recover his fountain pen? And, if he had to use criminal methods to recover the pen from the vault, why wait until the last possible moment before the anniversary of Agincourt?"

The inspector sucked at his pipe which he had lighted earlier. "Do you remember telling me how Mr. Howard had rambled on about his last meeting with Belcher? You were rather impatient, you told me, to ask how he had communicated with the absent heir."

"Yes. I remember. Howard was talking to Belcher about the Kylstone vault——" Terhune stopped abruptly.

Sampson chuckled. "Ah! Now you appreciate the significance of Howard's rambling conversation—probably you would have done so before but for your impatience to continue questioning him along your own lines. Remember this in future: always let people ramble; it is when they are least on guard that they divulge the most important information. But to get back to Belcher. You know what it is when you have lost something you cannot find; you can search for days on end without coming across what you want. Suddenly, a chance word jogs your memory. You say to yourself: 'That is where it may be.' You rush to that particular spot, and, hey presto! there it is.

"That is what I think happened in this instance. Gregory had lost his precious fountain pen—don't you think he might have treasured it because it was a token of one of the few decent acts he has performed during the whole of his life? He had long given it up as lost when Howard started speaking of the vault. Suddenly Gregory thought to himself: 'My God! That is where I lost it. In the Kylstone vault.' Of course, all this is pure supposition, but..." Sampson shrugged his shoulders. "It may yet prove to be justified.

"It is my belief, Terhune, that the first intimation Belcher had of the vault's being opened annually was at that time, when he was informed that it was due to be opened up in precisely two weeks' time. This news was a shock to him; firstly because it was to be opened up at all, and secondly, because, if it were, his pen might be discovered there. The next day, as we know from the date on the form, he went up to town and despatched the cable to Malatesta."

Terhune frowned his perplexity. "I still do not comprehend why he could not have waited for the twenty-fifth in order to get back his pen. There was no crime in his having dropped a fountain pen there."

"You assume that he dropped the pen there during a visit there on the previous anniversary?"

"Yes."

"Let us suppose that he did so. Right! Now if the pen had been, discovered, and proved to be his—remember that Kraszewski said that Blondie possessed an excessively cautious nature, which would have made him nervous of the pen's being identified as his—it would have been generally assumed that he had so dropped it on the previous anniversary. Do you agree?"

"Yes."

"Then that would have been positive proof that he had been in England on the previous twenty-fifth of October?"

"Yes," Terhune acknowledged for the third time.

Sampson sat upright and pointed a rigid forefinger at his companion. "But on that previous twenty-fifth of October Belcher was supposed to have been either in South Africa or on his way to England."

"I see your point," Terhune acknowledged. "But I have just remembered that a moment or so ago we were assuming that Belcher knew nothing of the vault's being opened annually."

"Exactly!" the Inspector exclaimed drily.

"Then how did the pen get into the vault?"

"In Belcher's coat, of course, from which it dropped out."

"But, Inspector, if Belcher was not in the vault on the day of the anniversary how did he get in? With the help of the key which was *lost* by Lady Kylstone's sister-in-law?"

"Of course."

"Then why, if he already possessed a key to open it, did he send for Malatesta to break into the vault?" Terhune asked triumphantly.

"Maybe because he had thrown the key into the deepest water he could find," the other man replied equably.

"One last question. What was Belcher's reason for entering the vault?"

Sampson leaned nearer to the fireplace to knock some ashes out of his pipe. "I once read a story of a murderer who concealed the body of his victim in a newly dug grave," he mentioned casually.

V

Terhune spent a happy Christmas—the happiest since childhood. Christmas Day itself he spent at Timberlands, with Lady Kylstone and Helena. He was one of many guests, for her eldest son, Sir Piers, miraculously arrived back in England in time for Christmas leave. Accompanied by his wife he journeyed from Lyndhurst to spend the holiday with his mother. Lady Kylstone's other daughter-in-law was also there, having, as usual, come down from Scotland especially for the occasion (Edmund, the second son, was in the West Indies). Alec Hamblin was also there, and Edward Pryce. Long before evening every member of the party was intoxicated with the gaiety of the occasion; they played every absurd game anyone of them could remember, and some none of them could remember. They were, all and every one of them, as childish as a grown man or woman could be, but nobody worried. Hadn't everybody prophesied that this was to be a Christmas of Christmases?

Boxing Day he spent with Julia. During the daylight hours they drove for many miles through the countryside; in the evening they went to a dance in Folkestone. It was nearly 4 a.m. before he tumbled into bed, tired but exhilarated with the zest of life. Perhaps he was too tired. Or too exhilarated. At any rate sleep eluded him as he tried to decide which of the two days he had enjoyed the more. Eventually he gave up the problem as hopeless—one might as well compare Chateau Yquem with Champagne. Or the 'Londonderry Air' with the 'Rhapsody in Blue'. Or Jeffrey Farnol with Ernest Hemingway.

So the Christmas holidays passed into the back of beyond, and the world resumed its normal life. A few nights later, just as the old year expired, and the new year gave its first post-natal howl, for the third time in as many months a number of shadowy men silently made their way through Willingham Churchyard, and presently clustered round the Kylstone family vault. This time, however, there was neither a breaking-in, nor an attempt. The door opened easily upon Sampson's inserting the key in the lock, whereupon he descended into the vault, followed by several other men, two of whom carried an extending ladder.

VI

"As I had anticipated, the remains of the poor devil were there, in the lower vault," the Inspector told Terhune later. "Only a post-mortem examination can prove the manner of his death, but there can be very little doubt about what happened. Seeing that Malatesta was in England last year I think we can assume that, on behalf of his paymaster, Belcher, the American murdered the first cousin once removed; the heir apparent to Jasper's fortune. Afterwards he and Gregory carried the body to the vault, which was opened by means of the key stolen from Mrs. Kylstone. The body was dropped into the lower vault, Belcher believing that the vault was not likely to be opened again before the death of Lady Kylstone, or one of her sons—by which time, he did not doubt, so many years would have gone by that any danger of pinning the murder upon him would have long since vanished. And that belief would have been justified, I am thinking, but for the existence of a certain amateur criminologist by the name of—let me see if I have a good memory?—Theodore Ichabod Terhune!

"Here's to you," concluded Sampson as he wearily raised his glass of whisky. "Coupled with the seven clues which searched for a crime—and found it. May the same happen again one day."

"Not likely," Terhune grinned. "Not in Bray. One crime in a century is one more than usual—for Bray."

"You never know your luck," Sampson mumbled as his eyes closed. He was very tired, was Sampson. Yet, unexpectedly, he opened them. "By the way," he added, "which girl are you going to marry?"

"I—I—that is another story," Terhune stammered.

"I suppose you mean another mystery—still to be solved?" the Inspector muttered, as he closed his eyes again.

THE END